John Simpson

Change of Course

novum ▲ pro

www.novum-publishing.co.uk

© 2021 novum publishing

ISBN 978-3-99107-483-0
Editing: Hugo Chandler, BA
Cover photos: Gabriel Araujo, Lcrms7, Fotoeye75 | Dreamstime.com
Cover design, layout & typesetting: novum publishing

www.novum-publishing.co.uk

Contents

PART 1

PART 2

PART 3

PART 4

PART 1

Chapter 1

We had got there as soon as we could. The doctor, who arrived after us, touched and probed with expert fingers before confirming what we all feared. We stood around for what had felt like hours at the time, milling aimlessly, saying nothing, not knowing what to do. We were in shock.

For thirty years this scene had played out thousands of times in my mind's eye. Parts of it were still clear but most had faded like degraded celluloid. Names and faces had blurred, conversations were muted, and time had compressed the incident to a thirty-second sight bite. I was happy with the deterioration: it was an example of time as a healer. Guilt and shame still threatened to overwhelm me sometimes when the memory made one of its unwelcome, but now infrequent, recurrences, but I no longer knew why.

All things considered; I was pleased that the memory had faded; until …

★★★

'Oi, wake up, mate.' The taxi driver's sharp nudge added urgency. 'Sorry about the beauty sleep, but which one's yours?' He seemed anxious to be rid of me and get his money. I could not blame him – the sound of the windscreen wipers had lulled me to sleep before we had even left Heathrow – I had not been good company.

'Just past that bus shelter on the left. Pull in behind that white Merc.'

Someone was sitting in the shelter, out of the rain. My first thought was that it was a child; very small. This impression was exacerbated by the green cagoule that was far too large. The person appeared to be writing.

We stopped in front of my 1930s semi-detached. I paid the driver, pulled up the hood of my jacket and retrieved my bags from the boot. The house seemed to have made a special effort to look its worst. The front lawn was overgrown and scattered with litter, the gutters were overflowing, and a mossy hue streaked the walls and path. It was a picture of damp and neglect.

I dragged my bags round to the back door where I spent ages looking for the keys, scrabbling around in my pockets. Eventually, I found them.

'Mr Young, David Young?' The call startled me, and I dropped the keys. I had not noticed the green cagoule following me up the path.

'Sorry! Here, let me get them.' It was not a child. The voice was a woman's. She picked up the keys, found the right one first time and unlocked the door.

'Bloody hood! It's like wearing blinkers – I didn't see you there. So, what is it you're after?' I asked abruptly. 'Survey? Plastic brushes? Cosmetics?'

'Nothing like that. Are you David Young?'

I nodded. Her voice was pleasantly low-pitched with a hint of an accent; the north-east, I judged. If this had been an unsolicited phone call, I would have ended it there but, instead, I opened the door and ushered her into the kitchen ahead of me. 'I'm sorry about the mess but ...'

'You've been away, I know. I've called round every day for the last ten days. I was about to leave you this ...' She brandished a business card with some handwriting on the back. 'Don't you talk to your neighbours? Tell them when you're away?'

I felt a sudden panic. Why would anyone want to see me so badly that they kept trying my door for ten days?

'Not if I can help it. They only ever whinge about the garden and ... are you the police or something? Has something happened ... someone died?'

'No, I'm not the police, and no one's ...' she hesitated. 'I guess someone did die, sort of.' She saw the concern on my face and carried on. 'I'd better explain. My name's Sophie Addison. You used to know my father.'

I shook my head; I could not remember any Addisons.

'Sorry,' she said. 'My father was James Lodge.'

'Jim Lodge?' That name had not escaped my lips in nearly thirty years. It was a shock. I shuddered; I felt the blood drain from my face. I turned away from her; I had to. Unwanted memories were stirring, and my mind was flooded with a medley of conversations, shared beers, work and ... No, this was rubbish. 'That's not possible. It's thirty years ago. And Jim had no kids; he couldn't have.'

'He died before I was born.'

This was ridiculous. Yes, Lodge had married on his final leave from Angola, but ... I turned back to face her. She had taken off the cagoule. Waves of rust-coloured hair framed her face. It was so like a face I used to know well. I stared like an idiot – dumb struck.

'Are you all right?' She sounded genuinely concerned.

I think I nodded. I was speechless.

She reached for the handbag she had put on the kitchen table. 'I've got some papers here. I can prove who I am.'

I waved them away; there was no need. I was still staring at her, believing the unbelievable.

'Did he look like me?' She sounded incredulous.

'Well, you look like him, more like.' I laughed nervously and she joined in, her face folding into a dazzling smile, Lodge's smile. It lifted my mood in an instant. I had not realised how tense we had both become, but the laughter relaxed us.

'I think you've answered one question, anyway,' she said, grabbing a handful of her hair. 'I didn't know where this came from.'

I felt my face reddening but fought off the urge to look away. Instead, I moved closer and scrutinised every detail of her face, comparing colours, shapes, and proportions with the mental portrait I had of Jim Lodge. She too blushed, embarrassed by the intensity of the examination, but she held her ground, knowing instinctively that this was an important part of the process, whatever that was.

'It's not just the hair ... You're incredibly like him.'

Her eye colour was Lodge's, the same shade of green. Her features were his too but softer, more feminine, and her hair had the same fiery brilliance as Lodge's. But it was her determination; that she had persisted until I'd turned up, which convinced me she was Lodge's daughter.

'Tell me about him. He's only a name to me; I want to know what he was like.'

I wanted to tell her something, but my mind was awash with disjointed snippets: not a single coherent fact. It could only give her a jumble of half-remembered half-truths, and I wanted to do better than that. I also needed to think about why I had chosen to forget that time. Did I have something to hide? I felt physically and psychologically drained. I needed time to rest and time to read and remember.

'Okay,' I said finally, 'but can you come back tomorrow? I've been on the go for hours; I need get myself together. Thirty years ... it's a long time.'

She looked disappointed. 'I was hoping ...'

I stifled a yawn.

She nodded reluctantly.

'At about three o'clock?' I suggested. I had to go into the office in the morning to report back and sort a few things out. We agreed on that and I offered to phone for a taxi. She shook her head and extracted a Mercedes-Benz key from her handbag.

★★★

The weather worsened to a storm as the evening progressed into night. Doors and windows rattled; the house seemed to shake. Broken branches, rubbish bins and other loose items clattered disturbingly. I had gone to bed early but could not sleep. I needed peace and a clear conscience, but I had neither. My mind was active but not analytical; memories hashed and rehashed, fact and fabrication merged and blurred. What had really happened? Had anything? Why was I so worried and why was I hesitating to root out the facts? I knew I had taken notes, but I had no idea why I had chosen to set it down: maybe there would be nothing useful. Images of Jim Lodge flickered around in my mind in a fruitless, frustrating loop. I could not trust my memory and I needed to do something about it if I was going to get any sleep. I got up. It was two in the morning. I started my research.

An old travel trunk in the attic was my repository for stuff I could neither throw away nor bring myself to look at again. The last time I had raised the lid was to put away the paperwork from my divorce and, before that, my father's death certificate. It was a catalogue of failure and melancholy.

I knew exactly where to find what I needed. The shoebox labelled 'Angola 1985-6' sent a shudder through me every time I saw it. I had not opened it since the day I put it away in the trunk thirty years ago, and I doubted if Rachel, my ex-wife, had ever pried; she was not the kind.

I steeled myself and took the lid off the shoebox. Its contents were unremarkable; some photographs and press clippings; a wad of Kwanzas, the local currency; another wad of permits for travel and work; and there were two notebooks; one for each of the two six-month contracts I completed in Angola. I have never kept a formal diary, but I have always made arbitrary notes about my work contracts just in case I ever have to refer back to something. I guessed I would have written plenty about Jim Lodge as his death had been a rite of passage for me; the first dead body I had ever seen. I wondered to what extent my recollection of events had been, or would be, coloured by that.

The first notebook was a disappointment. A quick skim told me little about Lodge. He was mentioned as a geologist, but he barely registered as a personality. I put it back in the shoebox and hoped for more from the second book, my second contract, during which Lodge had died. I took it, along with the press clippings and some photographs, down to the living room where I settled into my favourite armchair to read. My notes were a hangover from university, economical on sentences but rich on trigger words, a style that had always worked for me, making revision easy: Nocredo – Hercules – rains. Morgan – Thys Gerber – chopper – garimpeiros – Txicaca. It would have meant nothing to anyone else but me ...

★★★

I looked out from the window of the Hercules. It had begun its steep descent into Nocredo where the airstrip appeared as a bloody gash in the Angolan bush. The lushness and the lack of dust told me the rainy season had started while I had been away on leave.

The Hercules taxied to a corrugated steel shed that served as the airport building and workers swarmed around its tail, waiting for the door to drop. I saw two old men struggling towards us with some rickety steps, manhandling them to the front door so that I, the only passenger, could disembark, along with the crew.

I got up from my seat in the cargo hold and stretched; I was stiff. I adjusted my sweaty clothes and lugged my bags to the now open door where I stopped to look around for any faces I might recognise, to give me a lift to the mine. There was only one and he was a surprise.

A stocky, pugnacious-looking man detached himself from a small group and swaggered over, dragging another man in his wake. He grinned and offered his hand.

'Welcome back, lad. Good leave?' His accent betrayed his roots in the Rhondda valley.

'Great! Thanks Geoff. I wasn't expecting you. I can't believe you're my taxi.'

Geoff Morgan was the Mumbulo Mine Manager. 'Don't start,' he laughed, 'I had to come anyway ... with the chopper. I've got Jan's replacement with me. I'm showing him some of the illegal mining in the area.' A sly smile creased his face as he nodded towards his companion. I sensed I was convenient

14

to his plan; that I was going to have to work for my lift back to the mine. 'Did you meet Thys before you went on leave?' he continued.

I shook my head. 'I knew you had someone lined up, but ...'

'Thys has joined us from the South African Police. He's going to give us a policing approach to diamond security.'

The other man, tall and khaki-clad, with a terracotta tan, stepped forward and we shook hands; his grip was firm, but it tightened to a crush just before he released my hand. Was that a show of strength or a warning, I wondered.

Morgan glanced at his watch and gestured towards the helipad. The Alouette helicopter, a Perspex bubble on a flimsy steel skeleton, did not inspire confidence, nor did the pilot who leaned languidly against the fuel bowser smoking and chatting while refuelling took place.

As we approached, the pilot stubbed out his cigarette. He gave my smart new suitcase a contemptuous look before he snatched it from me and chucked it carelessly into the back of the cockpit. He then eyed the grubby, canvas bag that was slung over my shoulder. I hefted it to him and watched as he eased it carefully into a space behind the seats. That was a duty almost done. All that was left was for me to do was to sign in the bag at the mine office. I had picked it up at the company's office near Hatton Garden in London before getting a taxi to Heathrow. It was an inconvenience but one that no one would refuse to do. The bag contained not only all the business mail for the Mumbulo Mine but also all the personal mail. Without that bag, and similar ones, passing in and out with employees taking leave, the mine would not function. There was no telephone connection between the mine and its Head Office and, for personnel away from home for up to six months at a time, the weekly mail bag was the only link to home.

'É tudo?' he asked.

'That's all.' I nodded.

Morgan checked his watch again. 'Combustível? Have we enough fuel for the journey yet?'

'Sim chefe.' The pilot shrugged then set about getting his passengers strapped in and fitted with headsets.

We ascended vertically before heading towards the river, a fast-flowing torrent that etched a profound story into the landscape. It told, in a ratio of green to brown, where it ran and how it had been tamed. Huge blocky brown areas testified to man's interference as a diamond miner – ugly eyesores.

The racket from the rotors was deafening and I hated having to bellow to be understood. Even using the intercom, I had to shout and repeat myself several times, but Morgan felt no such reticence – he enjoyed shouting. He explained that he wanted my help to familiarize Thys with the activities of illegal miners: their numbers, their operations and their methods.

We flew high to maximise our range of vision and we had only been airborne for a few minutes when I saw a reddish-brown discolouration in the river water.

'Over there! Look!' I pointed towards it. 'We haven't any plants near there – it's got to be illegal washing, garimpeiros!'

Morgan, sitting next to the pilot, jabbed his finger towards the dirty water and nodded vigorously. The helicopter swooped like a peregrine and its prey panicked.

'Shit. There's hundreds of the bastards!' Thys shouted incredulously. Men, women and children scattered like shrapnel into the scrubby woodland, disappearing in seconds. All that remained were piles of muck, shovels, buckets and boxes.

Thys's request to land produced a withering stare from Morgan.

'They'll have AK-47s stashed close by. If we go down …' Morgan caught the pilot's eye and pointed up. I picked up flashes in my peripheral sight as the helicopter ascended rapidly: sun in the rotors, or was it a tracer? Either way, no one spoke for several minutes.

Eventually, Thys asked about the illegal miners. 'The garimpeiros? How many are there in the area?' he said.

'A couple of hundred,' Morgan replied.

I suppressed a laugh as my estimate was much higher. There might be two hundred men, but there were women and children too. I described to Thys how they dug gravel and dirt out of the riverbank and carried it to a washing area, usually upstream, in buckets and sacks. 'They shovel the muck into screens with wire mesh bottoms and immerse them in water to wash away the silt and sand. Any worthwhile diamonds are in the stones left behind; they sort through them and sometimes they get lucky.'

'All the illegals I've come across before have been after gold,' said Thys. 'That kit we saw … It looked the same as for gold to me. Are you sure they're after diamonds?'

'There is no gold around here. That's right isn't it, Geoff?' I said.

'Yeah, the geology's wrong,' Morgan confirmed.

'Anyway,' I continued, 'for gold, they'd use pans and sluice boxes. What we saw were screens; they're a different shape. Sluice boxes are troughs, much longer than screens, and they have carpet or sacking in them, as a lining. The gold gets caught in the lining. Sluice boxes are not the best way to recover diamonds, but they've been used for thousands of years for gold. They reckon Jason's Golden Fleece was probably a box lining.'

'Who's Jason?' asked Thys.

After a few more minutes Morgan bellowed into the intercom, 'I want to call in here.'

We were close to one of the Mumbulo Mine's open pits where we could see yellow machines, like a colony of termites, working at various tasks. Shallow-gradient roads skirted the pit, easing their way down to where the excavators and loaders worked, filling the trucks that supplied the pre-treatment plant.

A brown stain in the river, like an arrowhead, pointed accusingly at the Cambunda pre-treatment plant; I could see it was running. The plants were my responsibility.

'I want to show Thys the new river diversion,' said Morgan. 'It's just about finished, and we should be ready to start mining it in the next day or two. While we're there, David, you could make yourself useful by checking on the plant,' he added, wryly.

In the distance, we could see that the river split into two channels. One carried the flow and the other was almost dry. Morgan, a mining engineer himself, boasted about the mining department's achievement; completing the excavation of the new river course before the end of the dry season, and then breaking it through into the natural river. 'We've just about finished pumping out the old course,' he said. 'There should be a nice production bonus next month if Jim's instincts are right. I say instincts,' he mused, 'because all the other bloody geologists, with the same information, find next to nada. I reckon that bugger can smell diamonds.'

Morgan instructed the pilot. He landed us at the helipad two hundred yards from the plant. We all clambered out and shuffled around, stretching and kneading muscles to loosen up after being in the cramped cockpit. A mechanic was working at the plant workshop close by, servicing a haul truck. He wasn't using his Land Rover, so Morgan commandeered it to take Thys to the river diversion. I set off on foot to check on the Cambunda pre-treatment plant. The air smelled clean, refreshed by the rains; it had been heavy with dust when I went away.

A loader was shovelling ore from the stockpile and tipping it into the feed hopper where a jet of high-pressure water from the monitor gun drove it down into the plant. A little Angolan man, partially obscured by water spray, was operating the gun, carefully directing it for best effect. When he turned off the water, I recognised him as Armando, the shift foreman. I smiled and waved at him. Armando and I had established an instant rapport when we'd first met, six months earlier. He was eager to learn everything he could from me about the plants and he had made it his duty to help me with my Portuguese and teach me a few words of Chokwe, the local tribal language.

Armando gestured for a colleague to take over at the monitor, then he ran over to greet me, grinning hugely. We shook hands.

'Como está, Engineer David? Is your family well?' I nodded and confirmed that my parents were in good health then I asked after his family. He seemed to inflate with pride as he told me that his wife, Esther, was pregnant with their first child. He had known about it for some time but had said nothing before because she had previously miscarried several times.

'Congratulations,' I said warmly. We shook hands again, then I remembered something odd, '– but I thought you already had three sons.'

'Ah! Those are my brother's boys. In our society, my brothers' and sisters' children are my children, but …' he chuckled, 'some will be more mine than others.' Then his grin unfolded into something more sombre and he told me that one of his sons, a nephew really, had died of malaria a week before. I was saddened by the news. We talked about his excitement at the prospect of the new baby, and then I told him about some of my exploits while on leave. After a while, my conscience finally stirred me to suggest that we inspect the plant together.

We worked systematically down from the top, following the material flow, checking equipment for wear and tear. We had just reached the bottom and were checking the pumps when we heard a shout that told us Morgan was back from the river. We climbed back up the steps to where Morgan and Thys were standing yards apart, near the feed hopper. Morgan seemed very agitated. He was staring down at the plant screwing up his eyes, but I could tell he wasn't focusing on anything physical. I knew that any comment would only draw fire, so I kept quiet.

'There's fuck all in that river diversion!' he snarled, breaking his stare. 'Bedrock and sand, bugger all else; like an itchy arse, gritty, no real substance.'

I said nothing and Thys kept quiet too; he'd obviously read the situation accurately.

Morgan turned his back on us and wandered over to the stockpile; his manner did not invite company. I gave Thys an inquisitive look. He waited until Morgan was out of earshot before telling me that Morgan had been in high spirits on the short drive to the river, excited at the prospect of seeing for the first time what lay at the bottom of the new diversion.

His mood had changed as soon as they crested the hill overlooking it, and they had their first clear sight of it. He'd stopped the Land Rover and they both got out. All they could see were small patches of what looked like sand in expanses of grey bedrock. Morgan went silent, his face lost all colour, and he started hurling stones in the general direction of the river. When he had calmed down, they climbed back into the Land Rover and Morgan drove them the rest of the way to the river where he just sat and stared at it for several minutes without uttering a word. He eventually got out and spoke to the mining engineer supervising the pumping operations.

'River diversions are always hit or miss, a gamble,' I said. 'They are expensive and you never know what you'll get out of them until you start producing. Your description of the riverbed doesn't sound very promising, though. Maybe we should forget that production bonus.'

'Some gamble,' said Thys. 'It seems to me that it's one that Geoff didn't expect to lose, and he looks like a bad loser to me.'

Morgan seemed to have sorted his thoughts out and was strutting purposefully back towards us. 'We need to get back,' he said. 'I've got to talk to Lodge.' He moved towards the Land Rover then stopped abruptly. 'We'll need to run a test on the diversion material, David. Fix it for tomorrow morning.' It was not a good time for a discussion so I called Armando over immediately and told him that he should start preparing for an ore test as soon as he came on shift the following morning.

We drove the short distance back to the helipad where the pilot was asleep in the shade of the fuselage. Morgan rambled on about the diversion and concluded that Lodge must have been lucky in the past as he had certainly screwed up this time. 'David, I want you to run the test tomorrow, personally, and I'm going to make sure Lodge is there with you to see his fuck-up.'

***

The story felt real and fresh as though it had happened yesterday – my notes had done a good job. The faces, the places, the voices and even the smells seemed real, as though I was there again. I was hooked – I wanted to read on, but I was also frightened: there had to be a reason why I had chosen to forget. I knew that the more I read the greater would be the danger of digging up what I wanted to remain buried. I risked a few more pages then I skim-read the press cuttings before going up to bed.

My mind continued to churn as I tried to sleep, linking the past and the present. I'd never said much about my time in Angola, not even to Rachel, but now I was awakened to the massive influence it had been on my career, and Lodge was a key part of that Angolan experience.

Chapter 2

The storm had blown itself out by morning, albeit with a trail of debris left in its wake. Yet more rubbish littered the garden and broken branches were scattered around. It was a beautiful day, though, and I found myself smiling at the prospect of seeing Sophie again. I went to the office of Flourish, the charity where I worked, but spent little more than an hour there as I was unable to concentrate. I made the excuse of travel fatigue and skived off long before lunch.

I arrived home, intending to do more reading but my confidence deserted me. I saw my notes as a pathway to an unmapped minefield, so, instead of reading, I passed the time by dusting, polishing and tidying up. I was eager to make a good second impression. Time slowed as the appointed hour approached and I kept looking out of the front window every few minutes, hoping she would be early.

I started thinking about the previous day's brief encounter, analysing every word and action. Why had it taken thirty years for her to land on my doorstep and why was everything so urgent all of a sudden? It was also strange that she knew next to nothing about her father. Surely her mother would have told her something. But then she hadn't known where her hair colour had come from. Maybe she hadn't known her mother either. She was as much a mystery to me as her father was to her.

I spotted someone approaching in the distance, hair shining like a beacon in the sun – Lodge's colour – it could only be her. The baggy, shapeless clothes she'd been wearing when we first met had been replaced by figure-hugging jeans and a sweater. I had the door open before she had the chance to knock and I couldn't help staring in admiration as she stepped past me into the kitchen. There was fire in her green eyes and her smile was warm. She oozed good humour and zest for life; an irresistible combination.

She set about inspecting the kitchen, nodding approvingly at its transformation from yesterday's chaos to something approaching order. Then she checked the kettle for water, switched it on and took a carton of milk from her shoulder bag. 'I came prepared.' It was the first thing either of us said.

I pulled a cafetière and a couple of mugs down from a shelf and found the coffee. We talked about the storm of the previous night while we waited for the kettle, carefully avoiding any mention of Lodge. When we were ready, I led her through to the lightest room, the lounge, which had a south-facing French window and we sat facing one another over the coffee table.

'Where should we begin?' I asked.

'Maybe I owe you an explanation first,' she offered. 'I have rather dumped myself on you. I don't even know if I'm welcome.'

I assured her I was pleased she had come but I secretly wondered if I would feel that way in an hour or so. I was keen to hear her story though. 'All right, ladies first then.'

'Okay, from the beginning; my beginning. I was born in June 1985. My parents lived in Durham, so I always assumed that was where I was born. I never questioned it … I had no reason to.'

Sophie told me how Michael and Margaret Addison brought her up as if they were her biological parents. Michael was a school headmaster and Margaret an English teacher. Sophie's childhood was happy, and she loved her parents. She had excelled at school, favouring the arts, and had won a place at Cambridge to read Modern Languages when she was only seventeen. It was at the end of her first year, on her eighteenth birthday, when her parents told her that she was adopted, and she saw her birth certificate and the adoption papers for the first time.

'That must've been a hell of a shock, especially if you never suspected,' I said. 'I can't imagine how I'd have reacted – with anger, probably – but it's not something I've ever had to think about.'

23

'Yeah; shocked and stunned would be understating it. My life, who I was, my genes, everything; all that changed in an instant. I just stared at mum and dad, expecting them to have some explanation, but they didn't. I realised what unconditional love was that day. I tried really hard to hate them, but I couldn't; I still loved them – that hadn't changed. They'd always stood by me when I needed them, so I decided very quickly that they were still my mum and dad. They were the only parents I knew, and I had enough friends from broken homes to know that they were as good as I had any right to expect. Dad gave me the key to a drawer in his desk, which was always locked. He told me there was a file in there that contained everything they knew about my biological parents. I tried to give it straight back, but he wouldn't take it. I promised myself that I wouldn't look at the file until ... well, anyway. But back then, I was at university and I didn't want to be distracted from my studies.'

'Weren't you curious though? That must have been a dozen years ago or more.'

'Of course, I wouldn't be human otherwise. But I always keep my promises, even those I only make to myself.'

'But you're here now. That must mean ...' I looked away, realising I was probing into what was a deeply personal and painful subject.

'... that mum and dad are dead, yes.' She braced herself then said. 'I really miss them. I've only just started getting my life back together again.' She told me that they had been driving back to Durham after visiting her in Cambridge, where she had remained after her studies, and had been involved in an accident near Newark. They had both died from their injuries. That had been four months ago. She said that her world had fallen apart for a while and that she still felt guilty. 'I know it's stupid ...' She wiped a tear from the corner of her eye, '... but if they hadn't visited me that weekend, they'd still be alive. I was devastated. I wanted someone else to blame: another car, another driver. I even went to Newark, to the spot where it happened. I got witness names from the press and spoke to them all. It was a one-car accident. Just as well there wasn't anyone else; the way I felt I don't know what I'd have done.'

I said nothing but I couldn't help thinking that Jim Lodge would have behaved in the same way. 'Anyway,' she said, anxious to move on, 'this is what was in that drawer.' She reached down and withdrew a thin cardboard file from her shoulder bag and put it on the table in front of me. I caught her eye; she nodded.

I could see, before opening it, that there was very little in the file. The first few items were her birth certificate and papers relating to her adoption. The birth certificate named her mother as Gillian Lodge and her father as James Edgar Lodge (deceased), and she had been born in Whitby in North Yorkshire. The only surprise was Lodge's middle name; I had known he intended to settle in Whitby. There were photocopies of two death certificates: for Gillian Lodge who had died of pneumonia in Whitby on 15th December 1985, and James Edgar Lodge who had died of injuries received in a road traffic accident on 14th December 1984, in Angola. The latter had an endorsement from the British Embassy in Luanda. My tongue felt very dry.

The only other items in the file were three newspaper cuttings. Two were about the tragedy of a baby girl who had lost her father before she was even born and her mother before she was six months old. The other was about James Lodge's death. It was the same as a cutting in my shoebox except that Sophie's had a black and white photograph, which was missing from mine. It looked as though it had been taken at an end-of-week party, which fitted with the caption: 'Party – 13th December 1984 – James Lodge (second from left)'. His face was almost completely obscured by another one, mine. We looked to be in earnest conversation.

The report was very sketchy, and it told the story that had been agreed between the mine management and the British Embassy.

British Geologist Killed in Angola

Luanda, Angola, 18 December 1984. Sources at the British Embassy in Luanda have confirmed that a British geologist, James Lodge, 32, was killed at the weekend in a road accident in the north east of Angola, in the Lunda Norte province. He had been in charge of prospecting for a British diamond mining company. It is believed that the vehicle he was driving left the road and plunged into a river, killing him instantly. His body was found by a fellow worker, David Young, aged 25.

This is especially tragic as Lodge had married two months previously in Whitby, Yorkshire. His widow, Gillian, aged 25, has been informed.

His body will be repatriated for burial in Whitby.

'It's not much is it?' she said.

'No,' I muttered. I suddenly felt very cold and my mind seemed to be jumping around; we weren't supposed to be talking about this yet; I wasn't ready. I panicked. 'And it's bullshit.'

She had appeared quite relaxed until then, but I saw her stiffen, knitting her eyebrows in concentration. 'You mean ... it wasn't an accident?'

I hesitated, looking for a way out, 'It wasn't just me who found him; there was a crowd of us.'

'No!' She shook her head vigorously. 'I'm not buying that. You wouldn't say "it's bullshit" if that was all there was to it. Was it really an accident?'

Shit! I closed my eyes and squeezed the bridge of my nose. Not now! I'd planned to talk about Jim's life and to leave his death till the end, where it belonged, but I sensed that she would not let it go. I would have to wing it and hope it satisfied her.

'There was an accident and Jim, your dad, was involved ...'

She winced. 'Please don't call him my dad – father, yes – but Michael Addison will always be my dad.'

'Sorry. It was a Sunday. Your father was driving home, to Mumbulo, from a party in Nocredo. Mumbulo was the mining town where we worked and Nocredo was the administrative centre for several mining towns. He was alone, but there was another vehicle a few minutes behind him. He was using one of the mine roads. Someone stepped out into the road in front of him and he hit them. He did what you or I would have done here in England; he stopped to help. Kevin Dryden, who was driving the second vehicle, stopped to see what was going on. Apparently, there was a huge argument between your father and a group of Angolans, and it was turning nasty. Dryden said he tried to haul your father away to his car, but your father refused to move and fought to help the man he had hit.'

'I don't get it,' she said. 'He was trying to help. What was the argument about and …'? She hesitated. 'If he wasn't hurt in the accident, how come he died?'

'All I know is that Dryden got away and drove to my house where a bunch of us were having a drink. He was obviously very shaken up; and pretty incoherent. He kept babbling random stuff like "he was stoned", "he wouldn't come", "you have to go and help". It didn't make sense, but we could all see there was a problem and we had to do something. We got into whatever vehicles we had, everyone except Dryden, and we drove out to where he'd said. I can remember it being a very subdued drive. I had Carlos Pereira with me – he was a mining engineer – and we just kept on debating the phrase "he was stoned". Was he on drugs, was he drunk, or was he stoned in a more biblical sense? We didn't know what to expect. We were shitting ourselves. We didn't know if we'd have to fight or what. When we got to the place Dryden had described, the road was deserted except for the body, your father. His car had been pushed over the edge of the road into the river. We were too late.'

'Jesus,' she said. 'That must have been horrendous. Did you get counselling?'

I was surprised that she could even consider my state of mind after what I had just told her, even though her question was naive. I grunted and shook my head. 'No such thing then. Even if there had been, anyone having it would have been laughed out of camp. It was a different world; things have changed for the better now. We just went straight back to work the following day and got on with it. But I do get flashbacks. Your father was the first person I ever saw dead.'

'I'm sorry,' she said. 'But how did he die? Was he stoned to death?' Her face was a picture of horror.

'I guess so. There were some rocks lying around and there was what looked like blood on some of them. There was blood everywhere. I never thought it was anything else.'

She was silent for a while and there were tears in her eyes. I wondered if she was imagining her father's death or shedding tears for a love she should have known.

'What happened to the man he hit?' she asked.

The question hit me like a punch. Maybe the answer was in my notes, but I didn't think so. I don't think I had ever known. Had it even concerned me? I hoped so, but I couldn't be sure and that worried me. I don't think I had ever considered the other man. What had happened to him? 'I assume he died,' I said lamely.

'Don't you know?' She sounded incredulous.

'Why else would they have killed your father? It wouldn't make sense if the other man hadn't died.'

'I guess you're right, but I find it hard to believe you don't actually know.'

'Everyone was too traumatised and too focused on Jim to think about anyone else. We had a lot of theories, but I guess we mostly wanted to forget – it was too horrible. You might not believe me, but this is the first time I've spoken of this since about a month after it happened. We all just wanted to forget.'

'What if there wasn't another man … another body?' she said.

'There had to be. The Angolans would only have killed him if one of them had died, and there was a …' I stopped. I couldn't tell her that.

'A what?' she asked. 'You were going to say something. What was it?'

'Nothing,' I mumbled.

She smiled ruefully and shook her head slowly.

'All right,' I said. 'Everything seemed to suggest that an Angolan had died too: Jim's body and the car in the river.' It was as far as I could go.

'This is my biological father we're talking about. I wanted him to be more than a bashed-up body. I've only just got used to the idea that he existed, let alone died a violent death.'

I grabbed my opportunity. 'Look, this is hard for both of us, for different reasons. I'm not ready for this yet. Can we ease off for a while – calm down – then I'll tell you about your father – what he was really like – alive.'

To my relief, she nodded. But I knew we would be back.

Chapter 3

Sophie went through to the kitchen to make some more coffee; hoping, I think, that it would give me time to come up with a more convincing story about her father's death. Instead, I just sat and stared at the cover of the second notebook. It was identical to thousands of other notebooks except for the label: 'Angola – Second Contract: Oct 84 –'. The lack of an end-date hinted at unfinished business. My thoughts kept turning to Sophie. She had a right to know about her father but her questions about his death had unsettled me. By inviting her back to my home I'd tacitly agreed to tell her what I knew, or most of it. But there was something about Lodge's death that worried me profoundly; I had no idea what it was. It was like a splinter: I knew there was something there, but I couldn't get at it. Did the notebook hold the answer? I didn't know but I was reluctant to find out. In the end my procrastination earned me a reprieve. Sophie bustled back into the room with a tray of coffees and half a dozen biscuits that she must have ransacked the cupboards to find.

'Ready to go again?' she asked.

I nodded uncertainly. 'You hadn't quite finished your story.' I wanted to start the session on safer ground. 'What is it you do now? For a living, I mean. You're still in Cambridge?'

'Yes, I really love it there. After graduating, I stayed on and did a doctorate in social sciences. I really wanted to work in that field, but nothing came up that was quite right, or that paid enough, so I fell back on my first degree, languages, and I've been a freelance translator and interpreter for the last seven or eight years.'

'That sounds interesting. Who makes up most of your clients? Students, immigrants?'

'No not really, though I do some work for individuals, but I get most of my business from the high-tech companies in the science parks in and around Cambridge, helping them work with international clients and partner businesses; plus, I get involved in acquisitions of foreign companies. I enjoy it – I get to learn the business side of things too. What about you? You obviously still travel.'

'Yeah, too much I reckon. I'm a project worker with Flourish; it's a development charity. We focus mainly on Africa and, to a lesser extent, South America and Asia. My area's mining: I work with artisanal miners.'

'Artisanal?' She laughed. 'Sounds a bit up-market to me, very arts and crafts. You pay a premium for anything labelled "artisanal". Look at bread.'

I snorted. 'You're not even close. Some prefer to call them small-scale miners; they're subsistence miners really. They work independently, not for a mining company. They're often illegal. It's mining at its most basic: hammers, chisels, spades, pans, candles ... you name it – bloody lethal.' I told her about some of the mines I had visited in various African and South American countries. She blanched when I told her that I'd been down mine shafts forty or fifty metres deep without a rope: just bracing my back and feet against opposite sides of the shaft and walking down. She found it hard to believe that miners still use candles for light and that they worked with little or no ventilation.

'What do they mine?' she asked.

'Anything, but often gold – precious stuff.'

'Greed then. Why does a charity ...'

'It's not greed,' I interrupted. 'It's subsistence mining. Most of them barely make a living; even with gold. But it's a sensible thing to mine if you think about it: it's portable. A gram of gold is worth a significant amount; just over $ 30 at $ 1,000 an ounce. You'd need half a tonne of iron for the same return. I know which I'd rather carry around.'

'Yes, but what's wrong with farming? Surely that's a better option for pure survival?'

'Well, yes, if the land will grow anything. A lot of miners are, or were, farmers but droughts, floods and other shit like desertification has forced them onto plan B. If you can't grow your food, you need money to buy it – and that's where mining comes in. It's a straight choice: mine or starve. What would you do?'

'Start digging, I guess. It still doesn't seem like a typical charity area though – too many environmental issues. It must be a struggle to get funding,' she said. 'How many at Flourish work in mining?'

She wasn't surprised when I told her I was the only one and she couldn't hide her delight when she learned that we employed more than twenty social scientists as well as numerous specialists in other fields.

'Where is it you've just got back from?' she asked.

'Ghana; I was there for six weeks. Some field work – projects, and a bit of networking in Accra. I had some useful meetings with influential figures from government departments and other organisations.'

'What was the field work?'

'I've been working with one of the big mining companies in Tarkwa, persuading them to work with and help artisanal miners in the area. I also took a fact-finding trip to a place near the Burkina Faso border, to see a real live gold rush. What an eye-opener that was.'

'How so?' She was interested.

'It was so chaotic – a free-for-all – illegal, dangerous and criminally inefficient; an illustration of all that's bad in artisanal mining. Take for example the mercury. Some of the miners evaporate it off using the same pots they use for cooking!'

'You've got to be kidding. Surely they must know the dangers?'

'They do, but they ignore them.'

'Why?'

'They live from day to day, literally. They focus on what might kill them today not on what might kill them twenty years down the line. If you can't get through today, there is no twenty years.'

'That's really depressing.' Her face reflected her words.

'Yes, it is, it's heart-breaking. Providing the dream of a better future is one of the biggest challenges. Going back to the mercury though; much of it ends up in the rivers, which is where their food chain starts! There's just so much to do. There are other major problems too – AIDS and the sex trade not the least. I'm currently working on a funding proposal for a project to study the impact of AIDS in artisanal mining communities. But it'll be hard to make it attractive to the donors. They're falling over themselves to spend money on farming and microfinance projects, but mining ...'

'Funding,' she sighed. 'I had my fair share of frustrations with that too when I was in research. That's one side of research I don't miss.' After a pause she asked, 'Have you ever been back to Angola? Done any projects there?'

I'd been wondering how long it would take her to steer the conversation back there.

'No,' I said. 'I guess it's because our partners and donors – for Africa, anyway – focus on English-speaking countries. Ex-Portuguese colonies like Angola and Mozambique don't appear on our map, nor do any of French-speaking Africa.'

'Even though some of those, like Mozambique, are in the Commonwealth?'

'There's plenty to do in English-speaking places without complicating life with other languages and the baggage left behind by other colonial powers. Britain's past actions are hard enough to clear up.'

'That makes sense.' She stared at me, lips curled back between her teeth, deep in thought. 'Why did you change your career? You're like some sort of poacher turned gamekeeper.'

I laughed. 'Gamekeeper turned poacher, more like.'

Sophie looked baffled; her face demanded an explanation.

'It's simple really,' I said. 'Most people regard artisanal miners as the bad boys: working illegally and screwing up the environment.'

'Mercury?'

'Not to mention messing up riverbanks and destroying vegetation. Then there's child labour.'

'Bloody hell. If they're that bad, why do you support them? How can you justify it?'

'That's a big question, Sophie. Remember it's for subsistence; they only do it to survive. If they didn't mine, they'd either have to find some other way to get food or move on. The system, and the mining laws and the bureaucratic infrastructure, is rigged against them in favour of the mining companies. These people live where they have for generations, and they survive by whatever means they can, and as no one owned the land officially. They believe they can do what they want with it. Problems arise when one of them finds something valuable like gold, silver or precious stones and trades it to get money for food. It draws attention. Mining companies get wind of it and they snap up the mining rights, instantly making it illegal for the artisanal miners to mine their traditional land, as they are then on a mining company claim! They often can't even farm it, let alone mine it, after that.'

Sophie looked at me thoughtfully – she'd obviously never considered this before. While I had her captive, I continued on the subject close to my heart.

'Many of the world's biggest mines weren't found by geologists, like your father, but by the local people who happened upon something while working in their fields or fetching water from the river.'

'So why don't the ... artisanal miners you called them, just apply for the mining rights themselves; it would solve the problem surely?'

'Ah yes, but they have had no formal education and wouldn't know where to start with the bureaucracy! Many aren't even aware of the existence of mining rights – until it's too late – and the process for getting the rights requires you to go to a big city, typically the capital, which might be several days' walk away. Most simply can't afford the time or the legal costs. Mining rights are expensive. Artisanal miners stand no chance without some help.'

'So, do they just stop, or carry on somehow?'

'Well, it's a dangerous game. The mining companies often deploy armed forces to clear illegals off their property so there's a very high risk they'll get shot or injured in some other way. They can't even sell what they produce very easily. They're forced to use middlemen who rip them off. They're lucky if they get five dollars for a gram of gold. The middlemen will get upwards of twenty dollars for doing bugger all. The upshot is that artisanal miners have to produce a lot more gold to make a living than if they were legal. It means they have to cut corners and use whatever labour is available to them, and that means women and children.'

Sophie looked at me long and hard. 'I can understand all that but … You used to work for a mining company. You must have bought into what they stood for, including getting rid of artisanal miners. Something must have happened. You've changed sides and nobody changes sides without a good reason. What was yours?'

'I've never really thought about it,' I lied. 'I just sort of drifted into it.'

'For something you "just sort of drifted into" you're very passionate about it. Something must have stirred you up …?' She was very intuitive; it was unnerving and rather too close to the bone.

She must have noticed that I kept glancing at my notebook because she asked if she could take a look. After some hesitation, I passed it to her. There was no way she'd be able to make any sense of my notes. Triggers are useless if there's nothing to set them off.

As she thumbed through, her expression turned from excitement to frustration. 'You can't be serious,' she said. 'This doesn't say anything.'

'I've got loads like that – it works for me.' I held out my hand; she gave an exasperated sigh and passed it back to me.

'Let's go back to you and my father,' she said. 'How well did you know him?'

'We were friends, good friends. I'd known him for about eight or nine months, I think, by the time he died.' I told her that I had arrived in Mumbulo in early 1984, having been transferred from South Africa by the company. James Lodge had already been there for three or four years by the time I turned up. Sophie was both surprised and disturbed when she learnt that Lodge and I had barely known one another in my first contract.

At work, in the Mumbulo Mine offices, Lodge's Geology department had no direct dealings with my department, Metallurgy; plus, I was the shy, new boy, not yet fully integrated into the established social groupings.

'We shared a beer from time to time of course, but he was more comfortable with his usual cronies,' I explained.

'But you said you were good friends.'

'Don't look so worried. We became very good friends later on. I believe I knew him as well as anyone in Mumbulo did.'

Her face relaxed.

'It took me a long while to get used to Angola. I didn't adjust very well to begin with, and I found everything a struggle. Angola was completely different from here or South Africa: it was communist. There was a civil war going on and the poverty was in your face and far worse than anything I had ever seen in South Africa.'

'It never occurred to me that my father had worked in a civil war zone. What motivates people to work in these places?'

'I don't know about your father but, for me, there were three things: getting out of South Africa, I hated the politics, the apartheid; adventure, I was a young man and I wanted to see and do things that most young lads of my age would have no experience of; and then there was the money … It paid well. I guess a lot of that was danger money … but we never saw or heard any serious gunfire.'

'Serious? You mean there's … I don't know … casual gunfire?' She chuckled.

'Yes, sort of … The MPLA, that's the government army, had a barracks in town. They would often fire their AK–47s down the middle of the road after dark and we'd enjoy the tracer show while we supped our beers on the veranda. The civil war passed us by, as did the war with South Africa.'

'You couldn't have known that you'd be safe though, could you?' she asked.

'No, but we were young. We used to joke about mortality; it was like some abstract theoretical concept back then. Anyway, after I left, the civil war did reach the mining area and UNITA, the rebels, did capture some of the mining towns. I heard they took Mumbulo – that's where your father and I worked.'

Her slow head shake left me in little doubt that she thought we were mad. 'You said the civil war passed you by, but there must have been some effects of it?'

'Loads.' I told her that almost all supplies had had to be flown in; very little had come in by road. Angola's roads had been heavily land mined and any convoys that there were had to have a military escort. They were always getting ambushed or would run over land mines. Every item was ranked in priority and only absolute necessities ever made it in. Even diesel had been flown in. Mining equipment, food and booze had been top of the list so spares for cars, for example, had rarely made it. I told her how we had driven around in death traps, that my Land Rover had had no brakes, rubbish lights, and the tyres had been worn down to the canvas. 'It was all part of the fun of it,' I said.

'Some fun!' she chastised. 'Was that the cause of my father's accident? An un-roadworthy vehicle?'

'No, definitely not. He had a brand-new car; one of the few. It was a made-in-Mexico VW Beetle that came in on one of the convoys. The state of the cars had reached a crisis point – people couldn't do their jobs – they couldn't get about. So half-a-dozen VWs got bumped up the convoy list.'

'So, how come he got a new car, and you didn't?'

I ran my fingers through the greying vestiges of my hair, and chuckled. 'Because I was new back then. Your father was older and established. He was also someone the company would bend over backwards to please. He found them a lot of diamonds, made them a lot of money.'

'I'm pleased to hear that.' Her face lit up. 'But, back to your friendship; what changed between you on your second contract? A party or something?'

'No. We had some memorable parties … but it was a work situation that threw us together. It was right at the start of the contract.' I pointed at the notebook as though its title would validate everything I was about to say. I told her about the helicopter flight with Geoff Morgan and Thys Gerber, and how we'd landed at Cambunda so Geoff could take Thys to see the river diversion. 'The river diversion was your father's baby.'

'I understand babies, but river diversion?'

I explained that most of the diamonds mined in Angola were from alluvial deposits: riverbeds or former riverbeds. To mine the bottom of a river it's necessary first to dig a new course for it, then to redirect the flow before pumping out the original course. 'The pumping was just about finished with this one when Morgan went to see it with Thys – but it looked very unpromising. Morgan was furious – he got a bee in his bonnet that there was nothing in it. When he'd calmed down a bit, he ordered me to test the ore; put it through the plant, the next day.'

'And my father ...?'

'Morgan ordered him to do the test with me; as a penance for screwing up. I liked Morgan generally, but he had a nasty habit of rubbing people's noses in their mistakes.'

'Surely Morgan wasn't the only person to see the diversion. Did everyone think it was rubbish?'

I thought back to the previous night, to the last pages I'd read before going back to bed.

★★★

It was late afternoon when we landed at the helipad behind the mine offices in Mumbulo. I went to Geoff's office where I signed the mail bag over to his secretary. Thys then gave me a lift to the company house where I lived; it was known as 'the Madhouse' because it had the best courtyard for parties and often hosted them. The sun was setting, and it would be dark within half an hour. I didn't need my watch to know it was five-thirty p.m. give or take ten minutes.

The Portuguese had built Mumbulo on a grid. Two broad, mango tree-lined streets ran up the hill from the town's heart: the edifício público – the administration building – and the five-a-side football arena. A series of smaller streets linked with them every hundred metres or so. The houses in the main streets were all similar, built in the Portuguese colonial style. They were bungalows, set back about twenty metres from the road and all had five or six steps leading up from a path to a low-walled veranda. Each house had a spacious walled courtyard at the rear and small service roads ran behind the courtyards. The town had expanded over the years and the later additions deviated from the rigidity of the original footprint. The size and quality of the buildings also changed, deteriorating to shanty town dwellings, or bairros, as the locals called them, on the northern and western outskirts.

The mango trees lining the street provided a lush canopy and a profusion of pawpaw trees sprouted from improbable places, even from mortar courses in walls, softening the appearance of the town and lending it an untidy charm. Black and white goats were everywhere; they roamed where they liked, casually taking their pick of the choicest grass and the best viewpoints. One goat was standing on the veranda wall of the Madhouse as we pulled up and another was sprawling on the roof of the house next door. It was all good and familiar, but, although I was looking forward to getting back to work and seeing my colleagues again, my mood was subdued by the prospect of another six months before seeing home once more. It was a bit like a prison sentence except that it paid well. There were no cars parked in front of the house, so I guessed Carlos was still out at work. I went in, took a beer from the fridge, picked up a chair and went to relax on the veranda while I waited for my housemate to return.

I shared the Madhouse with Carlos Pereira, a mining engineer who looked after the mines north of Mumbulo, in the Nocredo direction. We had become good friends and we often shared transport as vehicles were in short supply and we covered the same geographical area.

The sun had just about gone. It was six o'clock; and a steady flow of vehicles washed along the street as workers returned home. Finally, a familiar Land Rover pulled up and Carlos bounded up to the veranda to greet me. Although he was Portuguese, his English was virtually faultless.

'The wanderer returns,' he said. 'It's good to have you back. Good leave?' We shook hands and hugged warmly.

'I wish I could say I was glad to be back, but you know how it is. Leave was great. It was good to see my parents, and friends. I did lots of travelling, lots of drinking, and I blew lots of money ... How were things here?' I asked tentatively.

'Well, they were okay until today. I spent most of the day repairing the dams at the Txicaca diversion so the pumps could hold the level down. Then when we saw the bottom of Txicaca for the first time, it looked to be a total washout. Sand, sand and more sand; a bit gritty maybe – very few rocks, at least, not that I could see. Basically, it's been months of wasted time and money. If we have to mine it, the volume targets will be buggered – you can't mine what isn't there. It's a nightmare. Bloody river diversions.'

'Yup. Geoff dumped me at the Cambunda plant today while he went to show Txicaca off to that new security guy. They'd picked me up at Nocredo with the chopper. He was seething when he got back; I was glad Thys was there. He copped the worst of it. Geoff wants me to test the stuff with Jim Lodge at Cambunda tomorrow. I don't envy Jim when Geoff finds him. He'll be looking for a scapegoat. I think he's shitting himself about what he'll report to London as he's probably been making exaggerated claims to them.'

'I'll keep my head down, I think. Morgan's unpredictable when pissed off, to put it mildly.'

I shook my can; it was nearly empty. 'You want a beer?'

He nodded and I fetched a couple of cans from the fridge.

'Steve's been looking forward to your return,' said Carlos, as he clicked open his icy can. 'Dryden's had him running around like a headless chicken, looking after your area as well as the south.' Kevin Dryden was the Metallurgical Manager, my boss, and Steve Vernon's. 'Steve's knackered. I don't understand why Dryden doesn't help you guys; he just sits on his arse in his office all day.'

'I think he'd get lost. It's probably better that he stays in and does the paperwork; he can't do any harm there. It beats me though how he keeps busy without any field work to occupy him.' I wasn't looking forward to seeing Dryden again. He could ruin a good day just by being in it.

'What about Jim Lodge?' I said. 'You're a big mate of his. What's he like to work with? And how's he going to take this?'

'He's easy to work with, if a little secretive; but Txicaca? He won't take that well; he's used to getting things right. I've always thought he

*was infallible with diamonds but maybe he's just been lucky, and his
luck's just run out.'*

*We supped our beers steadily and chatted idly for a while about my
leave and what had happened on the mine while I'd been away. It was
how we unwound most evenings before we showered and tidied ourselves
ready for the mess and our evening meal.*

★★★

'So, Carlos agreed? He thought it was a dud too?' said Sophie.

'Very much so and he'd spent a lot more time than Morgan
had at the diversion – he built it and pumped it out.'

'I'm not sure I want to hear about this test. Maybe I'll feel
better after eating something; I'm starving. I was so excited this
morning, I hardly ate anything. Have you got anything I can
cook up for us? I didn't see anything much.'

'Sorry. I didn't think. We could either go out, or phone for a
takeaway. There's a good Indian just up the road and they generally deliver within forty-five minutes.'

'That sounds good.'

I got the menu from next to the phone, told her what I wanted and left her to sort it out while I went back to staring at the
cover of the notebook again. I had to read on; I'd already told her
everything I'd read. I didn't want another session of winging it,
where I was forced to rely on my memory, which I knew to be
heavily self-censored. What I'd told her about her father's death,
I suspected wasn't exactly true. It was the version of events I'd
convinced myself about at the time, but until I'd looked at those
pages with objective eyes – something I'd managed to put off for
nearly thirty years – I'd never worked out what truly happened.
And as for what Sophie should learn …

I sighed and opened the book where I'd folded over the corner
of a page. At least there would be a bit more about the development of my friendship with Lodge … I owed it to Jim to do my
best for Sophie; I wanted to bring him to life for her.

Chapter 4

Sophie seemed quite happy sorting out our dinner, even though she was on my territory. She was bright enough to realise that the more she took on, the more time I would have for reading the notebook and the more I would feel obliged to tell her.

'I've been thinking about what you were saying,' she said as she set some pots of pickle and a plate of poppadums on the table between us. 'My father got that diversion wrong didn't he?'

'Let's leave that until after we've eaten,' I said, cutting her short. I put the notebook to one side and spooned some lime pickle onto my plate. 'Do you fancy some wine?' I was hoping alcohol might blunt her senses.

'If it's red, yes please. White's too subtle for curry. Besides, I know there's no wine in the fridge, and warm white wine? Ugh, I don't think so.'

'I'll get a bottle. I've got some very quaffable Rioja.'

'Sounds good.'

I got up and fetched a bottle from the cupboard under the stairs, opened it and poured us a large glass each.

'This should loosen your tongue nicely for talking about my father,' she joked. We each had very different hopes. 'To my father.' She raised her glass.

I hesitated then responded, 'To Jim Lodge, a fine man, a good friend, and a brilliant geologist.'

'Brilliant? I don't understand these mixed messages.'

'Your father was a great geologist, the best I ever met when it came to diamonds. He'd been in Mumbulo for about three years when I arrived, and the only reason he'd been sent there was to give it a final once-over before the mine was shut down. The powers-that-be had decided that it was no longer economic. He saved the mine. He re-examined everything, going through all the old sample data. He basically redrew the geological map with his estimates of the reserves, and he was right to do so. Single-handedly, he kept the whole Mumbulo mining area going. By the time I turned up, the area was back to being one of the company's top producers.'

'Thank you. That paints him in a much better light. At least it'll balance his failure a bit.'

'He was a clever blighter, but he could be difficult. A lot of people didn't like him or trust him because he was ...' I struggled for the right words, 'self-contained; he kept himself to himself.'

'Is that how you thought about him before you got to know him? Self-contained?'

'I guess so. I was a bit of a loner too – nowhere near as clever, of course. I felt fairly neutral about him. Our limited contacts gave me no reason to either like or dislike him. I can vaguely remember feeling a bit overawed, but that was his reputation not him. I think he was shy. Although he was very striking to look at, like you are, there was nothing flashy about him; he wasn't a show-off; but he did have something else – charisma maybe – people listened to him. That's why they built the Txicaca river diversion.'

'Did he have many friends?'

'He had a little group he socialised with. Until we got to know one another, I don't think I really registered with him at all. Geoff Morgan, Chris Howard – the Chief Engineer, and my house mate, Carlos Pereira, were his usual companions, but they'd all been in Mumbulo much longer than I had. He was also friendly with the Portuguese doctor, Maria.'

We finished our poppadums then I fetched in the main courses which we enjoyed in silence; both of us marshalling our thoughts.

'So!' she said when we had finished and cleared the table. 'You talked him up before. Now tell me more about the river diversion. Is that where your friendship grew from?' She took a swig of Rioja.

'Okay,' I began. 'We did that test the next day, the day after I got back. I went to the mine offices early and I found your father in his office, ready to go. I picked up what I needed from my office, which wasn't much: a notebook, a pen and calculator, then we set off for the Cambunda plant where I knew Armando – he was my plant foreman – would have started preparations ready for us.'

★★★

It was one of those wonderfully cool, fresh mornings that always seemed to follow overnight rain in Angola. It was the best time of the day; in an hour or two it would be hot, and the road would be dry and dusty. We were in Lodge's VW and he was driving. He was focused on the road, which made a pleasant change from Carlos Pereira, my usual companion, who detected potholes and ruts by feel. Lodge avoided the avoidable and minimised the impact of the unavoidable.

I really wanted to discuss what we had to do, but I felt nervous. The intensity of Lodge's concentration created an intimidating psychological barrier between us. I was in awe of his reputation and conscious that I had yet to establish my own. I was reluctant to break the silence.

I allowed my eyes and my mind to wander and I began to enjoy the scenery and the wildlife: the rolling scrubland, the river and the birds.

'So, what's the plan?' Lodge's question caught me off guard.

'For the test?' I immediately felt like an idiot.

'What else?' He laughed.

'We've got a procedure. Sterilise the plant, treat a known volume of test material then sterilise again. If we do it carefully, we can be sure which diamonds came from the test material.'

'How do you do the sterilisation?'

'We chuck loads of waste through the plant to flush out any diamonds still in there from the previous ore. Fifty or sixty cubic metres should be ample. Then we empty all the gravel bins of course. I've arranged for Chris to send one of his fitters out to give the plant a mechanical check before we start.'

'Okay. And security?' Lodge asked.

'I spoke to Morgan and Thys last night and Thys's organised for us to have two extra security guys: an Angolan and an expat. They'll ride shotgun on the ore trucks and ...'

'Mining's only going to send us one truckload,' he interrupted. 'I thought Morgan was going to take a swing at me when he barged into my office late yesterday. I just ignored him and let him rant on till he ran out of steam and stormed out. The "one" truck was his parting shot.' He turned towards me briefly and I was surprised to see that he was grinning.

'It'll be a nice quick test then,' I said. 'Only one truck … We might as well tip it straight into the feed hopper. That way we won't get any contamination from the stockpile through double-handling.'

'Good thinking.' Lodge nodded enthusiastically. I was bemused; I was more nervous than he seemed to be, yet it was his reputation not mine that was about to be tested.

'We'll send the gravel to the concentrator,' I continued, 'and run it through as a batch tomorrow morning. Then we'll batch-treat the concentrate at the sort house. We should have a result by close of play tomorrow.'

'It takes a while but I guess that's normal,' he said. 'Expecting any problems?'

'There are always problems. Every ore's different. Some have too many big rocks, some – too much clay, too much sand, not enough stones to break up the clays in the scrubber… the list's endless. I'm guessing that today's little challenge will be sand.'

We both laughed.

When we arrived at Cambunda, Armando was with the fitter checking the conveyor belts and screens, ensuring they were in good mechanical order. He gave a thumbs-up to indicate that all was well, and I gestured that we should get started. The loader went to a pile of waste material and began loading it into the feed hopper to begin the sterilisation. Lodge took over the monitor gun from the operator for a few minutes. He was like a child with a toy. He appeared fascinated by the power of the high-pressure water jet; how it could shift huge rocks and break up sticky clods of clay before blasting it all through the protective screen, the 'grizzly', into the scrubber below. I think he saw it like accelerated geology.

When we had treated about fifty cubic metres Lodge radioed the mine to tell them we would be ready for the test material in twenty to thirty minutes.

Half an hour later a dump truck slowly grumbled into the feed area of the plant. Armando held up his hand to stop the driver, and then climbed up to speak to him. The truck manoeuvred so that it could tip directly into the hopper where Lodge and I were watching with interest. The tipper slowly raised; the load was sand. There were some large rocks, and I could see some smaller stones, but I was left with an impression of sand.

I looked at Lodge, then chose my words carefully. 'This looks bad for the pumps. Everything'll go straight through with the water. We'll have to treat it very carefully or the pipes will block.' I looked for Armando, but he was already waving at the monitor gun operator to control the feeding.

Armando and I left Lodge at the hopper and we climbed down the steps, from the top of the plant to its processing levels, to check how much gravel was coming through. The pre-treatment of diamond-bearing river material is a simple process using vibrating screens, giant sieves, to separate the gravel from big rocks and from sand. I was fascinated by screens; I had always found them mesmerising. Stones and rocks bounce around in seemingly random ways before either disappearing through the mesh or going onto one of the gravel conveyors. I always tried to spot a diamond, but I never had. The sheer volume of stones, the mist from the water sprays and the constant up, down and forward movement made it very difficult.

Suddenly, the noise changed. The conveyors lost momentum and stopped. The regular rhythm of the screens changed to malarial convulsions before giving a final agonized jerk and coming to rest. Armando was shouting and getting information. A tell-tale wisp of smoke wafted up from the motor of the main conveyor belt and the electrical interlocks had stopped everything else.

I took a last glance at the screen before going to look at the problem. The shock was like a punch to the solar plexus. I struggled to breathe properly, and Armando just gawped. After what felt like an age, I regained some control and tapped Armando on the shoulder. 'Armando. Nobody's to go near that conveyor belt until we have security in place.' He nodded then shouted and waved his workers away from the conveyor.

I looked around for Lodge – he was still up by the feed hopper. I waved furiously for him to come down. He placed his hands on the handrails of the steps and slid gracefully down to where Armando and I were struggling to come to terms with what we were seeing. To see one diamond on a screen was rare, but here there were tens of them, mainly small, but some larger ones. Lodge grinned broadly; his hair blazed in the bright morning sun. I stared at him. 'You're not even surprised,' I said, shaking my head, 'you knew.'

He shrugged. 'I didn't know. I couldn't. But yes, I expected something.'

We called over two extra security men and we devised a plan to get the conveyor motor changed with the maximum possible speed and security.

When everything was arranged, I climbed back to the top of the plant where I knew I would be able to get a decent signal on my walkie-talkie. I called Morgan, Carlos Pereira and Thys Gerber, and asked them to come to the Cambunda plant as there was an issue that required their attention.

We never referred to diamonds on the radio, but everyone knew what Lodge and I were doing at Cambunda that morning. No one would be in any doubt that the diversion material was the 'issue'.

Morgan was livid when he arrived; his face was distorted with restrained anger – ready to explode. He stumbled down the steps then stopped to get his breath back; his finger pointing at Lodge, the focus of his rage.

I stepped between them and deflected Morgan's eyes towards the screen. His anger dissipated in an instant. After staring in awe for a good half-minute or so, he turned to Lodge and said, 'You, Jim, are a fucking genius,' with a huge grin on his face.

Lodge said nothing.

Morgan turned to me and asked, 'So, Boyo, what's the issue then?'

'Issues, plural,' I said. 'The first's in hand; the motor repair, but I need to know what to do with the gravel and I would imagine there are security issues at the diversion itself.'

'What's the problem with the gravel?'

'I think we should send it straight to the sort house as it looks a lot richer than any concentrate I've ever seen from the concentrator. Dryden'll never authorise it though if it's my suggestion.'

'Just do it,' Morgan said. 'Never mind Kevin, I'll clear it with him. Do what you think's right.' Morgan had his faults, but he was decisive and would trust the judgement of others and offer his backing. He would rant and rave if you got it wrong, but if you had him on your side, he was your best ally.

***

'So, my father was right.' Sophie hit my arm with a playful punch. 'You could have told me at the start. You've been toying with me, making me doubt him; making me think he screwed up.'

'Not really. It's just how everyone who saw the river diversion assessed it. You went along with it. You kept saying he was wrong. You never questioned it, and you're his daughter.'

'Very funny.' Her face told a different story.

'Sorry. It's not a joke, but I did want you to see how easy it is to get hooked into a point of view with the potential to destroy a reputation.'

'But you only gave me the one side ...'

'The same side everyone had. When they saw or heard about all that sand everyone forgot about his record, his successes.'

'So, it was a winner?'

'Oh yes. First impressions of Txicaca were soon forgotten. It was a tiny deposit, but it was so rich we only mined it sparingly to sweeten production at the end of each month. We did that for the rest of the time I was there and, I would guess, for a long time after that.'

Sophie was smiling broadly now, ecstatic that her father was still a hero. 'That still doesn't tell me much about the friendship between the two of you though.'

'I suppose not, but it's simple really. We just started talking to one another from then on, that was all, and we found we got on well and had a lot in common. I also granted him a favour; I took him into the sort house so he could help to pick the diamonds from the test; he'd never been in there before and he was interested to see how things were done. As a quid pro quo, he gave me a geological tour, including the Txicaca river diversion. We spent a lot of time with one another in the next few weeks. They turned out to be his last.'

Chapter 5

For once I was looking forward to going to the sort house. Normally I loathed, even dreaded, the place but I was carried along on the crest of Lodge's wave of enthusiasm. At the gate, I dealt with the bureaucracy for getting him a visitor's pass; then we went inside. The clang and thud of the door closing behind us was like a switch; Lodge's mood changed visibly. The sort house was a place that sounded good in conversation but in fact it was a dingy hellhole. It seemed to suck the ebullience out of Jim, like an austere poultice. There was no natural light, the place swarmed with flies and armed guards, and the atmosphere was oppressive: stagnant, hot and humid.

We passed through the second tier of security checks and I led Lodge to the changing room where we stripped naked under the CCTV cameras and donned the loose-fitting, pocket-less shirts and shorts that were the uniform for everyone with a hands-on role in the sort house.

'How can you work in here?' Lodge asked.

'I don't. I only come in when I have to: for the end-of-month production panic, the diamond exports and the routine checks that I do as rarely as I can get away with. The rest of the time, I'm out in the open like you.'

'You don't have quite the same freedom though. You're still on the plants; they're fixed locations. I have some tied responsibilities: mining blocks and river diversions, but most of the time I'm out in the bush; sometimes I just head off on a compass bearing. Tell you what; how about me giving you a tour around? Is Saturday okay with you? It'll be my pay back for this little treat.'

'Some treat,' I said, 'but yeah, you're on.'

I took him through the dismal labyrinth of corridors to the picking room.

'What's that din, David?' An irregular, staccato chattering like a misfiring machine gun echoed through the building.

'That's the x-ray sorters.'

'Blimey, they're a lot noisier than I expected.'

I told him that it was usually quieter; the rowdiness was because we were processing the Txicaca material. I explained that the sorters fired x-rays at the gravel, causing any diamonds to fluoresce. Sensors then detected the emitted light and fired compressed air at the source to blast everything around it into a concentrate bin – clever and remarkably effective. The amount of noise was proportional to the number of diamonds; the compressed air was firing almost constantly.

In the picking room I introduced Lodge to Diogo, the Chief Sorter, an Angolan who looked constantly amused. I explained to him that Lodge and I would be helping the pickers for an hour or so with the concentrate from the test. I liked Diogo. We had shared many a joke and kept one another going on long sessions through the night at the end of a month, getting every last stone into the production. I knew he would keep a close eye on Lodge and would speak out if he thought he was not up to the job. A bad picker meant more work for him as it was his job to check what the other pickers had finished with. On a good day, he would find nothing. I doubted Lodge would let the side down though.

The noise of the x-ray sorters stopped. Diogo nodded for three of the security guards to leave the room with him. They took two Angolan pickers with them and they returned a few minutes later lugging a concentrate bin, like a small milk churn. Diogo and one of the guards then unlocked the picking cabinet and lifted the bin inside before locking it again. The picking cabinet was a large glovebox; a long stainless-steel table isolated from the outside by a steel frame with Perspex windows. It had four pairs of holes along each side, a shoulder-width apart; each hole was fitted with an arm-length glove – a barrier between man and diamond.

Lodge and I sat side-by-side on steel stools and put our arms into the gloves. Diogo sat opposite me and opened the concentrate bin. He shovelled out a small quantity of gravel into an aluminium tray and slid it across to me, and then he did the same for Lodge and the five Angolan pickers who occupied the other stools.

I took a pair of tweezers and began to sort systematically through the stones in my tray, picking out any diamonds and dropping them into a stainless-steel beaker. I did a running commentary for Lodge's benefit and he was soon up to speed. He had started out worrying whether he would be able to distinguish a diamond from the rubbish but quickly learned that he could. Even the brownest, industrial-grade diamond has a quality that sets it apart from quartz and other shiny stones.

It took us less than an hour to pick all the stones from the test and the results were astounding. Lodge had recovered his excitement; he'd found four 'specials', diamonds weighing more than ten carats, and one of those was a beautiful, white octahedron with no obvious inclusions: it was just over 26 carats.

'We think we're lucky if we get two specials in a whole day,' I confided, 'but you picked four on your own, in an hour, and the rest of us found another thirteen. I'll be surprised if it's not a record for Mumbulo. It's certainly the best I've ever heard of.'

Even Morgan came to the sort house to watch me sizing, counting and weighing the stones. Before we left, I sealed them in a steel box, which Diogo and I, under the close supervision of three security guards, took down to the safe in the strong room. The picking room was oppressive, but the strong room only lacked shackles and blood stains to distinguish it from a dungeon; I was always glad to get out. Our production for the month up until then had been below target and we were going to struggle even to get close to it with only a few days left. This tiny volume of river material had yielded enough diamonds to take us well beyond our target and there were some big, beautiful stones in there too.

★★★

'How were the production targets set?' asked Sophie when I had finished recounting the sort house episode.

'They're related to selling prices inferred from historical data. As I remember, every mining area has an average price per carat based on the size, colour and clarity of the average stone from there. A ten-carat stone's worth much more than ten times that of a similar-quality one-carat stone.'

'So, something like Txicaca would really skew the targets if over-exploited?'

'You'd think so, wouldn't you? We got a beautiful ninety-carat stone once – that was from Txicaca – and it was worth a significant proportion of the value of the rest of the production; about 25,000 carats.'

'So, did the target change for the next month?'

I told her I couldn't remember, but I didn't think so. 'I certainly don't remember a production target ever going down.'

'Typical.' We both laughed.

We were quiet for a while, sipping our wine, quite relaxed in each other's company now. I reflected over my initial shock at seeing Sophie, with her uncanny likeness to Jim. I would have expected that spending some time with her and gaining familiarity with her character would provide her with a separate identity from Jim, and it had, but not completely. She not only had his looks, but she seemed also to have his intelligence, with her perceptive questioning and single-mindedness in getting the information she wanted. The fact that she was very obviously a woman was all that was stopping me from calling her Jim sometimes.

What more could I tell her with confidence? What was she thinking? What would she want to know? I was certain she would want to revisit her father's death – I knew I had not satisfied her on that. I decided to let my eyelids sag and feigned a yawn, hoping she would take the hint.

She leaned forward and tapped my arm to be sure I was not asleep. 'Who actually pronounced my father dead?' She stared at me as though she expected to see an imprint of her father's body on my retinae.

I felt the colour rise in my cheeks. 'The doctor,' I said.

'Did he do it there and then or …?'

'She,' I said. 'The doctor was a woman. Yes, she did it there. She arrived a few minutes after I did, and the others of course.'

'And she signed off what was written on that death certificate? "… injuries received in a road traffic accident"?'

'I doubt it. The documentation in Angola would have been in Portuguese. She, Maria, was Portuguese and she knew the circumstances at least as well as the rest of us did. No, I don't think she had anything to do with that.'

'Was she a competent doctor?'

'Very. She did a good stitching job on me once.' I rubbed my left eyebrow at the memory. 'And I know for certain that she saved the lives of Armando's wife and child.'

'Armando? The Angolan foreman?'

'Yes. His wife had problems with the birth of their baby boy. They would both have died without Maria. She had to perform an emergency caesarean in the surgery room at her house. She was as good as they come; your father thought so too. He was dead when she arrived. There was nothing she could do. They were friends; she would have saved him if she could.'

'Did anyone else check him before she arrived?'

I shrugged. 'What do you take us for?'

'I guess that did sound a bit off,' she smiled apologetically. 'I guess we're both tired. It's all been a bit weird, sort of surreal for me; bringing a father I never knew to life. And to death, I suppose.'

We agreed to leave it at that and arranged for her to come round again the following evening.

Chapter 6

'She's very attractive. Who is she?' Sophie enquired. She was holding a framed photograph she had taken down from the top of my bookcase. It was of a striking, auburn-haired woman.

'That's Rachel, my ex-wife,' I replied.

'I'm sorry. I hope you don't think I'm prying.'

'It's okay. We're still best friends. In fact, she's my boss at work.'

'Isn't that a bit awkward?'

'Not really. We always worked very well together and still do. Besides, it was Rachel who took me on at Flourish – she's always been my boss there. At home, she was in charge of the kitchen and I managed the shed: maintenance and stuff.' The state of the garden jarred my conscience. 'I've let it slip a bit lately, though,' I added lamely.

'Do you still love her?'

I did not answer. The truth was that I still wanted to love Rachel, but I wasn't sure that I ever really had. There should have been another face in that frame: one that haunted my dreams; the one who got away.

'Shall we get on with it?' I urged.

'All right, I can take a hint.' She replaced the photo then took a deep breath. 'I didn't sleep well last night. I was too excited: my imagination was more alive than I can ever remember. There was a man ... a ghost ... he had my face, my hair, and he had a beard. He was doing stuff with rocks: hitting them and breaking them; but it seemed like I was doing it. It was kind of weird, like a robotic game. I kept coming back to that nature or nurture question. How much of what I am was learned from mum and dad, and my upbringing, and how much is from my genes? I thought about how I do things: my thought processes and methods. I know about mum and dad, what their talents were, but I've no idea what my biological parents were good at, except for my father's geology. I had this strange feeling that I could just wander about in the bush, bashing rocks with a hammer, and find ore deposits. It's daft, but I need to know: was my father any good at languages?' She leaned forward, tensing visibly and I sensed she was searching my eyes. 'I must have got that from one of my biological parents because mum and dad, though they tried hard, never mastered anything other than English. I've always found languages easy.'

'Yes, his Portuguese was excellent,' I said, 'better than mine. To my ear he was almost fluent, and he also spoke a bit of the local tribal language, Chokwe. I always had a good relationship with the Angolans, but your father, because of the Chokwe, could always get closer to them. Portuguese was the colonial language; it was good for work, but it could also sometimes be a barrier. I reckon your father could have been a linguist if he'd chosen that route.'

She relaxed back into her chair. Her focus looked far away. 'Interesting,' she said eventually.

'You may have a lot in common with him, but I hope you never lay your hands on a geological hammer!' I joked. We both laughed. 'I do sometimes find it hard to look at you without seeing something of him, though. You were right about the beard, by the way. He often grew one. A lot of us did; easier than shaving when there's a dodgy water supply. As for how your father worked … I can't really comment because we didn't work together. His record: how he extended the life of Mumbulo, the river diversions … He was obviously doing something right, but I only ever saw him in action on a couple of occasions; once properly, when he showed me around, and told me a bit about the geology; the quid pro quo for the sort house trip.'

'Tell me about it anyway. You're the only source I've got.'

'To be honest, I wasn't really that keen to begin with, but Jim … your father was so enthusiastic I couldn't bring myself to disappoint him. Geology's one of those professions that's an extension of a hobby, a bit like being a professional sportsman. He had always loved rocks and could probably have made the gravel in my driveway sound interesting. I don't remember much of what he talked about now because it was so long ago. Also, a lot of it was quite technical and not my subject area.'

She looked at me eagerly; keen to hear anything that would augment the mental image she was building of her father.

★★★

The road was wet. Overnight rain had freshened the air, and the greenery was at its lushest. We were in Jim's VW again and he was driving. I chattered away blithely about my recent leave: telling him about my parents and friends, and how I had spent far too much money for no appreciable return on drunken escapades in expensive night clubs. Jim was quite happy to let me carry on, commenting politely and occasionally prompting for details. As he chuckled at one of my stories, I suddenly remembered that his last leave had been far more eventful than mine. I apologised for forgetting about his wedding and I asked him how it had gone.

He laughed. 'Don't worry. It was brilliant, thanks. Best thing I ever did. Gillian's ...' He sighed wistfully. 'It was only two months ago but it already feels like a lifetime.' He told me all about it and I have rarely seen anyone as happy as Jim was when talking about Gillian. His love for her was evident in every word.

'How did you meet her?' I asked when he had finished.

He chuckled at the memory. 'Pure chance; these things usually are, they tell me. I screwed up at Charles de Gaulle, after the UTA flight from here. I always set my watch to the time at my destination but, for some reason, I set it to London instead of Paris; it was an hour later than I thought. To cut a long story short, I was enjoying a coffee to kill the hour when I should have been boarding the plane. They paged my name and I had to run to the gate and board; they were holding the flight. When I went to my seat everyone was looking daggers at me for delaying them. Gillian had the seat next to mine. She gave me a proper ear lashing for being drunk and holding up the flight. You know how red I go; I can understand how she might have thought that.'

'And were you drunk?' I asked.

'Cold sober. I drink a lot here, but I give it a rest as soon as I leave camp. Anyway, we spent half the flight ignoring one another until she had to get up to go to the loo. Somehow, she got a bag strap tangled round the arm of my seat and we wound up laughing as it took rather longer to untangle it than it should have. We had one of those silly, very English bouts of mutual apologising when she returned to her seat: me for delaying the flight, and her for accusing me of being drunk. We both cracked up: I knew there and then that she was the one. I was going to hire a car and drive straight to my father's in Shropshire, but when she said she had to get a train to Darlington, for a connection to Whitby, I invented a friend in Middlesbrough and offered her a lift. When I finally owned up, somewhere on the A1, she told me she'd been wondering how long it would take me to come clean. I've never told her another lie; not even a white one.'

Neither of us spoke for a mile or so; each lost in our own thoughts. I envied Jim; he had found by chance what I had spent a fortune looking for without success. I guessed his thoughts were of Gillian.

'As you're in the business, I expect you know a little bit about diamonds,' he said, breaking the spell, 'but I'll start at the beginning anyway. They're pure carbon; their structure can only be produced at very high temperatures and pressure – conditions that exist in the Earth's mantle – they're brought to the surface by volcanic action. You find the primary ores, kimberlites, in volcanic pipes. Have you heard of Catoca?'

I nodded. 'I've heard the name, but beyond that ...'

'It's a small town a good way south of here, in Lunda Sul province, and it's the only place in Angola where they're actually mining kimberlite at the moment.'

I asked about kimberlite deposits near Mumbulo, as the diamonds we were mining had to have come to the surface somewhere. There were some, he told me, but no one had really investigated them as it was much easier to mine and process secondary ores.

'Kimberlite's a hard rock,' he explained. 'It's hard to mine and requires a lot of physical processing: crushing and milling, to release the diamonds. But with secondary ores, nature's already done that hard work; water and air have weathered, oxidised and broken up the rock. It's freed the diamonds for us. Then, over millions of years, the stones have been washed into the river systems and distributed along the riverbeds. If you understand rivers you can find secondary diamonds, and I think I understand rivers better than most.'

We talked about the possibility of mining kimberlite deposits in the future, but he assured me that it would never happen while the war was still going on. He pointed out that the crushers and mills we would need would require a lot of maintenance and we had enough problems getting spares to keep our current plant going; we were broken down most of the time. He was sure we would be mining alluvial diamonds for the foreseeable future.

'That said,' he winked. 'I do keep my eyes open for indications of kimberlite; purely academic, of course.'

'So, what are we actually going to see today?' I asked. 'No kimberlite, presumably.'

'Not knowingly,' he joked. 'I imagine you want to see Txicaca while there's still something to see; Carlos told me last night that they're about ready to pump water back in, to secure it. Hopefully, we'll get there before it's flooded, though. But there is another place, on the way, that I want to show you.'

The landscape – the hills, rocky outcrops, streams, even the vegetation – all took on a new life as we drove; I was getting an insight into the workings of a geologist's mind. When Jim talked about time, he didn't need a watch, he was dismissing centuries and millennia, as if they were seconds and minutes, and thinking in millions, even billions, of years. His love, and understanding, of rivers was obvious: his enthusiasm added credibility to every word of his explanation of how different rock types – whether hard or soft, water-soluble or insoluble – all contributed to the directional decision making of a river.

'What it boils down to is this,' he summarised. 'The river you see today is a very different beast from that of a million years ago, and even that would have been quite different from a million years before. The thing is: there are some sections that change more than others and I believe it's a combination of time and certain geological features that lead to higher concentrations of diamonds in some stretches of riverbed than others. I reckon the river course at Txicaca has been unchanged for just long enough to mop up a lot of diamonds, and its geology suggested to me the that it might contain plunge pools where denser materials, like diamonds, are likely to concentrate.'

He said he was investigating a couple of other possible diversion sites, but he still needed to check a few things before putting the wheels in motion.

'Anyway,' he continued; 'Diversions are only part of the story. We still get most of our diamonds from long-disappeared rivers and we need to dig bloody great holes to get at those. We're going to one of those now. We identify worthwhile areas, blocks, by digging trenches and drilling holes to get samples. Good sampling's essential or you can waste millions shifting topsoil and overburden for little return. When the samples point to a high probability of finding a decent number of stones, we demarcate the area as a mining block.'

He turned off the main mine road onto a track and stopped. 'This is interesting,' he said. 'We're only a short distance from Luomo Block 7; I'm going to show you how we found it.'

We got out and he led me along a narrow path into the scrub. We could hear the rumble of mining equipment operating nearby but we could not see anything; the view was obscured by thick scrubby vegetation. Very little grew taller than two or three metres, but it formed a good enough barrier to hide most things. The subtle, sweet smell of papaya drifted in from somewhere nearby and I licked my lips involuntarily. After about a hundred yards, the path opened out into a clearing pitted by holes, which looked as though they had been dug using hand tools. I waited for an explanation: I was confused.

'It was a garimpeiro mine,' he said. 'They'd been working here illegally for years until security cleared them out. I guess you could say they did my work for me.'

'Compensation?' I asked.

'No. Company policy's that they're working illegally on our, or more accurately, government property. Personally, I would pay them. They've probably saved us a lot more in prospecting and sampling costs than they've ever made from diamonds.'

'Has anyone ever suggested it? Surely, it would ease the tensions between us and the garimpeiros.'

'I did once, ages ago, but the company takes a hard line on it – they don't want to set any precedents. There's no chance.'

We walked on for another fifty yards to where the ground opened out into an open cast mine. Jim pointed out the characteristics of the ore deposit to me, but I was distracted; keen to get to the Txicaca river diversion. Besides, I had been to this sort of mine many times before, when sharing transport with Carlos Pereira. Jim did his best to make it sound exciting but my interest in geology had hit its limit.

I watched an excavator at the bottom of the pit load a couple of trucks while Jim went to speak to the block geologist who was sheltering from the sun under a canvas awning. When he had finished, we went back to the car and headed off to Txicaca. I had never seen it close-up before.

Jim drove us as close to the newly pumped-out channel as possible then we got out and walked. The mining department had built two small dams across the channel either side of a series of sand-filled troughs. We could see water gushing in from two large-diameter steel pipes. Geoff Morgan and Thys Gerber had decided that the best way to secure the diamonds in situ was to hide them under water. The mine had production targets both for ore treatment and for carat production. It would have been easy to mine all the ore from Txicaca in a few days but that would have upset the balance of the mine's production and shortened the overall life of the mine. The strategy was to use Txicaca as a sweetener, to make up any carat shortfall at the end of each month.

'We'd better be quick if we're going to see anything before the water covers it,' said Jim. Water was already running into one of the troughs, a plunge pool, in the bedrock, but we could still see the sands and gravels.

Jim drew my attention to the far bank and pointed out some exposed rock strata there; I could see that the rocks were folded. He told me how he had extrapolated that formation into the river and deduced that some soft rocks would have been exposed to the scouring effect of the flow. This would create plunge pools: perfect concentration features for diamonds.

'As you can see,' said Jim. 'There's no great science or secret to finding sections of river suitable for diversion, just observation and imagination.'

We watched until the water obscured the Txicaca treasure then Jim checked his watch and pointed towards the car. He wanted to take a quick look at something on the way back to town, on a stretch of road overlooking the river.

★★★

'That's about it.' I suppressed an involuntary shudder. 'We went back to town and normal life resumed.'

Sophie made a pensive clicking noise with her tongue. 'Do you remember any of the other geologists?' She scanned my eyes as though expecting to see names and addresses there. 'People who worked with him. Knew how he operated?'

I shook my head. 'Your father's team were all Portuguese, I think. There were three or four of them. It took me long enough to get to know your father, and he was English; I never really made the effort with the rest of his team. Most of us spoke decent Portuguese at work but we preferred to relax in English.'

She clicked her tongue again. 'Damn! Is there anyone else who would know these geologists, or who worked closely with my father?'

'The miners, I guess, Geoff Morgan and Carlos Pereira. There was another mining engineer, a Portuguese man, who looked after the southern area, but I can't remember his name – again, I didn't get to know him.'

'What was so different about Carlos? Surely he was Portuguese.'

'True, but he spoke English like a native speaker, and he preferred to socialise with us. Not only that, but he also lived in a Brit house, we shared the Madhouse.'

'Where's he now then?' she asked. 'Do you still keep in touch?'

'We did for several years but … we lapsed. He was teaching English in Porto the last I heard. That's at least ten years ago; probably nearer twenty.'

'And Morgan?'

'Not since the day I left.'

'This is all a bit disappointing,' she muttered. 'I had hoped you'd remember a bit more about them.'

'I'm sorry if you feel let down,' I bristled, 'but your expectations seem somewhat unrealistic to me. What do you remember from thirty years ago?'

'That's not fair; I wasn't even born.'

I smiled. 'And it was like a different life for me too.'

'Sorry, you're right,' she said, 'I'm being unreasonable. His accident ... Can you tell me about that again please, David? We've dipped in and out of it a couple of times without really covering the full story.'

Her habit of changing subjects caught me off guard again and I found myself trapped.

'As I understand it,' she said. 'He was driving back to Mumbulo after a party in Nocredo when he hit a pedestrian on the mine road.'

'That's right.'

'Then some guy, a few minutes behind, found him having a row with a crowd of Angolans, whilst trying to help the man he'd hit. This guy then drove on to your house to get help, and you went out with your friends to see what you could do.'

'That's about it. The guy was Kevin Dryden, my boss, by the way. We found your father's body. His car had been pushed over the edge of the road into the river.'

'You said you thought he'd been stoned. Why was that again?'

'Dryden said something about it and there were rocks with blood on them around his body.' I closed my eyes, trying to shut out the image, but it only served to sharpen it. I shuddered.

'Who else was there, at the scene of the accident?' she asked, clicking a ballpoint pen, and opening a notebook from her handbag.

'It's a long time,' I said.

'That excuse is getting a bit stale. I don't expect you to remember everyone but I'm willing to bet you remember most of them.'

'I can remember a fair few. I'll do my best,' I said. 'We were the first to get there: me and Carlos Pereira. Then another Land Rover with a couple of security guys arrived just after us. The security guys had guns; they checked around and secured the area. Morgan pitched up a few minutes later; I think Thys Gerber and maybe the doctor were with him. There were some others there too, but I couldn't swear to their names. I do know that Kevin Dryden wasn't there though; he stayed behind in Mumbulo.'

'Do you keep in touch with any of them? I know about Morgan and Carlos, but Thys and the other security guys? What were their names, by the way?'

'I can't remember. Er, one was Colin something but the other … I don't know, and I was never that close to Thys. We got on okay, but we had little in common.'

'And the doctor? Did you keep up contact?'

I shook my head. 'No,' I muttered.

'So, after you left, you pretty much cut yourself off from your friends? It sounded as though you and Morgan got on okay. Why didn't you keep in touch with him? He was the Mine Manager, perfect if you ever needed a reference for another job. Why lose contact with him? It only takes a Christmas card.'

'I had a falling-out with him; a difference of opinion on something, and neither of us would give way. There could only be one winner, and he was the boss. I left at the end of that six-month tour; I've never been back. My last few months were pretty miserable, and I couldn't wait to leave.'

'What did you fall out about that made such a difference? It must have been pretty major.'

'Much ado about nothing,' I said. 'I can't really remember. We were both stubborn and I guess we just came to an impasse over whatever it was.'

Sophie did not look convinced. 'Really?' she pushed. Her face was tense with anticipation but there was also a familiar half-smile; just like her father's when he'd been winning an argument.

My problem was that I still did not know what the grim truth was that I was protecting us from. I had forced myself to finish reading my notes after Sophie had left me the previous evening. There were some nasty details that I did not want to tell her, but there was nothing to worry me. Whatever it was that was bothering me, there was no record of it. Was it just my imagination?

She started again. 'Yesterday, you said that there was something about the way my father's body was arranged … or something to that effect … that made you sure that the man he had hit had died. Is that what you're not telling me?'

'Your father was stoned to death. I'm sure of that, and the Angolans wouldn't have killed him if he hadn't killed the other man.'

'I'm sure you were about to tell me something else, though, yesterday.'

I shrugged. I was not prepared to go any further.

'All right,' she said. 'What happened to my father's body after you found it and the doctor had finished with him?'

'We took him back to the garage at the back of the doctor's house in Mumbulo, in the back of the Land Rover. The doctor laid him out and cleaned him up before we sealed him in the lead-lined coffin that was kept for repatriating dead expatriates. We had a memorial service at the church in Mumbulo the next day, then we; Carlos and I, I think – drove the coffin to the Nocredo airstrip. I helped to carry him onto the Hercules, and he was flown to Luanda; then he was taken back to England for burial.'

'That's not quite what I meant. I could guess most of that, but was there an investigation? Was anyone caught? Was there even a crime under Angolan law?'

'There was an investigation … allegedly. And some people were punished for their alleged part in it.'

'Wow! You really didn't believe it did you? Allegedly, alleged … Why not? Did you have other evidence? Did you share it with the investigation?'

'No. I was unaware of any investigation until after the so-called sentence had been meted out. No one ever questioned me or asked my opinion. It wasn't thorough and I'm sure they punished the wrong people.'

'Is this what you fell out with Morgan over?'

I didn't need to say anything. She could see from my reaction that she was right. 'So, how did you know they'd got it wrong? Did you know who really did it?'

'No, but I know who didn't do it, someone I would have trusted with my life.'

'Give me a clue.'

'Armando.'

'The plant foreman? Why would you trust him above those who did the investigation? Did they think he killed my father?'

'No, they didn't,' I said.

'Now I'm really confused.'

'I don't think the investigation found anything. The mine management, including Morgan, and the authorities – the police and the community leaders – all wanted the case closed. I think they just made up something vaguely plausible, doled out the retribution and drew a line under it.'

'Wow! That's a pretty serious allegation. I assume you had evidence, or was it just Armando's word? You never said why you trusted him so much, anyway.'

'That's my business,' I said, 'but he is central to it.'

Sophie looked away; I could tell she wanted to lay into me for not giving her the full story, but she was holding herself in check. I felt remorseful.

'All right, it was like this,' I started. 'It was a Sunday morning. I was lying in. It was my only day off in the week.'

'When was this?' she asked – 'How long after my father was killed?'

'A month, six weeks, maybe. I'm not absolutely sure.'

'Quite a while though; enough time for the investigation.'

I gave a derisive snort before carrying on. 'I think it was about ten when the doorbell rang. I hoped Carlos would answer it, but he didn't so I had to get up.'

★★★

The front door of the Madhouse was a mosaic of glass and boarded-up panes but there was enough glass for me to see that it was Armando ringing the bell. It was only the second time he had ever been to my house; the first was after the birth of his child. I was concerned that something had happened to his wife or the baby, so I opened up without hesitation.

The blow caught me under the chin and sent me reeling backwards, with surprise as much as the power, onto one of the rickety, wood-framed armchairs. He came at me and dragged me to my feet before pounding my stomach and ribs with a barrage of punches. When I finally managed to grab his hands to stop him, he subsided to the floor, sobbing. I was angry, hurting and wanting revenge but I kept my self-control. I held his arms behind his back and waited for him to recover his composure.

'What did I do to deserve that?' I asked angrily. The words were a bit slurred as I had bitten my tongue when he hit me on the chin. It was bleeding and felt swollen.

'Don't pretend you don't know. You must know. Everyone was there. You let them do it!'

'You're not making any sense. Do what? What are you talking about? Is it Esther? The baby?'

'It's the village ....' he said. He was staring intently into my eyes. 'You don't know do you?' He had seen the truth. 'I'm so sorry.' The tension fell away from his body and I released his arms. He slumped onto the floor.

'You'd better tell me what happened,' I said. I moved to sit on one of the chairs, checking for injuries as I sat down. My chin was sore, and my tongue was going to be a problem for a few days.

He told how he had been woken early that morning by the sound of a megaphone.

★★★

It had taken Armando a while to come to his senses; the village was often noisy, but this was beyond the ordinary. In addition to the megaphone there was a deep rumbling noise that seemed familiar in a different context. He did not recognise it at first. Esther and their baby slept on; night feeding set its own schedule. He got up and threw on a shirt and shorts before going out to investigate. The bare earth was cold under his feet.

Men, women and children were looking out from other huts. Some were running around, shouting and screaming. Nothing made any sense. Armando felt dazed. He rubbed his eyes, trying to focus. He was picking up signals, but they were foreign, beyond his experience and expectation.

What he saw made even less sense than what he had heard. There was a crowd of armed men walking slowly towards the centre of the village. Some were wearing police uniforms. They were followed by what looked like two D9 bulldozers. What was happening, and why? His ears were getting used to the din and he started to filter out the village noise to make out what the megaphone was saying. He heard the message once then listened harder as it was repeated; he must have misheard it.

'This is the police,' it began. 'We have investigated the murder of the British geologist and we know the killers live here, in this village. You have fifteen minutes to hand them over or action will be taken against all of you; the village will be flattened. This action will be carried out by the army, assisted by the mining company.' The message was repeated every minute. Time was counting down.

All around, parents had started collecting their children and their possessions and abandoning their homes for the bush. It was a very tight community with many family linkages. There were no big secrets here. If anyone here had killed James Lodge, Armando was sure he would know who it was. He had to explain.

He walked towards the advancing army.

'Stop there!' The megaphone boomed. Armando was twenty metres from them; several rifles were pointed at his chest.

'Do you have any information about the murderers?' The man's uniform had gold braid and polished buttons. Armando had little doubt that this was the man in charge.

'Sim,' said Armando. 'Yes, this is a mistake. Nobody ...'

The policeman cut him off. 'Do you know who killed the geologist?'

'Não, não sei. Nobody ...'

'You're wasting time. We know the murderers are here.' The policeman looked at his watch and raised the megaphone to his mouth again. 'The clock is running. You now have twelve minutes.'

Armando held his ground. He could see Geoff Morgan and some other senior mine personnel standing at the back of the group.

'Senhor Morgan,' he shouted, 'you know me ...'

Again, the policeman interrupted. 'If you work on the mine you have two reasons to hand the culprits over: to keep your home and to keep your job. Think about it.'

Armando could feel tears of frustration building. He turned and walked back to his home. When he got there, Esther was up. She flung her arms around him. She was frightened but she was resilient like most Angolans. Civil war had affected everyone in the country. This was not a new experience; it was just another sorry chapter that had to be endured. She had already got the baby and their few valuables together. They were ready to leave.

Esther picked up the baby, and Armando loaded himself with baggage and cooking pots, then they joined the exodus to the periphery of the village where they sat in shock and watched what happened.

The operation took less than fifteen minutes. The bulldozers moved forward, twenty metres apart, and steered a parallel course through the village with a heavy steel chain strung between them. The unfired mud-and-straw brick constructions offered little resistance to the might of the diesel-powered monsters and the huts that escaped their direct onslaught were toppled and smashed by the chains. A litter of broken adobe, thatch, wood and mutilated corrugated iron marked the site. Nothing there would ever be used again.

The bulldozers withdrew to their low loaders to be taken back to the mines. The security force kept watch until all was clear, then they all disappeared in a convoy of Land Rovers.

★★★

I was flabbergasted. 'Jesus! I don't know what to say. I honestly had no idea, but I promise you this; if I had, I would have argued. It would probably still have happened, but I would have warned you.'

'That'll be why you weren't told,' said Armando.

I had thought myself to be part of the inner circle, especially after Txicaca. It was a shock to realise that I wasn't trusted.

'So, what will you do now, Armando? Where will you go? What about Esther and the baby?'

'I don't know. I've been sacked. I'll have to find some other way to make a living.'

★★★

'What happened to Armando after that?' Sophie asked when I had finished telling the story.

'I don't know. I never saw him again. I don't know where he went or what he did. I did make some enquiries in the surrounding villages, but nobody seemed to know of him.'

'You've got a pretty poor record for keeping in touch with people, haven't you? If I ever wanted to talk to Armando, how would I find him?' asked Sophie.

'I haven't the foggiest. He might even be dead by now.' I felt sickened by the thought. 'Life expectancy was extremely low; the civil war further intensified; and the AIDS epidemic ...'

'I'll have to go to Angola myself at this rate,' she said. 'What happened after that anyway? What did Morgan have to say about it? Surely he must have told you what evidence they had.'

'I was so angry I could hardly speak. I remember opening a bottle of scotch and swigging a good proportion of it down. I didn't want my anger to subside, but I also didn't want my nerve to go when I faced up to them.'

'So, you had a showdown? I don't mean to offend, but you don't strike me as the "showdown" kind,' she chuckled. 'This I must hear.'

I told her how I had walked the long way round to Morgan's house, getting my ideas organised and building up a head of steam. Everyone would be there as he had a regular Sunday morning social fixture.

★★★

I could hear voices drifting over the wall from Morgan's courtyard; happy, excited voices. The talk was loud enough for me to hear that it was about the clearing of the village. They obviously considered the operation to have been a success.

I checked the time. It was after eleven-thirty. I was later than usual thanks to Armando's visit and the time I had taken mulling over what he had told me. Morgan's front door was open as always. I walked in and picked up an armful of beer cans from the fridge – old habits die hard – before going to the courtyard door. I stopped and surveyed the scene. People stood around talking, drinking, and enjoying themselves. I knew everybody there, but now they seemed like strangers. Didn't they know what had happened that morning? Of course, they did – it was the only subject of conversation. They all seemed happy that suitable punishment

69

had been administered for what happened to Jim Lodge. Justice had been done and they could get on with their lives.

Morgan was talking to Kevin Dryden. They made a strange pair: Morgan was short and powerfully built, and Dryden towered and swayed like a flimsy flagpole over him. As I walked over to them, Dryden's shadow seemed to pass through me like a spear.

'Bom dia, Boyo. You're a bit late today,' said Morgan, in high spirits.

'I didn't get up as early as you this morning.'

'Ah! You've heard then. Have a beer – great, you've brought some out. We're just celebrating a job well done; a satisfactory outcome. We got even with the bastards.'

'What?' My voice was shrill with anger and disbelief. 'Is that really the way you see it?'

'Of course. The police from Nocredo investigated Jim's murder and we acted together on their conclusions.'

'Which were?'

'That the killers came from that village. We gave the village the chance to surrender the killers. They chose not to, so we ploughed it into the ground as we told them we would.'

'What if the killers weren't from there? Have you thought about that? Armando came to see me this morning. He lived in that village. He assured me that the killers weren't from there. He would know.'

'Armando, always bloody Armando with you. You seem to think the sun shines out his scrawny arse. Well, he got what he deserved.'

'Armando's fired,' Dryden cut in. 'I don't want to hear of him anywhere near any of our plants ever again. He's guilty by association at the very least.'

'He's not guilty of anything!' I shouted. 'What's the evidence?'

'It's all in a confidential report, but the investigation was thorough,' said Morgan.

'So, why wasn't I questioned? Or Carlos? We were the first to arrive at the body.'

'Because you didn't see what happened. Kevin was questioned,' Morgan waved at a nodding Dryden, 'because he saw Jim being stoned.'

'So, you recognised the killers, did you?' I stared up at Dryden's eyes. His expression was as close to hatred as any I had ever seen directed at me.

70

Morgan answered for him. 'Kevin was able to supply some useful information which, with other evidence, pointed at that village.'

'So, what is this other evidence? That it's the nearest village to where the body was found? You'd have your next-door neighbour arrested if you were burgled?'

'It's more than that, but I can't tell you. If it becomes public, it'll be obvious where the information came from and there would be personal safety issues. You have to take my word for it. Trust me.'

'I'm not sure I can do that. "Personal safety issues" is a bit bloody convenient.'

Everybody in the courtyard had gathered round to listen. 'Come on David,' someone shouted, 'just accept it that the case is closed and get on with your life.'

'That's right,' said Morgan. 'We've no room for conspiracy theories here. It's too small a community. It can't be tolerated. I know you're upset. I suggest you go away and think about it and we'll have another talk when you've calmed down.'

'Yes, when you've calmed down, we can start talking about your next contract.' This was Dryden; his implication was clear.

'Piss off, Dryden! What you bastards did this morning was fucking barbaric. Medieval! I thought we were civilised. Even if someone there was guilty, it's still no reason to bulldoze the whole village into the ground.'

'Steady on!' It was Morgan again. 'They're all guilty. If they don't hand over the killers, they're guilty themselves, by association. And we've dealt with them once and for all.'

'And another thing,' I said, 'how come everyone seemed to know what you were going to do except me? Why was I left in the dark? You talk about conspiracy theories, but …'

'I think you've just answered that one,' said Morgan. 'We knew you'd warn Armando.'

I was lost for words.

I picked up a can of beer and downed it in one. That was better. 'Dryden, there'll be a letter on your desk in the morning.'

***

71

'You resigned?'

'I completed my tour, but I never went back. It was the longest three months of my life. I was a pariah. It was all right during work hours; everyone was professional. But after work, I was ignored. It would have been unbearable except for ...'

'Except for what?'

'It's not important. I kept myself amused.'

'So, who do you think killed my father?'

'I really don't know. But I'm sure in my own mind that no one from Armando's village had anything to do with it. I trusted Armando and I don't believe he would have lied to me.'

'Maybe he just didn't know.'

'I'm sure he would have. I think it would've been virtually impossible to keep a secret in that village. You couldn't break wind without everyone knowing.'

'Do you know what happened to Morgan and Dryden? Where they went? Are they still alive, even? I want to talk to them.'

'I've no idea. If I see either of them again, I doubt we'll share a drink. You'll be on your own if you go looking for them.'

PART 2

Chapter 7

I recognised the caller's voice without the need for introduction; the tone and the trace of Durham were unmistakeable. I quickly forgot my irritation at the disturbance; the funding proposals could wait. It was several months since we had last spoken. Sophie had phoned my home a few times in the couple of weeks after she went back to Cambridge, but nothing recently. I had thought about her often, but I was beginning to think she had exhausted me as a source of information. Maybe, she had shifted her focus to her mother's life; I knew she intended to explore that too.

'I want to go to Angola,' she said when we had finished the pleasantries, 'to see where my father died.'

'What?' My thoughts froze. I struggled to respond.

'I want to see where my father died,' she repeated.

'Yeah, I heard, but that's not going to be easy.' I felt sick, panicky. 'What is it you need from me? A map?'

'Not exactly. I want you to go with me, to show me; take me to the exact place where it happened.'

I laughed nervously. 'Angola's not a tourist destination … at least, not outside Luanda. You can't just walk into the mining areas; you need permits. And then there's transport …'

'I've thought of all that. We're going to work our passage.'

'You seem to be forgetting that I've got a job and I can't just leave it at the drop of a hat, much as I'd love to help you. I'm working on projects and funding applications now. Without those, I don't have a job. I can't do it.'

'Speak to Rachel,' she said.

'What's she got to do with it? What've you been up to? How do you know Rachel?' We had hardly mentioned Rachel in our earlier meetings.

'Just speak to her,' Sophie insisted.

She refused to be drawn, referring me to Rachel every time I tried to prise anything from her. Our conversation moved on to more general subjects, but her parting shot was that we would talk again soon. I guessed she must have phoned Rachel in the last day or so and suggested to her that we develop a project that would take us to Angola. I had to laugh because I knew Rachel; I could have told Sophie exactly how Rachel would react to the idea of me gallivanting around Angola on a nostalgia trip. I felt confident that I had nothing to worry about.

★★★

'Ah, the very person.' It was Rachel; her office door was open. I had to walk past it to get to Accounts, my destination. She smiled. 'Come in and sit down. I've got something to show you.' She waved a folder at me.

'What is it? I'm up to my neck in proposals and I need to discuss some budget details with Dave in Accounts. I can't really spare the time to vet other sections' stuff right now.'

'No. This is for you; call it a present. I've been approached by a social scientist from Cambridge, a Doctor Addison. She says she knows you and is keen to work with you. Must be mad,' she chuckled.

'Wwwhat? Is that a project proposal?' I realised I had underestimated Sophie.

'It's more than that. It's virtually a cert for funding ... from that new EU money-pot we were talking about, for building capacity in former war zones. It'll have to go through the full EU assessment, but she's been liaising closely with the Fund Director and she's got the nod that it'll be funded, provided she can get a credible mining expert to take responsibility for the technical aspects.'

I felt sick. 'It's in Angola isn't it?'

She nodded. 'So, she did talk to you ... as I suggested.'

I felt trapped. 'Only vaguely. How much is it for, and what's the time scale?'

'More than 300,000 euros over two years. You'd better read it; to my eye it's pretty damned good.' She brandished the folder again and I took it reluctantly. 'With minimal input from you, it'll secure your position for the next couple of years; stop your whinge-ing about writing proposals. Now, what was it you came in for?'

'Nothing. If you remember, I wasn't coming here, I was go-ing to Accounts. As a matter of interest, have you actually met Doctor Addison – Sophie?'

'Yes, we had dinner together last night after the interview.'

'Interview?'

'Yes. We had a vacancy for a social scientist. It's been open so long you've probably forgotten about it, or maybe you never no-ticed – it is social science after all. Besides, she's delightful. Just your type, I'd have thought. Don't tell me you object.'

'No, but …' I had mixed feelings. 'I assume you've taken her on.'

'She's seems perfect, almost too good to be true: qualifications, personality … She's committed and she can write a bloody good project proposal. She'll be on the usual probation of course, and there's the formality of references, but … she said she had a fam-ily connection with you.'

'That's stretching it a bit. I used to know her father. Anyway, when does she start?'

'In a couple of weeks, officially, but she's here now. We're cutting corners. She's having her induction now and she'll be working as a volunteer for the next two weeks, until she starts properly. I want you to spend time together on this proposal – I'm sure you'll like it as she's done your job for you; the part you don't like; you can't object.'

'But it's Angola …'

'What is it with you and Angola? You never talked to me about it, always changed the subject. You need to face up to whatever happened there and get over it. Work with her and work it out. It's a terrific proposal and it'll be a goer if you put your back into it. Think of the benefits; you're always preaching about how arti-sanal miners are neglected so don't duck a Godsent opportunity.'

I felt cornered. Angola seemed inevitable.

★★★

I slept badly that night. I'd read Sophie's proposal thoroughly several times, looking for that fatal flaw that would scupper it, but it was excellent; not perfect but as good as these things ever got with all the editing and compromising required to satisfy the donors. It was not only a very good idea, but it also fitted in closely with the EU's requirements. It was cleverly written too, showing that I was the only option as a technical advisor on mining issues. No one else that I knew of, or that she could find, could speak Portuguese or knew anything about diamond mining.

She had researched how the civil war in Angola had affected the north east of the country. She had identified the companies now operating the mines in the area and had found evidence of their intolerance of artisanal mining. The main aim of her project was very similar to many that I'd done before; working with mining companies and artisanal miners, finding ways to ease the conflict between them and enabling them to work together to benefit both sides. Sophie's project was unique for its focus on the effects of the civil war. Almost everyone had a gun, knew how to use it and would not hesitate to do so if given the slightest excuse. This had led to lawlessness and the mining companies were employing private armies to protect their workers and to flush out any groups perceived to be a threat. Although Angola's civil war was over, local conflicts, exacerbated by mine security forces, still threatened to trigger local battles, especially when the mines were owned indirectly by a government that was not to everybody's taste.

I dreaded going back to Angola, but I loved and valued my job. Sophie's proposal would secure that for another two years at least, but it required me to face up to my anxieties about the past. What was I to do? There was little choice; I would have to man up and go.

★★★

I am an early starter but when I entered the office Sophie was already sitting by my desk. She looked happy and her smile almost floored me; it was so like her father's.

'Welcome to Flourish,' I said. 'I see you've made yourself at home.' She had a mug of coffee parked on my coaster. 'At least you didn't nick my mug.'

'Sorry,' she said. 'I hope you don't mind me sitting here. The receptionist – I've so many names to learn – showed me to your desk.'

We talked about what we'd done since we last met and she told me how her proposal, *Diamonds for Good Not Blood; Rebuilding Confidence and Capacity in War-Ravaged Communities in North-Eastern Angola*, had been developed from a suggestion for further work she had made in her PhD thesis.

'Handy,' I said.

'Yes. My PhD focused on the loss of skills, capable people and infrastructure in the former Yugoslavian republics after the various civil wars there. A lot of the ideas are transferable, with minor tweaks, to most post-civil-war situations. You might not think it, but Africa has a lot in common with the Balkans: aggregates of mismatched parts, bubbling with feelings of resentment, injustice and the belief that some groups are lording it over others. The religions, languages and other cultural aspects are different in Angola, but the underlying principles are much the same.'

'I noticed your thesis was listed in the references, but I didn't check to see where it was cited, so I didn't quite twig the relationship. It does explain, though, why the proposal seems so well thought through. It's far better than most.'

'Thank you.' Her face lit up. 'You probably saw some of your own papers in the references too. They're very good too. It made the writing relatively easy once I'd found a suitable funding possibility.'

'You could give us all lessons. In general, we hate writing proposals, and the fundraising department has too much to do to give every proposal the time it really needs to maximise its chances.'

'I've learned from a lot of failures. I tried to get money for some research ideas after my PhD, but perhaps I wasn't as interested as I ought to have been and I guess it showed. I failed. This, on the other hand, had my full concentration and effort. Maybe that's why some ideas don't work. The author doesn't really believe in them.'

I nodded, thinking of some of the rambling, poorly argued efforts I had failed with in the past. She was at least partly right but I was keen to be seen to be adding value. 'There are one or two bits that aren't quite right; that need beefing up a bit. I've stuck in some post-its.' I passed her my copy of the proposal. 'There's not much, but I think it'll be better for the changes. See what you think.'

She forced a smile but said nothing. I sensed she wanted to rip into me but was too unsure of her position as yet. She did not take well to any hint that her work could be improved. If we continued to work together, I knew she wouldn't hold back if we had a similar discussion in the future.

'Don't worry, Sophie. It's excellent. It's only stuff you couldn't have known.'

'Don't patronise me. I researched it thoroughly and you're telling me I got some of it wrong. I don't do wrong.'

'That's a bit harsh. It really is just minor changes.' I hurriedly changed the subject. 'I ought to see if we can find you a desk. In the meantime, you can take that one.' I pointed to one just across the office. 'It's Janet's; she's the micro-credit expert, she's away for a couple of weeks in South America; Colombia I think.'

Sophie made herself at home at Janet's desk before settling down to work. I introduced her to the others in the office as they arrived; she was very amiable and fitted in well.

Rachel came in shortly after lunch and suggested that the three of us had dinner at her house that evening, if we were not too tired. We agreed on seven-thirty p.m. My ex-wife was as excellent at cooking as she was at almost everything else; we would be well fed. We were still close but there had been something destructive about our marriage; our relationship had become less productive than it had been before. We were both uncompromising in our work, but in our marriage we both compromised on virtually everything. As a result, neither of us ever did what we really wanted to do. I guess it is possible to try too hard.

★★★

It was still a mystery to me how Rachel performed her domestic miracles. She had worked a full day and she still managed to put an excellent three-course dinner on the table by seven-thirty.

We talked about Sophie's proposal as we ate, and Rachel and I recounted tales from projects that we had done together over the years. Sophie listened avidly and interrogated Rachel in depth about social baseline studies and stakeholder engagement. I had helped Rachel, and other social scientists, many times with workshops and questionnaires but this was not my territory. Although it was the most important aspect of Flourish's work, social science was always secondary to the technical issues for me. I think this was why Rachel and I worked so well together. We helped one another, but neither of us would interfere in the other's territory unless we spotted a glaring mistake.

We agreed that Rachel and I would do a final check on the proposal in the morning. I would then pass it on to the fundraising department for them to submit it to the EU. The final date for submission was still two weeks away but it always felt good to be early. The Fund Director had told Sophie that all proposals would be assessed in about six weeks and that he would give us official notification in about two months. He had also promised to call her if there was a problem. On the back of the positive feedback, he had already given Sophie, Rachel agreed to release an advance from Flourish's funds to enable us to start preliminary work, contacting organisations and ministries in Angola. The two women oozed enthusiasm, and, despite my fear, I felt excited at the prospect of getting the project started.

It was after midnight when I gave Sophie a lift back to her bed and breakfast.

'It's all starting to come together,' she said as she was getting out of the car. 'I can dream about Angola now.'

Dream was one word for it.

Chapter 8

A blast of hot, humid air engulfed us as soon as the cabin crew opened the door. Welcome to Luanda! I was uncomfortable. Within minutes my clothes were damp, my waistband chafed and sweat flooded my eyes, making them sore. Sophie looked relatively cool but preoccupied. She had not said a word since the pilot had announced the start of our descent into Luanda's airport. She had the window seat and her eyes had locked onto Africa as its detail gradually sharpened. She was still staring out and I suspected she was thinking about Jim Lodge.

'Did they fly my father's body out from here?' She confirmed my suspicion.

'I should think so. It's the only international airport in Luanda, and he left Nocredo in a Hercules coming here. I don't know what they did with the coffin here though: whether they put it straight on the next Europe-bound flight or stored it for a day or two.'

'I'm just trying to picture his last journey.'

'I did something similar when I finally left here thirty years ago. It was only a few months after he died … I remember wondering what it would be like to be dead – weird; I think it was the first time I acknowledged that I would die myself one day.'

'Let's stop being morbid,' she smiled. 'Once we've got through the formalities, we can have a drink in the hotel. How does anyone do anything in this heat? We're not even off the plane yet.'

'Well, you look remarkably cool and dry to me. I could wring my shirt out. I always hated Luanda for the climate, but it's wonderful up in the mining area. Being inland and at altitude it's cooler and drier.'

Nothing about the airport was familiar when we got inside. Either my memory was flawed, or it had been redeveloped after the civil war. Much of the surrounding area had looked, from the plane, as though it had been rebuilt. There were still a lot of shanties, but there was also a lot of money evident. Things had changed.

We collected our baggage, cleared the airport bureaucracy and got a taxi to the Hotel Presidente as quickly as we could.

'I can't wait for a lovely, cold shower,' I said, 'then we'll get something to eat and drink, and plan our meeting with the Mining Ministry tomorrow. It's mainly a courtesy but they'll also sort out our guias de trânsito, our passes, to the mining area. I don't know what Angola's like now, so we'll have to play some things by ear.'

'Such as?'

'Business. Oiling the wheels. We might have to offer them something to get what we want.'

'A bribe? You're going to bribe the Mining Ministry?' She scowled her contempt. 'An offer they can't refuse?'

'Don't be such a drama queen. Like I said, I'll play it by ear. I'm not comfortable with it, but it might be how things work here now, I don't know. It's why I bought to the maximum of both our duty-free allowances at Heathrow.'

'And there was me thinking you were an alcoholic chimney. It looks like I've got a lot to learn. I'll just sit and watch if it comes to that tomorrow.'

'It pays to have good relationships with those in high places: things tend to run more smoothly.'

'Is it so corrupt here though? Is this why you were so coy about that miscellaneous expenses line you added to my project budget?'

I nodded. 'Better safe than sorry. Thirty years ago, the odd dollar bill used to help but it wasn't essential.'

'I'm already starting to dislike Luanda,' she said. 'I can't wait to get to Nocredo and Mumbulo, to see what my father used to see every day; and to see where … Oh bugger, I'm getting morbid again.' She smiled sadly.

'It'll be behind us soon enough and I'm hoping it'll be a cathartic experience. Anyway, remember why we're here. First and foremost, we're here for the project; that's our priority, not the hidden agenda. If we find anything out about that, it's a bonus.'

★★★

The meeting with the Ministry went well and we came away with the necessary permits to go to the Lunda Norte province, to Nocredo and Mumbulo; and to Lucapa, Nzagi and Cafunfo if we needed a change of plan. I'd translated a presentation about the project into Portuguese and they were impressed that we'd taken the trouble. Before we left them, they said they would arrange for someone from Diangola, the government-owned diamond mining company, to meet us at Nocredo airport. They also booked us two seats in the supply Hercules that was going to Nocredo the following day. It was starting to happen very quickly. When we left, my briefcase was lighter by a bottle of malt whisky, a carton of cigarettes and some expensive perfume.

Back at the hotel, Sophie was excited by our rate of progress and she kept asking me questions about what Nocredo and Mumbulo were like. I had shown her some photographs from my box of memories, and a few more that I'd found on the internet, but I had no idea how the civil war had affected the two towns. I knew Mumbulo had been captured by UNITA rebels, but I had no idea whether Nocredo had suffered the same fate. It had been a nasty war – I knew that much – but I did not know whether the towns had been destroyed or simply taken over.

Over the intervening years, I had occasionally wondered about Armando and the other Angolans I'd known. Had they survived? Had their families survived? I was sure that very few Angolans would have come through the civil war without losing someone close to them. If the civil war was not enough, there was also malaria, AIDS, malnutrition, and numerous other ways of dying or being seriously impaired.

I resolved to make Armando a priority; he had been important to me thirty years ago, but I had allowed myself to forget him. Was he still alive? What about Esther, and their son? Did they have other children? I hoped they were a big, happy, healthy family, but my head told me to expect otherwise. I had no idea how I would find them or even if they were there to be found. I could not remember the family name and Armando was so common I would definitely need it.

Chapter 9

From the Hercules, on the descent into Nocredo, I scanned the area for familiar landmarks, but everything looked different. Even the river seemed to be going somewhere else. It took me a while to realise that we were flying into a new airstrip, not the one I had known in my half-forgotten past. The runway was of red laterite just like the old one – it looked the same, but it was as though someone had cheated with a jigsaw puzzle, forcing pieces into the wrong places.

'Wow! It's really beautiful,' said Sophie. 'I always imagined it'd be brown and ugly, but it's wonderfully green; unbelievably lush. The town looks a bit of a mess but the scenery …'

'It always looked great in the wet season but … All that green feels temporary to me: the vegetation's all scrubby and low-lying, and the roots are shallow. It looks totally different in the dry; as though it's given up the ghost.'

'Kill joy!' she said, but she was still smiling. 'And my father; did he like it here?'

'I'm not sure. We never talked much about it. He was colour-blind, so I know he didn't have the same appreciation of the birds that I had but, as for the rest …'

'I'm sure he liked it. I love it, so he must have.' She was so like Lodge that I almost believed her flawed logic.

'Well, he liked it enough to spend quite a few years here.'

'Where are the mines from here?' she asked.

I was completely disoriented by our approach and though I knew the river was aligned roughly north south, the sun, which was directly overhead, wasn't offering much help.

'Erm, I think it's that way,' I said, pointing along the river, 'or maybe …'

'I thought you knew this place.'

'I did, but this is a new airstrip and I've lost my bearings. I'm pretty sure it's that way,' I said, pointing in my original direction. 'It looks vaguely familiar, but the town has changed completely. It used to be only on the west side of the river, but now it's spread to both sides. I wouldn't have known we were in Nocredo if it wasn't the only stop for the plane. And that bloody big sign, of course.'

'Mmmm.' She did not sound impressed. 'So, do you know where we're supposed to go now, we're here?'

'No, I haven't the foggiest, but I hope it doesn't matter. I spoke to a guy called Manuel Silva on the phone yesterday. He's the Diangola man, the one the Ministry contacted. He should be picking us up and taking us to the casa de trânsito – that's a sort of hotel …'

'You forget I speak Spanish and it's not very different from Portuguese. How will we recognise him?'

I laughed. 'We're the only strangers here, the only passengers on this plane in fact; I don't think he'll need to be Sherlock Holmes.'

A stocky man of about my age with bronze-coloured skin and a black beard stepped out of the shade of the terminal shed and moved towards us as we disembarked. His smile and outstretched hand confirmed his identity.

'O senhor Young, a doutora Addison?'

'Sim, David e Sophie' I said. 'O senhor Silva?'

'Manuel.' We exchanged greetings. He apologised for not being able to speak English but my rusty Portuguese and Sophie's Portunhol; adapted Spanish, served us well, especially Sophie's. I think she could have said anything in any language and Manuel would have pretended to understand.

The roads in the town were deeply rutted and we had to hang on to the grab handles in Manuel's Land Cruiser to stop our heads bashing into the roof. The journey took us across the river bridge into what looked like an older part of the town where some of the streets looked vaguely familiar, but I couldn't identify any specific building. Sophie and I talked to Manuel in broad terms about our project and he, in turn, explained that he was the chief logistics administrator for Diangola, responsible for stores, transport and some personnel issues. He was based in Nocredo at Diangola's main regional office, but he spent a lot of his time in Mumbulo at the mine.

The casa de trânsito was a shock. It was a chunk of the past thrust unexpectedly into my present. It was the same large, Portuguese colonial-style house that we had used all those years ago. It was where I had spent my very last night in the diamond area. I felt slightly unsettled by it. Although I had only spent the odd night there, it was a bridge to the distant past, continuity of a kind.

The layout of the house, the bedrooms and the bathrooms all came flooding back, and I did not need to be shown where the dining room was.

Manuel was surprised when I started to show Sophie around. 'How did you know where the dining room is?' he asked.

'It hasn't changed in thirty years. It's been repainted and the furniture's new, but it's the same building.'

'You were here during the war years, Senhor Young?'

'Yes. But the war didn't come to Lunda Norte until after I left. I was in Mumbulo as a metallurgist in the diamond mines.'

'That's all there is there; all there ever was. Nocredo's the same; it's still the administration centre for the whole area. Anything here that isn't mining supports mining. I'm Portuguese but I was born here, and diamond mining is all I know,' he said.

'Were you here when UNITA took Mumbulo?' I asked.

'No. And they took Nocredo too. Most of us could see how things were going and we got out through what was then Zaire and escaped to Portugal. I stayed there for six years until after Jonas Savimbi was killed, then I returned.'

'And your family?' Sophie asked.

'We all came back together, except my sister. Her work as a nurse was very important. She stayed on in Mumbulo throughout the civil war. I'll visit her tomorrow when I take you to Mumbulo.'

'How long has your sister lived there?' Sophie never missed an opportunity.

'Since the early eighties, I think,' said Manuel.

I realised she must have been there during my stay and wondered which of the young Portuguese girls she had been. We had not mixed much but it didn't stop us looking.

'How much artisanal mining is there in the Mumbulo area now?' I asked, keen to move the conversation to the business of our visit.

Manuel paused and sucked his bottom lip, as though performing a tricky calculation, before he said, 'a lot,' which fell short of my expectation.

'A hundred? A thousand? Ten thousand?' I tried.

'Probably thousands. It's hard to say. We get lots of reports of activity. We scare them away and then we get reports from other places. Are they the same miners operating in many locations or are there different miners in different areas? Even one's too many. They cost us a fortune in security. We need to get rid of them,' he said.

One of the first things we needed to do was estimate their numbers and talk to some of them. It would give us some idea of how big our job was going to be. We also needed to persuade people like Manuel, who clearly believed artisanal miners to be little better than vermin, that Diangola and other organisations could benefit by changing their stance.

Manuel left us to settle in and told us he would pick us up early in the morning to go to Mumbulo. He also told us that he had already set up meetings with representatives of ARDCO and Diangola. ARDCO was the British company that had operated the mines since the end of the civil war, on behalf of Diangola, the government mining company. We ate our dinner on the veranda, in front of the dining room. We talked about the project and who was going to do what in the meetings the next day, and then we relaxed with a couple of cans of cold beer.

'You never did tell me where your passion for artisanal mining came from,' Sophie had a knack for spotting when my guard was down. 'It can't be the technical side; it isn't challenging enough. And it can't be the money – Flourish pays well for a charity but I'm sure you'd get a lot more if you were working for this ARDCO outfit here. Armando's about the only Angolan you ever mentioned by name. It has to be something to do with him, but I don't understand how he fits in. As far as I can work out, he worked for the mining company; he wasn't an artisanal miner.'

'True,' I said, 'but when his village was razed to the ground and he was fired, he might well have become one. I really don't know.'

'That's not enough though is it? You don't suddenly commit your life to something on the suspicion that someone you once knew might or might not be doing that something.'

I smiled. I was enjoying her thought processes for the moment. 'Does my motive have to come from Angola? I've worked in other places.'

'I think the roots of it are here. Angola scares you, or somewhere in Angola does. Rachel alluded to that, too. You're not stressed here in Nocredo though, so it's not Nocredo that scares you.' I tried not to blink as she searched my face for a clue.

'My passion, as you call it, for the plight of artisanal miners came about over many years, from experiences in lots of different countries. There was no "road to Damascus" moment for me.'

'Not Damascus maybe, but what about Mumbulo?' she said very quietly.

PART 3

Chapter 10

An early start augured a long day; it would be the first of many. Manuel picked us up at six-thirty a.m., as we had agreed, and he was driving us to Mumbulo for the first of the two meetings he'd arranged for us before lunch. He was proving to be very useful. He said he had arranged transport for us to go to the mines in the afternoon. He also offered to fix it so he would work in Mumbulo rather than Nocredo for the next few days so he could ferry us back and forth from our accommodation. I accepted his offer, but it crossed my mind that he might not have been so helpful if I'd been alone. It meant we had no immediate transport worries, and, with luck, we might find somewhere to stay in Mumbulo if things turned out well.

The road to Mumbulo was not the obstacle course I remembered. The route had not changed much but the pot-holed and corrugated dirt surface had been replaced by a smooth tarmac one. Sophie was lost in thought and I guessed the project was not the main thing on her mind.

My suspicion was confirmed when she said, 'My father died on the road from Nocredo to Mumbulo didn't he? Is this the same road?'

'No, there's a back road, a mine road, or there was then. This is the public road.' She managed to look both relieved and disappointed at the same time. She was eager to face her monster, but at a time of her choosing. I, on the other hand, was happy to defer my monster indefinitely.

I took out my project notebook to check the times of our meetings. At eight a.m. we had a meeting with ARDCO, the Angolan River Diamond Company and at ten-thirty a.m. we were due to meet with Diangola. The Mumbulo mining area was run by a partnership of Diangola and ARDCO. ARDCO provided the expertise, equipment, and a commitment to develop the local people and infrastructure whilst Diangola provided the labour and held the licence for the mine. Without Diangola, ARDCO could not operate. It was a similar relationship to that which had existed more than thirty years ago except the names had changed. Manuel told us that he would attend the Diangola meeting but not the ARDCO one. He said he would take the chance to visit his sister while we were with ARDCO.

I felt a tingle of anticipation as we reached the crest of a small hill; I knew exactly where we were and that I was about to see Mumbulo for the first time in thirty years; and there it was, where I expected, sprawling in the middle-distance; it looked much bigger than I remembered. Manuel explained that, during the war, many people had moved into the towns from the rural areas, swelling the bairros or favelas, the shanty suburbs. I pressed him about the migration, whether it was safer in the towns, but he just shrugged. I knew it was a subject close to Sophie's heart – she had told me migration was a strong theme in her PhD thesis – and I expected her to pick up my questioning, but she remained silent; her mind was on another road.

The mine offices were where they had been thirty years before, but they were quite different. The old colonial-style buildings were gone; replaced by a confusing, interlocking array of sea containers which had been converted into offices.

Manuel guided us through the maze to a pair of side-by-side containers that had been cut through into one and furnished luxuriously in the style of a boardroom. The air conditioning was quietly effective. I had primed Sophie not to mention her ulterior motive to anyone that day, on the basis that it was better to keep things purely professional until we had our feet under the table. If we were forced to go to a different mining area, she would lose the opportunity of finding anything out about her father.

There were three ARDCO people waiting for us: mining engineer Harry Finding, a deeply tanned, balding Yorkshireman;

geologist Constance van Niekerk, a tall, blonde South African woman; and metallurgist Mitch Fenton, a dour Australian with a straggly beard. I introduced myself and Sophie and gave a very brief overview of our project before yielding the floor to Sophie. She delivered our PowerPoint presentation of what we intended to do and what we needed from a cooperating mining company – in this case: ARDCO. I kept a close eye on everyone, trying to gauge their interest and identify who would be the easiest to work with. Who could we sway? The men were totally engrossed, but I suspect that was more due to Sophie than the content of her presentation. Constance was also interested, and I felt that she was a better yardstick than the other two.

'So, in a nutshell, what is it you want from us?' asked Harry when Sophie had finished.

I recapped what Sophie had said about establishing a dialogue between the different stakeholder groups. 'You and the artisanal miners, what you call garimpeiros, represent two of those stakeholder groups. Women, children and workers in service industries are others, but we need to talk to the local people to get a comprehensive list. What we need from you, in the first instance, is a commitment to sit down at the same table and engage with the other stakeholder groups, including the artisanal miners.'

'Garimpeiros, you mean! You're taking the piss,' said Mitch. 'We have to use an armoured car to get close to those bastards.'

'Look,' I said. 'They're scared of you and you're scared of them, but if we can establish peace, all that'll be a thing of the past.'

'It can't work. They're illegals. They'll always be illegals. They'll steal even more diamonds if we don't clear them out. How can it work?' This was Harry.

'Who do they sell their diamonds to?' I asked. 'How much do they get? And most importantly, why do they steal diamonds in the first place? For money of course ...'

'Yeah, our money,' shouted Mitch. 'Do you really expect us to help them to rob us? You must be joking.'

Harry held his hands up in a gesture for calm. 'Let's listen to what they've got to say before we judge them.' Constance nodded her agreement and Mitch sat back with an expression that oozed negativity.

'Artisanal miners, what you call garimpeiros, have always been an issue here,' I started. 'Their problem is that the mining companies control every square millimetre of land. They think it's their land because they were born here, and they used to be able to do what they liked with it. Now, they can't even plant cassava or pineapples ... The bottom line? – unless someone in a family has a job with Diangola or ARDCO, they can't survive without breaking the law. All that most of them want is to be able to support their families.'

'All they have to do is bugger off somewhere else then. Easy peasy,' said Mitch. 'Why don't you just help them to move?'

'Because this is where they belong. More so than you or Harry or Constance or ...' I gestured at myself and Sophie.

'But it's the Angolan Government that passes the laws, not us,' said Constance. 'They also own the mines, so technically they own the diamonds too. Surely you'd be better off starting with them.'

'We are. We've got a meeting with Diangola straight after this,' said Sophie.

Harry and Constance nodded their approval, but Mitch was still combative. 'Do you seriously reckon they'll want their diamonds pinched any more than we do?'

'This isn't about theft.' Sophie was bristling. 'You'd know that if you'd been listening to my presentation instead of ...'

'You'd better tell that part again,' I interrupted.

'All right.' She exhaled noisily. 'We acknowledge that there is theft, but it's theft for a reason. Our aim is to eliminate that reason by working with you, Diangola and representatives of the artisanal miners to find areas of agreement. As you know, many of the mines here weren't found by your geologists but by the so-called garimpeiros.'

I was pleased to see that Constance, the geologist, was nodding in agreement.

Sophie pressed on. 'They have, in effect, done a lot of your prospecting for you. We're not asking for you to pay them retrospectively but to view them more sympathetically. We'll only know precisely how after we've held some meetings and workshops, but some of the possible actions are: permitting agriculture, subcontracting the mining of certain areas to the artisanal miners, fair trade, buying the artisanal production from the miners at a fair price and selling them tools at a fair retail price.'

'You forget,' said Constance, 'that part of the problem is the sale of the illegal diamonds. The garimpeiros sell to traders from over the border in the Democratic Republic of Congo, the DRC. Those traders won't react well.'

'You may be right but that's a border control issue, surely; and the way I understand the marketing here is that the Angolan Selling Corporation, ASCORP, now takes all the production and deals with it. I don't know what happens in the DRC, but I bet they don't sell back to Angola, so Angola would gain by tightening the border controls and buying at a fair price from the artisanal miners.'

'That's about right,' said Constance. 'The old hands still talk about de Beers' Central Selling Organisation, CSO, but Angola took over its own marketing after the civil war. I believe it was an effort to get away from the stain that UNITA put on the industry. We don't produce "blood" or "conflict" diamonds here.'

'But you still have a private army,' said Sophie.

I gave her a hard stare to encourage her to cool it. If she managed to antagonise Constance, I didn't want to think about what might be going on in Mitch's head.

'It's not all one way,' said Constance defensively. 'The garimpeiros have AK–47s and rocket-propelled grenades. They often attack our workers. We have to send them to work in convoys with armoured cars in front and behind to protect them.'

'All the more reason to talk to them,' I said. 'It still sounds like a war out there, and wars don't end themselves. Somewhere along the line either one side surrenders, always at a huge cost in lives and money, or people take it upon themselves to start talking. You can look upon us as mediators in that process if it makes it easier for you.'

Harry and Constance both looked thoughtful and receptive to the idea, but Mitch wore a look of contempt. 'I prefer the surrender idea,' he put in. 'If we shoot the lot of them, there's no longer a problem. The only good garimpeiro is a dead one,' he sneered. It was a statement we had to ignore although I could see from Sophie's face that she was struggling, as I was.

Constance spoke up. 'I think it's worth a try. We've nothing to lose and, provided Diangola are okay with it – the legal aspects are their area – I think we should give you a week or two to see what comes of it. What do you think, Harry?'

Harry nodded. 'That sounds sensible to me, so …' Mitch's opinion was not canvassed; it was obvious what he thought from his scowl, but we already had a majority if it came to a show of hands.

'I'll get you a map of the area,' said Constance, 'and we'll mark where we know there's been recent illegal mining activity. I can't guarantee what you'll find anywhere as the heavies go in every so often and clear them out.' She glared at Mitch and I sensed that he was a prime mover behind any such actions.

We finished the meeting and agreed to meet again in a few days, to discuss our progress.

Diangola had their offices in the same complex and Harry guided us to a pair of containers, similar to ARDCO's meeting room. Manuel was waiting outside. We thanked Harry and followed Manuel into the room where he introduced us to two Angolans: Luis Martins and Eusebio Agostinho. Neither looked enthusiastic.

I did the presentation this time as my Portuguese was still better than Sophie's. Manuel helped me out on a few occasions, and it was clear from some of the comments that he had already briefed his colleagues thoroughly before Sophie and I arrived. The two men were political appointments, employed to look after the interests of the Angolan government which owned the diamond mines. I pounced on the opportunity to emphasise that the government was getting nothing from the sale of illegal diamonds at the moment as the miners were forced to sell to buyers who traded over the border in the DRC. I told them that, if the artisanal miners could be licensed or subcontracted to produce diamonds then the government would benefit in two ways; they would get all the diamonds and they would also be able to claim taxes from the miners. I also pointed out that the world at large would take a dim view of the methods currently employed to clear the area of illegal miners.

'But that's ARDCO not us,' said Luis.

'It's their private army, yes, but they wouldn't do it if they didn't have your agreement. Or if you didn't turn a blind eye.'

'We don't like it but it's fighting fire with fire,' said Eusebio. 'The civil war's over but the guns and landmines and other weapons are still out there. It's necessary to use guns against the miners simply because they have guns, and they're not afraid to use them.'

'That's why we want to go in, under a white flag, and talk to them,' I said. 'If we can get everyone around a table, I believe we can come up with a solution that will benefit the Angolan government, ARDCO and the artisanal miners, the garimpeiros. We would appreciate your backing to conduct some initial investigations. We want to identify one or two pilot groups who might be willing to participate, then we need to organise a meeting, again under a white flag, and see if we can find some points of agreement. If that works, we'll try to draw in other groups and broaden the scope.'

'How can we be sure they still won't sell their diamonds to Congolese dealers?'

'That's for the meeting, but if you're fair; if you pay a fair price, they'll sell to you because they certainly don't get a fair price from the dealers. They sell to them because there's no choice. And by a fair price, I mean one that still has some margin in it for you, but which reflects the market value of the stones and the effort put into producing them.'

'Okay,' said Luis, who appeared to be the senior of the two. 'When would you expect to be ready for the first meeting?'

'I don't know. I'll have a better idea when we've been out in the field and spoken to some of the miners. Without them, there is no meeting. It might not happen, but I hope and believe it will.'

Luis asked Sophie and me to leave the room for a short while to allow him to have a private talk with Eusebio and Manuel. When we were called back in, we were told that we had a week to find a suitable group of miners. We were asked to liaise with Manuel, and he would organise the meeting for us when we were ready. He would be responsible for booking the edificio público, publicising the meeting, and he would also advertise for attendees from other stakeholder groups.

We came away from the two meetings feeling happier with the outcomes than we had expected. We had anticipated more resistance, but the only negative voice had been Mitch's and he'd been outnumbered. I had one tiny concern, that we had not met any of ARDCO's most senior management, but Constance, Harry and Mitch had assured us that they had the necessary authority. I went over everything that had happened in my mind; it all seemed too easy. Was I missing something? If so, what was it? Who had we met? What had been said and what had been agreed? Everything seemed okay except ... yes, the senior management of ARDCO. Sophie had produced detailed dossiers on everyone and everything we were likely to encounter. Her thoroughness had left me in no doubt that the dossiers were complete and accurate. But were they? No matter how hard I tried, I could not conjure up the name of anyone in the senior management of ARDCO. I asked Sophie if she could remember any names, but she just shrugged and said she would check the files when we got back to Nocredo in the evening.

Chapter 11

Sophie was in high spirits, like a little girl, swinging her arms and threatening to break into a skip, as we walked into Mumbulo from the mine offices. We had accepted gratefully when Manuel invited us to have lunch at his sister's house, but we turned down the offer of a lift as Sophie wanted to see the town on foot. He gave us directions and drew us a simple map, showing the offices, the principal streets and his sister's house. As we progressed, the town became more familiar to me.

Familiarity aside, I began to feel more and more uneasy as we neared and then reached the street where I had once lived. Mango trees still lined both sides of it but there were now more gaps; aftermaths of the war I supposed. Goats still ran freely on the grass that fronted the houses and they still perched on improbable vantage points. The children still wore colourful clothes but now the shirts were branded: Manchester United, Chelsea and Barcelona. My old house, the Madhouse, was still there too, I could see it further up the hill, and we were getting closer to it. My thoughts blurred; time was confused; had thirty years really passed? I don't know whether Sophie sensed my feelings or whether her own thoughts were running a parallel course, but she had also gone quiet. Perhaps she was experiencing trans-generational déjà vu.

'Where did my father live? Was it in this street?' she asked. Her appearance added to my unease. Her hair was tucked away inside a khaki sun hat, but her green eyes and the set of her features were clear in the bright sun; she looked uncannily like her father. I had walked these streets with Jim on many occasions in the last weeks before his death. What was our fate to be?

I shook my head and pointed. 'No, It's in the next street across. I think that's the back of it you can see through the gap there.

It's either that one or the next one along. This is where I used to live.' I stopped and looked up the path that ran from the road to the veranda steps of what had been the Madhouse. The veranda was now secured with elaborate wrought ironwork, including a gate. It was familiar but different.

'Isn't this Manuel's sister's house now?' she asked, pointing at the sketch map.

'No, not quite ...' I felt my insides gurgling ominously as I turned my head a few degrees to the next house. It had been re-painted dark green, and it too had acquired wrought iron security but, despite the superficial changes, something felt the same. I had once known that house as well as I had known the Madhouse.

★★★

It was a Friday, late afternoon, the week after the Txicaca test. The sun was getting ready to duck below the horizon and I was driving back to Mumbulo from a remote plant. I planned to go straight home, to the Madhouse, have a quick shower and then walk round to Morgan's for the end of week party.

The wind seemed to blow up from nowhere, dragging a dark curtain of cloud over what was left of the sun. The day was ending prematurely. A distant, blinding flash fractured the darkness. It was quiet, very quiet. A sudden cracking noise. Then a louder crackle. A rumble. Louder, louder, louder, an explosive crescendo. Another flash, then another. Noise overlaying noise. Then the rain started. Huge, heavy drops hammered down on the car roof in a drum roll of gathering intensity. I had to stop as the road was lost under water. I loved these thunderstorms and I looked forward to what was coming; it would be a pyrotechnic treat. Light and sound converged and synchronised as the storm closed in. The noise of the rain was deafening, and I could see nothing but the erratic alternation of blinding light and impenetrable black clouds. I just had to wait.

An explosion shook the car and I ducked instinctively. I was momentarily blinded and deafened. I thought I was dead. Angola was full of landmines. It took a while to realise that it was lightning: a strike or a near miss. The storm slowly receded. I recovered slowly: my vision returned. The bridge of my nose throbbed painfully. I felt around my face. It was sticky with blood which dribbled down and soaked my shirt. I laughed ironically; I liked to look my best on a Friday night.

An hour later, I completed my drive into Mumbulo where the streets were steaming, and the grass gleamed under the streetlights. Black and white goats eyed me curiously for a while but quickly decided that grass was more interesting.

Carlos's car wasn't outside the Madhouse, so I guessed he'd driven directly to Morgan's. I went to the bathroom where I threw off my bloody clothes and manoeuvred myself under the feeble dribble of the shower until I felt cleaner. I was still bleeding, and the water trickled red to the plug hole. I checked in the mirror and saw that some of the blood was from my nose, but most was from a gash in my left eyebrow. I daubed Vaseline on it and shoved toilet paper up my nostrils to control the bleeding while I got dressed. I eventually set off for Morgan's holding an old T-shirt to my head.

Morgan's front door was wide open and welcoming. Two of Thys Gerber's mine security men sat on the veranda supping lager from cans. I exchanged pleasantries with them and went through to the kitchen, stopping at the fridge to pick up a six-pack of cold beers. The party in the back yard was in full swing and must have been going for over an hour. We had a session every Friday at sundown, and all expatriate personnel would meet for a beer at one of their houses. Chris, the Chief Engineer, should have been today's host, but Morgan had decided to hold a special party, with food as well as drink, to celebrate the Txicaca success.

I looked around the courtyard. Where should I start? It always surprised me how well this peculiar mix of people, mainly men, got on together. The mine camp was like a prison so we all had to make the best of it, compromising and rubbing along with many we would not normally choose as friends. Looking around there were not many I would spend time with in a normal life. Morgan, Carlos Pereira and Steve Vernon were about the only ones, and Jim Lodge after the last couple of days of course. Then there was Maria … I sighed wistfully. On the other side there was Kevin Dryden; why did he always have to be there? He was my boss; we had never got on and never would. He had given me a dressing down that very morning for not consulting him over something trivial. He was a pen-pusher, and I am sure he resented my involvement in the success of Txicaca; he was missing out on the glory. I had no particular favourite drinking mates as talk nearly always gravitated to work: the only common ground most of us shared. How long would I be able to avoid that tonight? Geoff spotted me and greeted me as he walked over.

'You're a bit late, Boyo. Did you get caught out in it? Bloody hell! You been in a fight? What happened?' Morgan looked closely at my seeping eyebrow. 'You might need stitches in that. You'd better see the doc.'

He dragged me over to a group under the central mango tree, where the doctor was the centre of attention. 'Maria, would you take a quick look at David's head, please? Try and sort it out.'

'She's not a psychiatrist,' someone quipped. Maria gently mopped the blood away with the T-shirt before taking a closer look.

'It looks clean,' she said, 'but I'll need to stitch it to stop it opening up again. How did you do this?'

I told her about the lightning: how I had ducked and bashed my head on the steering wheel.

Morgan burst out laughing. 'Forget the sympathy; not for a self-inflicted wound.'

'Come on,' Maria said, grabbing my arm and pulling me towards the house. I had studied her from afar many times, never quite having the nerve to talk to her. As the doctor, she had always seemed out of reach, untouchable. She was not a conventional beauty, but her features could certainly hold the attention. Her eyes were big, brown and expressive; her mouth: full-lipped and up-tilted, ready to laugh, but it was her character: bubbly and intelligent, that set her apart from the rest. It was my first time alone with her. Inspiration dried with my tongue. I desperately wanted to say something clever and witty but all I could do was nod and grunt. 'I'll get my bag from the car,' she said. 'I just hope I remembered to put the razor in as I'll have to shave the eyebrow. I'll see you in the bathroom.'

When she returned, she put her bag down and closed the bathroom door, bolting it behind her. She then walked over to the wash basin where I was cleaning myself up from the latest escape of blood. She turned my face towards hers to assess the injury then washed it gently with cotton wool and antiseptic. She cut the hairs short with scissors before shaving around the gash. Her face was closer to mine than I had ever dreamed; warm and smiling. I was so engrossed I hardly noticed the needle as she stitched me up. I did not want it to end.

'All done,' she chuckled. 'Don't look in the mirror for a couple of weeks, though.'

She put her hands on my shoulders as though admiring her handiwork but then she leant in and kissed my eyebrow like a mother kissing a child better. I found myself laughing and my tongue miraculously untied itself. 'Is that standard treatment?'

She shook her head then reached up and stroked my face, looking me in the eyes. I pulled her to me, and we kissed; a long, urgent kiss. I had never been happier.

There was a bang on the door. We sprang apart like naughty children. 'Haven't you finished darning him up yet, doc? There's a lot of beer being drunk out here and ... well ... I could do with relieving myself ...' It was Morgan's Rhondda Valley baritone.

'We're just tidying up. We won't be long.' Maria wiped the corner of my mouth with a piece of cotton wool and held it up for me to see, lipstick.

Morgan grumbled something about his bladder and went away.

'Make some excuse and go home,' whispered Maria. 'I'll get out as soon as I can. Come to my house. The back door.'

The back door of the house where Manuel's sister now lived.

★★★

A shout brought me back to the present. It was Manuel. He had seen us and was waving from his sister's house. 'Esta casa,' he shouted.

Sophie smiled and waved back. Her carefree mood had returned. As she scampered off towards him my feet felt weighed down, anchored by history.

'Come on!' shouted Sophie over her shoulder from the veranda, 'it's a fantastic spread; delicious-looking salad, interesting meats, and there's wine too.'

I steeled myself and hefted my feet into a reluctant walk.

'My sister sends her apologies,' said Manuel as I joined him on the veranda. 'She had to go out for a while, to look in on a sick friend, but she said she'd try to get back before you have to go.'

He steered me to a table where Sophie was already loading a plate with cold meats and salad. It should have looked appetising, but the past was like a finger in my throat. I was conscious of appearing ungrateful as I picked around without enthusiasm.

'I'm sorry,' I said, rubbing my stomach, 'but I seem to have a slight ...'

'Just take what you can eat.' Manuel smiled sympathetically, but Sophie's look was more quizzical.

'Excuse me a moment please,' I said, anxious to give credibility to my excuse. I dashed inside and crossed the living room to the corridor which gave access to all the other rooms. The doors were all ajar and I could not resist taking a sneaky peek as I passed each one. The whole house had been completely refitted. The décor was all different: new furniture and floor coverings, modern light fittings, and there was a television. The room that had been used as a surgery and emergency room was now a study-cum-library. I was just beginning to relax when I saw it. A photograph. Yet another reminder of a past I did not feel ready to face up to yet. I reached the bathroom at the end of the corridor where I sat down to recover my composure. After an appropriate time, I flushed the toilet and headed back through the house and returned to the veranda.

I tried to eat some lunch and struggled to make polite conversation. After about half an hour, I reckoned we could reasonably take our leave.

'I'm sorry we missed your sister, Manuel; we'd really like to meet her,' I said, 'to thank her for all this. It was very good and thoughtful of her to prepare it. But we do need to get out into the field to look for some artisanal miners.'

'Not just yet,' said Sophie. 'We haven't even got transport yet.'

Manuel had arranged for us to have an unmarked vehicle for the afternoon so we could drive around without frightening anyone who might have a guilty conscience. He would stay here, at his sister's, until we returned, then he would take us back to Nocredo.

Sophie stood up decisively. 'Manuel, would you mind if David and I went for a short walk? Just around the block to help our food settle.'

Manuel smiled and nodded. Anything Sophie suggested was okay with him. He said he would chase up the vehicle while we were away. We thanked him and set off.

'I just want to look at where my father lived,' she said. 'Manuel's face was a picture when you went to the loo. I think he thinks you're psychic. You seem to know your way around every house, without directions.'

'Well, I did tell him I'd worked here before, and I have been in a lot of these houses. The Company had use of most of them in these two streets thirty years ago. I doubt if anyone'll remember me though.' That photograph! 'Besides, I've changed a lot. I used to have more hair and a beard.'

We walked around the corner into the street where Jim Lodge had lived. Sophie stopped. 'Which one was it?'

I carried on ahead of her and stopped at the end of a path. 'This one.' A goat jumped down from the roof.

'How do they get up there?' she asked.

We stood side by side, quietly staring at the house. It was like all the others: set back from the road in a swathe of grass. It had the usual raised veranda with artistic wrought iron for security and it had its own unique colour scheme. Where Manuel's sister's place was mainly dark green with lighter green adornments, and the Madhouse was terracotta and white, this was royal blue and yellow.

'Did it look like this when he was here?'

'Pretty much. I don't think it was blue and yellow then though, but it might just have been faded. It was certainly a lot tattier. They all were except for Manuel's sister's.'

'Who lived there then? Who was your next-door neighbour?'

I had not thought of anyone else since I set eyes on it again. 'I think it was the doctor.'

'The one who certified my father's death?'

'The Portuguese version. Yes.'

We finished our walk in silence. Just as we got back, an old Land Rover pulled up and an Angolan driver got out. Manuel shouted from the veranda for him to give me the key, which he promptly did.

Before setting out we spent a few minutes studying the map that Constance had given us. She'd marked a few crosses on it at locations where illegal mining was suspected. One or two of the old plants were still marked on the map, including Cambunda, but they were my only points of reference; everything else had changed. Lodge had saved the mine thirty years ago, so I was surprised to see how much recent mining there had been. I wondered if they were still mining the reserves that Lodge had identified. The map showed roads that bore no relation to any I remembered and there were many more river diversions than there had been. I realised the changes would make it difficult to locate exactly where Lodge had died. I might yet be spared facing that.

Sophie noticed a change in my demeanour. 'You've brightened up, all of a sudden. What's made you so cheerful? You've been a right grump.' She looked at the map suspiciously. 'Which is the road my father died on?'

'I don't think it's marked.' I put my finger on where I genuinely thought it should be but there was no road there anymore. The river split into two channels with an island about a kilometre long between them. 'It looks as though it's in a mine. See this – it's a river diversion.'

'We can still go there, can't we?' she said.

'We can try but I doubt if we'll be able to pinpoint the place. It might even be under water.' I felt so confident we would not find anything that I suggested we went to that area first. 'There are a couple of possible illegal mines nearby so let's go and check it out. Do you want to drive, or shall I?'

'You'd better,' she said. 'You're more experienced at driving on the right, not to mention mine roads.' She took the map off me and studied it for a few minutes to get her bearings before folding it to show only the part relevant to our journey.

We set off. Mumbulo, as my first impressions had informed me, had grown a lot and it took longer than I expected to get away to open country. The roads were unfamiliar, and the lush green landscape did not wear the wounds of mining lightly. It was as though someone had stuck giant reddish-orange plasters randomly all over it. Although I had seen the mines marked on the map, the reality was shocking. Tens of years of near-continuous mining activity made Sophie's role of navigator more necessary than either of us had expected. More than once we took dead-end turns to mined-out blocks. It was hot and dry, and we had to stop twice to allow the red fog of dust, kicked up by passing trucks, to settle before continuing.

After about half an hour Sophie tapped the map and said, 'I think we're somewhere close.'

I pulled into the side of the road and we checked the map against the visible landmarks together. We were about two hundred yards from the river on a stretch of road running approximately parallel to it. The map showed the river dividing into two, creating an island; it was the river diversion I had identified as being close to where Lodge had died. The diversion course had a single kink in it where a hill, a rocky outcrop on the island, bulged into it. I recognised the hill. The vestige of what appeared to be an old road skirted the lower contours on its upstream side and ran out of sight behind it; no road was marked on the map. My blood ran cold; I shivered.

'That's where it happened, isn't it?'

'I'm not sure,' I said, but I was.

'We'll need a boat,' said Sophie.

Chapter 12

Sophie leaned forward; her bottom was braced against the Land Rover. She was staring at the island, deep in thought. I knew she was scheming. Logic said she could not force me to go there if I did not want to, but she had already outmanoeuvred me to get me to Angola.

'Come on!' I reached for the map. 'Let's go and find some artisanal miners.'

Constance's marks were colour-coded by the probability of us finding anything; a red cross meant a confirmed sighting, but blue was only suspected activity. We were close to two crosses, a red and a blue. The blue was very close by.

'We ought to go on to the next marker, the red one,' I said. 'It's more likely we'll find something there and it's not far, only a couple of miles.' I wanted to put some distance between us and the island.

'All right,' she conceded, 'but we'll have to come back here some time.'

We followed the river north, in the general direction of Nocredo. After the river channels recombined at the end of the island, the river's full power was concentrated into a single stream fifty yards or so across: a huge volume of water.

'Where does it go?' asked Sophie. 'It's flowing north isn't it? The wrong direction for the Atlantic and it can't go to the Med can it? There's the Sahara.'

'I'm pretty sure it finishes up in the Congo River, but I can't remember if it joins another river before then.'

'The Congo must be huge if it's got many rivers like this feeding it.'

'It is. I was on a flight that refuelled in Kinshasa once, that's on the Congo and the river looked to be at least three or four miles ·

across between Kinshasa and Brazzaville on the other side. I think your father once told me it was the deepest river in the world.'

'Are there diamonds in it?' she asked.

'I don't know but I would expect so. They would be a bugger to mine though. It's not a river to divert; it would have to involve some kind of deep dredging.'

We were close to where Constance had marked the map with the red cross. I turned off the main mine road onto a narrow track only slightly wider than the Land Rover. The grass and scrub grew in tight, trying to reclaim the track into the bush. When it got too dense, I stopped, and we got out.

'Are there snakes here, David?'

'It's Africa,' I said, 'cobras, puff adders, mambas and pythons at the very least, but it's crocs and hippos that worry me. They're far more likely to attack.'

'Shouldn't we have something then?'

'Such as?'

'I don't know, a gun maybe?'

'Well, we haven't got one and I've never carried one.' I shuddered at a fleeting memory. 'No one I knew was ever bitten or injured by the wildlife. We had a few scares, but …'

'Do you ever get nervous in places like this?'

'Always. Shit scared would be more accurate,' I said. 'But not of snakes and things … I've been to more artisanal mining sites than I can remember, and it doesn't get any less scary, especially when you arrive alone, without someone they know and trust. Remember … what they're doing is illegal, so anyone dropping by is unlikely to be a friend.'

'A gun's a good idea then, surely? Self-protection.'

'Don't ever make that mistake. If they see a white face with a gun, they'll probably shoot first and ask questions later.'

'Do you really think there's a serious risk here?'

'I don't know but it's a good idea to consider that possibility. It's a bit late now to start rethinking things – it's your idea that put us here anyway,' I reminded her. 'Let's get it over with, come on.'

111

I checked around in the Land Rover until I found what I expected, a panga machete, under the driver's seat: useful for cutting back vegetation.

We followed the track until the scrub eventually won the battle and it petered out completely. Grass grew tall around us and the spiky branches of stunted trees nibbled and scratched at our exposed arms and legs. It was no more than two hundred yards to the river, but I doubted we would reach it exactly where the miners were working, if indeed they were working. We would almost certainly have to walk along the bank for a while.

'Do you know any songs?' I asked.

'Why?'

'Either you sing, or I whistle. If there's anyone here I want to give them ample warning. People behave better if they're not surprised.'

'You'd better whistle then. I can't sing to save my life – they'd probably shoot to shut me up.'

We made slow progress with me hacking back the vegetation. I was so engrossed that I did not notice that Sophie was no longer just behind me until I turned to tell her something. I guessed she'd taken a comfort break, so I decided to do the same; give her a chance to catch up. I was just zipping up when I heard a crack just behind me; I thought it was Sophie and I vaguely remember trying to make up a toilet joke just before my head seemed to explode with pain. I sagged forward on my knees, stunned and uncomprehending. As my head cleared, I could see that I was surrounded by men with weapons: guns, pickaxes and machetes; I wondered what had hit me. Sophie was standing with them. She was gagged and I could not see her hands; I guessed they were tied behind her back.

A young man, who seemed to be the leader, grabbed my shoulder. 'Levante-se! Stand up!' he said.

It was a struggle as my hands were bound behind me. I had not noticed them do it so I must have been unconscious for a short while after being hit. Sophie looked terrified. We were prodded and cajoled through some thick bush for a short distance before we broke through into a path that was obviously in regular use. The sound of fast-flowing water grew louder as we walked. When I tried to turn to look at Sophie, I was given a sharp prod in the back and was told to keep going.

They took us to a clearing by the river where they shoved us both to the ground and bound our feet. Two men stood guard over us with automatic rifles; we were not going anywhere in a hurry.

I tried to move but a pain in my shoulder caused me to cry out.

It must have been an odd scene. Men, women and children continued to work close by, washing and sorting gravel, as though nothing had happened; they glanced across at us from time to time but they showed no emotion. A small group of men, the ones who had captured us, stood away from the workers; they were deep in discussion. I tried not to think about what they might be deciding, but I failed dismally. I could only imagine they were discussing how they were going to kill us and dispose of our bodies. I was sure we were going to die. My only unselfish thought was that I hoped they would not rape Sophie before they killed her.

The young man, the leader, detached himself from the group and came over to us.

'Why did you come here? What did you want?' he asked in Portuguese. He held up our map and pointed at the red cross that marked where we were. 'You came looking for this place. Why?'

'Please don't harm her,' I said, meaning 'us'. 'We were looking for you to offer you help. We're from a British charity.'

'Who are we then? If you were looking for us, you'd know who we are.'

'You're a group of miners. You're working illegally at the moment, but we want to do something about that. I don't know exactly who you are; that doesn't matter.'

He gave me a sharp kick in the ribs. 'That's right,' he said. 'We don't matter to anyone except when they want to kill us or move us on. That's why you're really here isn't it? Some sort of trick.' He shook his head in disgust and went back to the group. There was a lot of head shaking before an older man came over.

He looked about sixty; fit and wiry in appearance, but it was his expression that bothered me: I had never seen such hatred in a face before. He stared at me as though he thought his look alone could kill me. Then he looked at Sophie and his expression changed; I feared the worst for her. His brow furrowed and he bent over her and ripped the gag from her mouth. He smiled lasciviously.

'Please let us go,' Sophie pleaded. 'We really did come to help you. We mean you no harm.'

'Who are you?' he asked.

'I'm Doctor Sophie Addison and this is my boss, David Young. We work for Flourish. It's a British charity that helps people like you.'

The man turned his attention from Sophie back to me. He crouched down and stared at my face; he said nothing. After a minute or so he stood up and went to re-join the group.

Chapter 13

'Are they going to kill us?' Sophie sobbed from her curled-up position in the dirt. 'I didn't expect to die here, so close to where my father …'

It was hard to give her my honest opinion. 'I don't know,' I said. 'I don't think they will. They'd have done it by now if they were going to.'

I did not even convince myself, but my efforts to comfort her took my mind off my headache and the searing pain in my right shoulder. I had a horrible feeling though that the pain would end all too soon.

The old man had come back to us without me noticing. He stared at me again, nodded, and started to untie Sophie's hands and feet. Why was he doing that? Easier access?

'No!' I shouted.

He laughed. 'Untie him,' he said to Sophie and he looked me in the eyes again. 'Do you remember me?' he said. I shook my head.

'My name's Sylvestre. Now do you remember me?'

For the first time, I saw past my fear and his hatred. I saw his face in a new light. Yes, it was vaguely familiar. My mind stripped it of wrinkles and blackened his silver hair and I was taken back thirty years. It was the eyes, eyes I had stared at then, eyes that had not trusted me at first, but eyes that had ultimately taken a chance. Yes, I remembered Sylvestre.

★★★

I had tried to wriggle out of the security operation, but Kevin Dryden and Morgan had insisted that I went. It was the end of my third week back from leave and I was to show Colin and Jug, two former soldiers, exactly where the illegal river mining operations were that we had seen from the helicopter on my return from leave. Dryden had smirked maliciously as he argued the case for my involvement: I was familiar with the area and knew how to find the location from the road.

Jug hid the Land Rover well off the road, about a half a mile from where Morgan, Thys Gerber and I had seen the garimpeiros, and we set off on foot. The two men made an odd pairing: Colin was tall and thin while Jug, as his nickname hinted, was shorter and stockier, but both were able to move swiftly and quietly; they didn't bother to hide their irritation at having to wait for me to catch up every fifty yards or so.

We reached a point where we had sight of a clearing. It was roughly oval, about sixty yards long by forty yards at its widest. The reddish orange soil was scattered with piles of dirt and rocks, and felled vegetation was stacked untidily at one end. A man-made trench brought a trickle of water in at the far end, which then split into tributaries to feed several small ponds. It was a place where I could imagine garimpeiros washing gravel and looking for diamonds. Colin stopped and raised his hand, signalling for quiet. He edged forward slowly then crouched behind a bush, watching and listening. He waved for me to stay where I was but ushered Jug forward to a position about thirty yards to his right. They waited until both were satisfied, then they raised their automatic rifles and advanced.

I waited where I was and listened, dreading the sound of gunfire. There was none. After what seemed like an hour, but was probably more like five minutes, they reappeared, one either side of an Angolan they had captured. Jug waved me forward into the clearing. Colin thrust a pistol into my hand and barked instructions at me: 'Don't let the bastard escape,' he said, gesturing to the Angolan. 'The safety's off – just point it and squeeze the trigger if he tries to run – it's dead easy.'

I was too stunned to argue. They disappeared, leaving me on guard.

I looked across at my prisoner. He was a Chokwe: short, in his late twenties, thin and wiry. His eyes flicked back and forth between the gun and my eyes; I was sure he was sizing me up and weighing his chances.

I wanted to talk to him, to gain his trust, but I knew that was unrealistic. I could not imagine how he felt but I felt like a prisoner to the gun I was holding. I would be much happier if he just ran – there was no way I would shoot him. I would be called a wimp, or worse, and I would probably be disciplined but my conscience would be clear. For me, the gun was purely a deterrent; it was to deter him from attacking me. I had to try to get him to trust me not to shoot him if he ran away.

'Sou David Young. Como se chama?' I tried.

'Sylvestre,' he replied quietly.

I asked him where he lived, and he told me he came from many kilometres away. It was a naive question. No one suspected of illegal mining was going to tell you where to go looking for them. I asked about his family, but he regarded every question with suspicion, and our conversation was one-sided and not very revealing. I did not have the Portuguese vocabulary to talk about much apart from mining, family and food so my strategy was doomed.

Time was passing and I did not know how long Colin and Jug would be gone. How would they treat their prisoners when they got them back to town? Probably give them a good beating. I had to get Sylvestre to run for his own good as well as for mine.

If I told him to run, he would most likely think it was a trap and expect to be shot and I did not trust him enough to put the gun down. I caught his eye and gestured towards the end of the clearing with the felled vegetation, opposite to where Colin and Jug had disappeared. He looked worried, searching for a trap. I kept my eyes locked on his and pointed the pistol away from him. I nodded. He got up slowly and moved towards the felled vegetation; his eyes flicking between mine and the pistol. When he reached the end of the clearing I nodded again and fired a shot away from him. A look of understanding lit up his eyes and he turned and ran into the bush. I dashed to where he had disappeared and fired a shot to authenticate my effort to stop him then I returned to where I'd been sitting. I had a pee against a nearby tree.

I waited and the longer I waited the more frightened I became. Had I drawn attention to where I was? Would I be captured or shot by the garimpeiros? I had not thought my plan through. Would my shots influence Colin and Jug's operation? Would they have to abort? Had they already done what they needed to do? How would they react to my gun shots? Oh shit!

I found a secluded spot outside of the clearing, but which offered a good view of it. Being here should give me a chance of getting away if things turned out wrong, or so I thought. Suddenly, my right arm was twisted *up behind my back, the gun was prised from my hand; a hand clamped over my mouth, gagging me, and then I was free.*

'You should see your face,' laughed Colin as he pocketed the pistol. 'I guess he got away then. It's a good job we got three more, so it won't matter too much. What happened?'

'My bladder was killing me. I had to have a piss and, while I was preoccupied, he did a runner. I'd no idea those things were so inaccurate.' I nodded at the pistol.

'No worse than your dick by the look of things,' Jug laughed and pointed at some splashes that had not yet dried on my boots. I blushed but I was secretly glad of this accidental corroboration.

They led me to where three Angolans were tied up. We took them back to town.

★★★

'Yes, I remember a young man called Sylvestre. It was a long time ago,' I said quietly.

He nodded thoughtfully. 'I trusted you then,' he said. 'You didn't have to let me go free. In fact, I'm sure you disobeyed orders. After today we're quits. I'm letting you go, but if I see you again …'

'Sylvestre,' I said. 'We were telling the truth. We do very much want to help you.'

I could see from the way he was screwing his face up that he was weighing things up, much as he had thirty years before. Then he shook his head. 'No. Those other bastards are still here. You wouldn't be here without their permission. We can't even think about talking until they've gone.'

'Who are you talking about? I don't understand.'

'Come on.' He was still shaking his head. 'Those two you were with before: the tall one and the fat bastard.'

It was my turn to shake my head. Sophie looked confused; she had no idea what was going on.

We said no more and Sylvestre led us back through the scrub to where the Land Rover was parked. I made a mental checklist of names. I hadn't expected to know many people in Mumbulo, but the list was growing. Colin and Jug had all but faded from my memory, but they were apparently still in Mumbulo, then there was the face in the photo. My past was invading and occupying the present; I felt sick.

Obrigado, Sylvestre,' I said when we reached the car, 'I hope we do meet again, and I hope you'll welcome us next time.'

He laughed. 'A lot must change. Be careful and don't come back while …' He gave me back the machete, then on the point of turning away, he hesitated. He pointed at Sophie. 'I've only seen one other with hair like that. It was around the time …'

'She's his daughter,' I said.

Sylvestre nodded. 'I didn't know him, but he was known to be fair-minded. I knew many who liked him.' With that, he turned and headed back towards the river without a further word.

Sophie had to drive because the pain in my shoulder made it difficult for me and I was feeling slightly dizzy from the blow I had taken.

'What was all that about? Something very strange happened there. One minute I thought we were going to die. I was about to start begging, then … he realised he knew you. I think it was your name; he knew it, but he hadn't recognised you until he heard your name. How did you know him?'

I told her the story.

'So those two guys: Colin and Jug, they're still here?' she said.

'It seems like it. I wonder what they're doing. They could be a real problem for us; they were only ever happy when they were out playing soldiers. They won't be best pleased about what we're trying to do. Sylvestre's probably right not to trust us because we could easily be set up to draw the miners out and make them more vulnerable.'

'That's taking it a bit far isn't it?'

'I don't know,' I said. 'I didn't really know them that well, but their presence could screw up the project. It's certainly something we need to think about.' I closed my eyes for a moment; the afternoon's encounter flashed through my mind and I had to clasp my hands together to stop them shaking. 'Bloody hell! What a day, eh?' I muttered. 'Talk about lucky.'

'I've never been so scared.' She laughed tremulously. 'Whose silly idea was this anyway?'

'My head's bloody killing me, and my shoulder. If we need to explain this to anyone, let's just say I fell into a hole. Okay?'

'You should see a doctor,' said Sophie.

Mumbulo. That house. That photograph. I really did not want to see a doctor the way things were going. I felt utterly exhausted. Adrenaline had kept me going for the last half hour, but it seemed to drain away in an instant and all my energy went with it.

'Can you drop me at the mine offices?' I said 'I want to have a word with Harry and Constance. You can take the car back to Manuel then pick me up when you're ready.'

'What is it with you?' she said. 'Everything's had an element of mystery in it since we got to Mumbulo. You don't want to go back to that house, do you? You were quite rude in your haste to get away after lunch; you couldn't wait. Is it Manuel's sister? Don't you want to meet her?'

I said nothing.

'She's obviously very kind, she didn't have to invite us for lunch. She put a lot of effort into it. The least we can do is to thank her personally.'

'You're right, of course.' The more I thought about it the more I realised I did not really want to go to the offices either. A lot of people there would already know about us and what we wanted to do. My name was bound to come up in a conversation somewhere and the afternoon had already demonstrated the longevity of memory. I might as well face the inevitable. 'Okay, Manuel's sister's it is.'

Chapter 14

Sophie's driving style was like her father's had been, careful and efficient. Nonetheless my shoulder was sensitive to every bump and I was feeling nauseous. When I wasn't preoccupied with my discomfort, I kept seeing that photograph in my mind's eye. I really did not want to go back to that house, but I had to get it over with – rather today than tomorrow or the day after.

An informal market had sprung up near the edge of Mumbulo since we had left, and Sophie was forced to slow to a virtual stand-still to negotiate a course through the sea of multi-coloured, milling humanity. Eventually, she pulled the Land Rover to a stop by the kerb in front of Manuel's sister's house, the house that I still thought of as Maria's. I braced myself mentally before getting out and following Sophie up the path. Manuel opened the wrought iron gate and welcomed Sophie like a long-lost friend before turning to greet me with less enthusiasm. A sturdy woman with a friendly face and dark hair was standing on the veranda. Manuel introduced her as his sister, Teresa. I recognised her from the photograph. The other person in the photograph, a wedding picture, was sitting where I had sat to eat my lunch. He rose but did not offer his hand to either Sophie or me. He gave me a cursory glance before staring long and hard at Sophie. I often stared at her myself, but I had forgotten my first reaction to her. This man knew who she was too, without introduction, and he looked as though he had seen a ghost. He was as tall as I remembered, but now he had a slight stoop.

'Hello Kevin,' I said, avoiding any hypocritical embellishment.

'I always swore I'd have you kicked out of town if I ever saw you again, Young. As for her, I can see she's Lodge's. What's she doing here?' Sophie looked as though she'd been slapped, and I could see she was fighting to keep control.

'I'm not overjoyed to see you again either. You don't seem to have changed much – probably still need a map to get to Nocredo.' It was as though we were carrying on a conversation, we'd started thirty years ago. I could see nothing that I liked any better now in Kevin Dryden than I had then.

'Insults aren't a good idea. I'm the General Manager of Mumbulo, and the number two in ARDCO. I have influence.' He forced a grin.

I glanced at Sophie, remembering the question I had asked her earlier about the ARDCO senior management dossier. She looked sheepish.

'I hope you're not going to let our past differences get in the way,' I said. 'I assume you know why we're here.'

'I know why you say you're here. Mitch gave me the run down earlier. I must admit I was surprised to hear your name again after all this time. Her name meant nothing of course.' He jabbed a finger in Sophie's direction without looking at her, 'but, now I can see who she is, I want to know why you're really here.'

'To do what Mitch told you. We want to build bridges between you and the artisanal miners.'

'Garimpeiros, you mean. Well, rope and hanging are two words that go well together. From what Mitch said you'll find plenty of rope. I don't think you've got a clue what you're dealing with. Or maybe you have.' Dryden smiled maliciously. 'You look as though someone's given you a good beating already. Expect more of the same … if you're lucky.'

'So, you're not going to stand in our way?' I was surprised.

He shook his head. 'Carry on.' He made a hanging gesture with his hands.

Sophie tapped Manuel on the arm. 'Come on,' she said. 'Let's get back to Nocredo.'

Sophie and I thanked Teresa for the lunch, and I struggled not to say something unpleasant to Dryden.

On the way back Manuel was furious. 'Why didn't you tell me you knew my brother-in-law? He went berserk when he heard your name this afternoon. I thought he was going to hit me.'

'I didn't know Kevin Dryden was here until I saw a photograph in the house at lunch time. I certainly didn't know that he was married to your sister until then and I was too shocked to say anything. Besides, it was so long ago that I thought everything would have changed.'

'Well, it hasn't, has it?'

I did not answer. I thought back to something Dryden had said. 'If Kevin's the number two in ARDCO, who's in charge?' I asked.

'A man called Geoff Morgan.'

I laughed; there was an inevitability to it. My shoulder was too painful for me to turn and look at Sophie in the back seat, but I hoped she would not miss the little shake of my head.

'Is Morgan based in Angola?' I asked.

'Yes, but he doesn't live in Mumbulo.'

Sophie – not one to be cowed by a guilty conscience – had been following our exchanges closely. 'Where then?' she asked. 'Nocredo?'

'No. Luanda. Although ARDCO's only operation is in Mumbulo, they keep an office in Luanda to be close to Diangola and the Mining Ministry,' Manuel explained. 'Senhor Morgan spends most of his time there.'

We continued in silence for a while as Sophie and I each considered this latest piece of information.

'What does all this mean for us?' Sophie asked me, now in English.

I told her the truth, that I had no idea. I had liked Morgan until things had turned sour between us in the aftermath of her father's death. Morgan and Dryden were very different animals. Dryden and I had loathed each other from our very first meeting. The two men did, however, have one thing in common – a dislike of garimpeiros. I wondered if their views had mellowed over the years. Dryden's did not appear to have done, but what about Morgan's? And what about Sophie's quest? I was ambivalent about it. I wanted answers but I did not want the pain that would go with finding them; the pain that had already started.

I apologised to Manuel for not telling him anything. It had been unfair of me. He didn't deserve the afternoon he had had; Dryden's reaction to my name and then the vitriolic exchange between Dryden and me. He said it was okay, then he shook his head and spat out of the window. 'The man's a complete arsehole anyway.'

After Manuel dropped us off at the casa de trânsito, Sophie sighed noisily. 'Wow!' she said. 'So that was Kevin Dryden. Was he always like that? I can't remember anyone I've ever disliked as much, on first meeting him.'

I laughed for the first time in a couple of hours. 'He was on his best behaviour there.'

'He recognised me just like you did. It's really weird the way you both looked at me when you first saw me. You still stare sometimes, you know. It's as though you're looking at, or is it looking for, my father. People often look at me; I'm used to it, but Dryden unnerved me. And his comments were horrible, as though my father was worthless.'

'Forget it,' I smiled encouragingly. 'The one I feel sorry for is Teresa. Imagine being married to him.'

'I'm starting to wish we'd never come. It's only our first day and I've already thought I was going to die, then that man ...'

'Yes, I've been trying to forget Kevin Dryden for thirty years. But you knew he'd be here, didn't you? Why did you leave him and Morgan out of the dossier?'

'I'm really sorry, David, but I thought you wouldn't come here if you knew. I thought you'd make sure we worked in one of the other areas: Cafunfo or Lucapa or somewhere.'

'You're right. I probably would have. But we're here now ...' I sighed; I could not change anything. 'It worries me that Dryden's not trying to stop us.' I continued. 'Something seems wrong.'

'Like what?'

'No idea. It's just out of character. The Kevin Dryden I remember would've said no to anything I wanted to do just to prove he was the boss. Maybe he has softened with age, but somehow I don't think so; he's still a nasty piece of work.'

'What about the others? The two you were with when ... Sylvestre, you know.'

'Colin and Jug? The only thing they knew anything about was playing soldiers. I expect they're doing the same now, if indeed they are still here. One thing I do remember about them though ... They were there when we found your father. They were the ones who checked around for threats and secured the area.'

Sophie's eyes lit up. 'I hope Sylvestre's right then, that they are still here.' She was no longer sorry we had come; she had a possible new line of enquiry. 'They might remember something you can't.'

'I wouldn't pin my hopes on that if I were you. Your father's death would have been a pretty low-key event in their eyes – nothing went bang. They're far more likely to remember action with guns-a-blazing and knives out.'

'And Geoff Morgan? I wonder how often he visits Mumbulo. Maybe he'll visit while we're here – that would be helpful. Failing that, we can find him in Luanda when we go back out.'

I smiled ruefully. The list of names and places she most wanted to see was remarkably like my list that I never wanted to see again. I wondered whose wish would come true.

Chapter 15

'How should we approach things today?' Sophie's voice lacked its usual confidence. She was picking at her breakfast without enthusiasm. The assertiveness that had brought us both to Angola was gone. There were dark shadows under her eyes; the previous day had taken its toll.

'We've got two options.' I took a sip of coffee and looked her in the eye. 'Either we pack our bags and bugger off home, or we get the map out and decide where we're going to find some artisanal miners. As we're being paid to do the latter, I vote for that, but ... let's be more careful and make sure we're carrying a good stock of aspirin.'

Sophie spluttered, sending a mouthful of coffee over her toast. 'I thought you'd want to leave,' she said. 'You never wanted to come here.'

'True, but as we are here, let's make the most of it. What happened yesterday afternoon was something I've been expecting to happen for years. The way I see it, it's taken nearly fifteen years of working for Flourish and hundreds of site visits before I got clobbered. It might happen again today, or it might be another fifteen years – the odds haven't changed much, if at all.'

Sophie had Constance's map out of her bag so quickly, I had the impression that she thought I might change my mind if she did not act fast. She passed me the map.

A good night's sleep had done wonders for my head, but my shoulder had stiffened badly. I winced as I tried to open the map. 'Let's learn from our mistakes,' I said. 'Let's not get caught with a map again, not with an incriminating X marking the spot. You can't blame Sylvestre's group for not trusting us.'

'Manuel said we could have that Land Rover again today,' said Sophie. 'I think it's a good job he works for Diangola and not ARDCO. I'm sure Dryden would have vetoed us using one of their vehicles.' She looked at her watch. 'What time is he picking us up?'

'About seven, I think. We'd better hurry up and decide where we want to go today. He'll be here in ten minutes.'

Manuel was alert and smiling when he arrived. He was not a man who bore a grudge and I liked him all the more for that. He confirmed that we could have the Land Rover from about nine o'clock or nine-thirty, as it would be used to collect some office supplies before that.

Sophie would have to drive again, at least until I got some relatively pain-free movement back in my shoulder. I had tried to draw Sophie's attention to some red crosses on the map, to the south of Mumbulo, but she just smiled and plonked her finger on the blue cross near the island in the river.

'As I'm driving, I call the shots,' she said. She reasoned that it might be good to start somewhere where we were less likely to encounter hostile miners, to get our confidence back.

'But that defeats the object,' I argued.

'We have to go there sometime and, if Dryden gets obstructive, it might be our only chance.'

I couldn't disagree with her logic, but her objectives and priorities were different from mine – I didn't want to go anywhere near that island – for once I would have welcomed an intervention from Dryden.

We had some time to kill at the mine offices while we waited for the Land Rover but neither of us wanted to run into Dryden. We had nowhere to go so we waited in Manuel's car, keeping our heads low until our Land Rover turned up. We watched as people came and left, looking for any familiar faces. Alas we did spot Kevin Dryden and he us; his eyes seemed to lock on to Manuel's car and a 'gotcha' smirk flickered across his face. I pointed out two distant figures to Sophie, walking between offices; they were too far away for a definite identification, but their shapes, sizes and juxtaposition left me in little doubt that Colin and Jug were indeed still in Mumbulo.

It was a relief when our transport arrived, and we could stop behaving furtively. We took the same route as the previous day to get to the river diversion, including some of the same wrong turnings.

The mine roads were just wide enough for two trucks to pass but not without them making a mess of the vegetation on the fringes. It was best therefore to park off the road to avoid any possibility of being clipped by a passing truck. We found a little track where we could pull off safely.

We took one last look at the map before hiding it under the driver's seat. I found the machete again and took a couple of practice swings with my right hand. My shoulder was getting better but not that much better. I would have to hack our route left-handed so progress would be slow. Sophie volunteered to blaze the trail, but I could tell she was not keen. We would see how it went and, if I was struggling, she could have a go.

The track we had parked in was similar to the one I'd used the previous day. It headed towards the river and quickly narrowed. I guessed its only purpose was for letting mine trucks pass. We set off towards the river and I had to start using the machete within fifty yards. My left-handed action carried most of the power but little of the accuracy and coordination of my right; I soon switched the machete to my right hand. After some initial pain, the shoulder improved dramatically – it was what it needed. The river was no more than a hundred and fifty yards from the car but it took longer than I expected to reach it. Eventually, we broke through.

'Looks like Constance was right.' I was squatting, examining the riverbank. 'Someone's been digging around here recently. The bank's a mess but the water's clear.'

'Does that mean they've gone?' Sophie sounded hopeful but her face was tense.

'Not necessarily. It's just that, if they are here, they're downstream not up. There would probably be some colouration in the

river if they were washing upstream. Come on.' I set off downstream and I could hear her reluctantly start to follow.

Going downstream suited me; it put the island behind us
where it was less likely to be a conversation piece. I started whistling and this time Sophie joined in; the memory of the day before was still fresh in both of our minds. The bank was uneven
and fell quite steeply towards the river in places, but progress was
still much easier than hacking through vegetation.

After about three hundred yards we came to an area where
the scrub had been cut back from the river to about sixty yards.
It was deserted. It was a typical washing area with small piles of
rocks and soil scattered around; some were darker than others –
fresh. And I could see dark, wet patches on the ground. The hairs
on my arms stood on end. Someone had been here very recently.

I held my hand up to warn Sophie not to do anything rash
then I put the machete down and shouted, 'Bom dia!' It was all
I could think of.

We waited. I was shaking and I was sure I could hear Sophie's
teeth rattling behind me. I shouted again, 'Hola!' which was better than good morning but not much.

'Hola, senhor.' The voice: male, neither hostile nor friendly,
was very close, somewhere behind me. I relaxed slightly – we
were talking at least.

'Hola, senhor,' I said.

There was a rustling and thirty or so men emerged from the
cover of the trees into the clearing facing us. Many of them held
rifles and were pointing them at us. I guessed the man behind
us must have given a signal that we could not see.

A pair of hands ran up and down me, checking for a weapon. He moved around to face us, and Sophie held up her arms,
expecting to be frisked too, but her action only elicited a laugh.
'Senhora, I would see if you were carrying a weapon. I will check
your bag though.' She handed it over. He gave it a cursory look
and passed it back.

'So, what are you doing here? Are you lost?' His Portuguese
was surprisingly refined to my ear.

'No, we're not lost. We hoped to find some friendly miners.' I gestured at the piles of ore and tools dotted around the area.

The man laughed. He was short and wiry, and his dark skin, though it looked healthy, bore many scars. 'And what makes you think we might be friendly? I haven't seen either of your faces before and I would certainly remember the senhora; the hair's unusual.'

'We work for a British charity, Flourish.' I gave the short speech I had rehearsed in my mind as I hacked through the scrub. 'We're looking at ways to enable cooperation between groups like yours, artisanal miners, and companies like ARDCO. Our hopes are to end the conflict and to get you a better deal, to sell your diamonds at a fair price. In short, we're here to help you.'

'At least you didn't call us garimpeiros,' he said. 'But no one's ever helped us before. They didn't help my father, or my grandfather and I've never expected anyone to help me. I don't believe you. What are you really doing here?'

'Just what I said, to help. The civil war's over. That shows that any conflict can be stopped if all the parties are willing to compromise. We've had meetings with both ARDCO and Diangola and they're prepared to talk. We want to start a dialogue between them and you, or someone like you.'

He shook his head and laughed. 'Dialogue? That's funny. Do you think we're stupid? The mining companies have never tried to talk to us. They just send in their army, so-called security. They threaten us and sometimes they flatten our homes. Why should they change now and why should we trust them? Why should we trust you?'

'Because we can offer hope for your children.' Sophie spoke for the first time. She moved past me with her hand out to him. 'I'm Dr Sophie Addison and this is my colleague David Young.' I offered my hand too. He shook hands with Sophie first then he looked hard at me before shaking mine.

'Muachaquima,' he said. It was a fairly common Angolan name; I'd heard it many times in the past.

He waved the guns away and signalled that it was safe for everyone to go back to what they were doing. Women and children slowly emerged from the scrub, joining the men, and settling down to work. Muachaquima led us away from the river towards some logs at the far end of the clearing and gestured for us to sit. He offered us water, which we politely declined, then he began to question us. His questions were incisive and intelligent; I could not help wondering what he could have been in another life.

After interrogating us for about ten minutes, he sighed. 'Why should you care about us? Nobody else does. The world doesn't seem to know we even exist.' He concentrated on me, ignoring Sophie even though it was she who had somehow broken the tension and brought about the change in Muachaquima's attitude towards us.

'We're interested in communities recovering after wars,' I replied, 'how people can improve their standard of life: what they do, how they work and, most importantly, what the obstacles are. We know you're classed as illegal miners, but we believe we can change that. If you were legal you could sell your diamonds through the mining company, at a fair price, and you wouldn't have to worry about their security forces.'

He gave an ironic laugh. 'You're living in a dream world. What are we supposed to do? Just walk into Mumbulo and say "here we are, we're garimpeiros and we want to sell you some diamonds." Those bastards at ARDCO would think it was their birthday. They'd take the diamonds, beat us up then put us in that hellhole of a gaol. It would save them coming to look for us. I think you're genuine, but I don't trust anyone at ARDCO.'

'If I could guarantee your safety, would you consider meeting with ARDCO and Diangola?'

'Of course, because what you describe is a world I visit every night, in my dreams. The problem is that I don't believe you can give such a guarantee. Let me put it another way; I believe they'll tell you that we'll be safe, but I think it'll be a trap.' Muachaquima scratched his head and screwed up his face in thought. 'I also dream that, if I have children, they will go to school and university, but, as it is, they will have to work here with me or we

131

wouldn't make enough to live. I want to trust you, but this situation isn't a result of the war; it goes back further than that. It was people like us who found diamonds here. We farmed the land and lived on it long before the Portuguese and the British came along and claimed it. We've been ripped off ever since. What do they stand to gain from working with us? I'm sure you mean well but I can't trust those people.'

I sensed that Sophie was struggling a bit with the Portuguese, but she had understood enough. 'So, you're happy to continue being moved on and having your camps broken up. Surely there's no future in that. You want children; you said so. How many children work here? Where do they go to school? Do they go to school at all?'

'I teach them myself, here. I'm the schoolteacher.'

'Where is your school then?' she asked.

'Right here. These logs are my school.'

'I don't doubt that you're a good teacher,' she glared at him, 'but it's not good enough is it? The children deserve better than this. They deserve to be educated somewhere that feels secure, where they can learn with confidence. Looking over their shoulders wondering when their father will be arrested or shot isn't conducive to learning. You have to look to the future.'

He switched to English, which was almost faultless and sounded as though it had been learnt in Johannesburg. 'Yes, I am a good teacher. Yes, we do need to break this cycle, but the problem is trust. I know this man is trustworthy.' He pointed at me. 'And I trust you because he trusts you.'

I looked at Sophie and her expression was as mystified as I knew mine was. Did this man know me? Had he spoken to Sylvestre? How had he decided so surely that I was indeed trustworthy?

He mooched around the school area for several minutes, wringing his hands, agonising over what he was going to say next. Suddenly he stopped and relaxed: his decision was made. 'We need to change. I'm going to take a chance with you, for the children, for their future. I'll speak to everyone; explain what you've said to me then you'll need to earn their trust. You must deliver on any promises you make, and that includes any guarantee of safety. I believe we get one chance in our lives and I'm going to trust you with my chance.'

'And what have I done to earn your trust?' I asked. 'I expected this to be a much more difficult process.'

'I trust my senses. Let's just leave it at that for the moment. And don't kid yourself that this is going to be easy. I'm on your side and I have some influence in this group but, if they don't like the idea, it won't happen. We've had years, generations, of abuse so the distrust of the mining companies is deeply rooted, and not without reason. Remember that.'

'Would you like me to talk to everyone now?' I asked.

'No. I want to speak to them individually. They're hard to control as a group. One will speak against it and the others will follow because it's the line they've always taken; they don't do change very easily. Where are you staying? Mumbulo?'

'The casa de trânsito in Nocredo.'

He nodded. 'It'll probably take me two or three days to convince the group, but ...'

'Brilliant! Thank you Muachaquima. We'll carry on with ARDCO and Diangola, and we'll come back to see how you got on and to let you know what we've arranged. Can you contact any of the other groups?'

'One other, maybe. One thing you might not realise is that things are still polarised here. Although the civil war's over, there are still long memories. There were many atrocities. Some people supported the MPLA and others, UNITA. You're lucky you came to us. If you'd suggested getting a UNITA group to talk to Diangola – they're MPLA – who knows? Maybe those other groups have changed, but I still don't trust them. They're another reason we keep the AK–47s.'

'Do you know Sylvestre?' Sophie asked. 'He seems to be one of the senior men in another group just downstream.'

'Yes, but I wouldn't advise going to that lot. They've been known to attack mine transports. They give ARDCO their excuse to keep the security force. Shoot first and ask questions later.' I rubbed my shoulder at the memory. Muachaquima smiled. 'Ah! You already made that mistake then.'

We laughed and, without thinking, I clapped him on the back like an old friend. He did not seem to mind.

We talked for a while. Muachaquima told us how his mother had taken him away from the war as a child, over the border to Zaire, and how they had worked their way south through Zambia and Zimbabwe, over a couple of years, until they reached Johannesburg. His mother had done casual work – cleaning and stacking shelves – for money to keep them fed. His father stayed in Angola and had fought against Jonas Savimbi's UNITA in the civil war that had flared up again after the failed elections of 1992.

We shook hands with Muachaquima and were about to head back to the car when Sophie said, 'That island in the river diversion. I really want to go there. Does anyone have a boat we could borrow?'

Muachaquima was silent for a moment but eventually he nodded. 'Tomorrow is Saturday; it'll be quiet in the afternoon. Come here then and I'll sort something out.'

Sophie agreed provided she could get transport. She smiled at me; triumphant; and I knew she would go whether I did or not. Muachaquima said nothing more but his eyes carried a message I could not quite grasp.

Sophie drove us back to Mumbulo where we had a late lunch with Manuel and Teresa. Kevin Dryden was not there as he always ate his lunch in the ARDCO mess. Manuel had been summoned to a three-thirty p.m. meeting in Nocredo, so we had to go back with him, somewhat earlier than we would have liked. On the way, Sophie managed to persuade him to lend her his car for the following afternoon.

We spent the rest of the afternoon catching up with emails and writing up the events of our first two days in the mining area.

Chapter 16

An early night had done me good: I was well rested. Nature's choral repertoire of buzzes and chirps had lulled me to sleep in minutes. I'd almost forgotten this relaxing aspect of Africa, but the last couple of nights had refreshed my memory. A flash of iridescent turquoise caught Sophie's eye and her face lit up, enchanted by the beauty of a bee-eater. We sat together in companionable silence on the veranda of the casa de trânsito, watching the birds outmanoeuvre the flies with a spectacular aerobatic display. We were the only guests, so we were using the veranda as an alfresco office.

'I'm wondering how I should question Kevin Dryden.' It never took Sophie long to get back to one or other of her pet topics. 'He scares me. And I don't think he liked my father much, judging by those snide comments.'

'Well, I'm not the best person to ask. I've never had a proper conversation with him. The only time I didn't dislike him was when he came to the Madhouse in a panic after your father was killed. But he soon reverted to type … and my view of him reverted with it.'

'What about Morgan?'

'You'll be able to talk to him okay. He's quite charming in a rugged kind of way, but I don't know how much you'll get out of him. He's shrewd. He'll say what he wants you to know and you'll probably believe he's told you everything, but he won't have.'

'Oh, I'm an expert at spotting evasion. You, for instance.' She smiled lopsidedly. 'I think I'll ask Manuel about Morgan; whether he's coming to Mumbulo soon. I really want to talk to him – get his views. He should know what evidence tied the Angolans to my father's murder. Failing that, I'll try and catch him in Luanda on our way back out.'

'Just be careful,' I said. 'The project's the priority and it has to look that way too. Dryden already has his suspicions. Remember? If either Dryden or Morgan thinks that you're showing more interest in your father's death than in the Flourish work, they'll find a reason to get us out with no return ticket. They'll expect you to show some curiosity; that's only natural; but they won't expect the Spanish Inquisition.'

'Don't worry. I can be subtle when I try.'

I remembered how she'd got information out of me. Maybe she'd manage it again.

'Going back to Dryden,' I said. 'Maybe Teresa's your way in. God knows what she's doing with Kevin, but she must have some influence over him. If you can befriend her ...'

She reflected on this for a moment then she clicked her fingers decisively. 'Did you find yesterday as weird as I did?' Her sudden change of subject caught me off guard, as it was probably meant to. 'I expected to have to work much harder than that to get somebody on our side, but Muachaquima decided to trust us ... well you. It was as though he knew you, just like with Sylvestre, but he's too young. I guess he's about my age.' She studied my face intently.

'I've never met him before,' I answered the question posed by her eyes. 'I'm sure of that. As you said, he's about your age; he probably wasn't even born when I left. It's just about conceivable that he's heard my name, but I doubt it. I certainly don't remember the names of many Angolans from thirty years ago, so I wouldn't expect them to remember mine.'

She nodded slowly. 'But it was after we introduced ourselves that he changed his attitude; Twice in two days. What is it about your name? You seem to have left an indelible impression, whether you wanted to or not.'

I shivered. The hairs stood up on my arms and on the back of my neck. That was it!

'I think his full name might be David Muachaquima,' I said slowly.

She gawped. 'David?'

My eyes moistened. Another piece of the past crashed in on me. I took a deep breath and told her.

★★★

It was the middle of the night but the piercing trill of the phone prodded me awake. I was tired; I just wanted to sleep on. I got up, wearing an evil mood, and answered it.

'Bom dia, chefe.' It was Gabriel, the concentrator foreman. He sounded nervous.

'What do you mean, good morning? It's two a.m. It's not a good morning.' Fortunately, he knew me and carried on.

'Chefe, there's a problem at Cambunda. They need you to go there.'

I tried to extract more information from him, but it was very vague. A truck driver had brought a hand-written note from the Cambunda foreman, Armando. It requested that Gabriel should contact me urgently as I was needed. The Cambunda radio was out of order so I couldn't call back and check the details. I was very surprised that Armando was on shift as I thought he was on days. Whatever the problem, I couldn't ignore it and the only way to find out what was wrong was to drive out to Cambunda.

It was twenty-five kilometres of bumpy dirt road in a rickety Land Rover with only one headlight. It was not a journey I'd volunteer for at night, but it gave me plenty of time to rehearse what I was going to say and do if it turned out to be a wild goose chase.

★★★

An hour or so later, I could almost feel her pain. Her screams needled my nerves, stirring me to imagine agonies beyond my experience. What was she suffering? Was she going to die? I desperately hoped not. The Land Rover was overheating; the radiator had a leak and I'd forgotten to top it up in my haste. My hands were shaking, and I felt helpless. The burden of responsibility for her life was dragging me to the edge of panic. The temperature gauge was silently shouting for me to stop, and I didn't even know the road or where I'd get water round here; I hadn't even known where Armando's village was before tonight. I was lost in the middle of nowhere at half past three in the morning.

'Armando,' I shouted, 'A agua ... the car's overheating. We need water now.'

Armando was in the back, comforting his wife, Esther, but he understood the urgency instantly. He had one big advantage over me; he knew this track and he knew where to find people. I stopped and he got out and disappeared into the night.

While he was away, I climbed into the back and held Esther's hand. I had no idea what to do, so I just mumbled softly and tried to be comforting. I hoped she wasn't going to die and certainly not before Armando returned. Where was Armando? Every minute felt like an hour and Esther's screams had subsided to a moan. Her screams held life, but the fading of her moans sounded like her life was ebbing away with the blood which was pooling on the floor of the car. Her labour had gone seriously wrong, but no one knew what to do. She needed a doctor urgently.

I reflected guiltily on the anger I'd felt when I'd first arrived at the plant. I had seen gravel and waste pouring off the conveyor belts into the bins; it was running well, and I'd felt duped. I'd lost valuable hours of sleep. Armando had rushed over to the Land Rover and jumped in before I had a chance to get out. He was obviously upset but I yelled at him to get out and stop wasting my time; my anger was simmering on as I begrudged him every second of lost sleep. He quickly convinced me that Esther was very ill and needed to get from their village to hospital, and then it had all changed. I was now totally committed, rooting for Esther, desperate for her to live and desperate for her baby to live too.

I suppose Armando had only been away for about ten minutes, but it felt much longer. He came back with two plastic containers of water. Blood glinted on his arms and legs where the grass had cut him. Despite his exertions, all I could see was fear on his face. Tears were streaming from his eyes. I was cradling Esther's head in my lap and she was quiet.

'Armando! Thank God! Have you got the water?' I asked.

'Is she ...?'

I realised he thought she was dead.

'She's just sleeping. We need to be quick. She's very weak.' I told Armando to take over caring for Esther, and I set about filling the radiator. Fortunately, the engine temperature had had time to fall a little and some other men had arrived with more water; enough to give us a reserve.

We set off again.

I was sure that Esther would die before we could get to the hospital. My only hope was Maria, so I drove straight to her house where she had a medical room from which she ran her surgery. My faith was vindicated; Maria performed an emergency caesarean section on Esther and saved both her and the baby. The baby was fit and well, but Esther was very weak and had to spend a few days recovering in the hospital.

★★★

My arms fizzed with goose bumps at the memory, and my eyes were blurred. It was one of the few things I'd ever done for which I felt justifiably proud. It was the only time I'd ever helped to save a life, perhaps two lives. Armando had trusted me to do my best and I'd not let him down despite my initial reaction. I was honoured by Armando naming his son after me.

'If Muachaquima really is Armando's son, then maybe Armando and Esther are here too,' said Sophie, echoing my thoughts.

'I would hope so,' I said. 'But life expectancy's not good here and Muachaquima said his father fought in the civil war. He might easily have been killed.'

'But he also said that his mother took him away to South Africa. Surely, she would have come back to look for her husband. She's probably here even if Armando isn't.'

'I only met Esther once and I doubt if she registered what I looked like; she was delirious. It's Armando I really want to see.' My resistance collapsed and tears streamed down my cheeks. 'Armando, please be alive,' I blubbed.

Sophie gave me time to recover, a look of understanding and concern on her face.

'It looks as though there are more people here than I expected who knew my father; more than I even hoped,' she said. 'Kevin Dryden, Morgan and possibly Armando.'

'Armando wouldn't have known your father well. He met him, of course, but I doubt if they ever had a conversation. And we don't know whether Armando is here or not yet. We don't even know for sure that Muachaquima is his son.'

'I have a feeling he is, though,' she said. 'And Armando sounds like a good man from all you've said, and he's important to my father's story even if they never knew each other personally. I want to meet him if possible.' Sophie's old confidence was back. She was going to milk the recent turn of events for everything she could get.

'I'm going with you this afternoon,' I said. 'I have to see that place again, and ...'

'I knew you'd want to come.' Sophie smiled.

I thought about that parting look Muachaquima had given me. I knew he was David.

Chapter 17

Manuel brought the car round much earlier than I expected; I had forgotten that he normally worked in Nocredo, not Mumbulo. As we had plenty of time, I invited him to eat lunch with us at the casa de trânsito and I was happy to put it on my account there. It was some sort of pay back for all his help. The chef had cooked an excellent feijoada – end-of-the-week Brazilian cuisine had arrived in Angola. I thoroughly enjoyed the rich, leftover-pork and bean dish but Sophie was not so keen – she picked at it like bony fish – I should never have told her there might be pigs' ears in it.

Manuel drew us a map showing us the best way out of Nocredo to get onto the mine road to Mumbulo. Although we knew the public road, it would be a long way round to use that and then take the mine road back towards Nocredo. Sophie was gung-ho to get to the island, but my main motivation was to see Muachaquima again, to find out if he really was Armando's son. I was desperate to know if Armando was still alive, and to see him if he was. And what about Esther?

I knew Muachaquima to be a man I could work with, but, if he was David, why hadn't he told me who he was? That seemed odd to me. Most people, when they see a link, raise it so that it can be confirmed or disproved, but not Muachaquima. Was his identity as David just a fantasy I had cooked up with Sophie to explain his willingness to work with us, or did he want to speak to his father before telling us who he was? If so, why? If we found Armando, would he be able to tell Sophie anything about her father's death? Did he know anything about the man Lodge had hit with his car and the biggest question of all; who killed Jim Lodge? If it was not people from Armando's village, then who was it? Someone from another village? Why had Lodge insisted on staying at the accident site when Dryden said he had offered a way out? Why had I not demanded answers to these questions at the time? Why had I convinced myself of the cut-and-dried version Dryden and Morgan had so firmly backed? Was it recalling some of the details I had forgotten, coupled with a new set of instincts, Sophie's, that had now made me suspicious? Or had a guilty conscience driven me to bury the whole incident because I was more comfortable with it that way?

A tap on the shoulder brought me back to the here and now; it was Sophie. 'You okay?' she asked. 'I thought you were on another planet.'

'Yeah. I'm fine. I was thinking, that's all. Are you ready to roll?'

'When you are.'

Manuel's Land Cruiser was in better condition than the car we had borrowed from him in Mumbulo. The only problem was that it carried Diangola markings which were likely to scare off any illegal miners if they had look-outs by the roads, and I suspected they did.

I drove. My shoulder still ached but exercise was proving to be the best therapy for it. Sophie was subdued and I asked her what was bothering her.

'This is the road my father was driving on from Nocredo, isn't it: when he was killed? We're seeing the last things he would ever have seen, aren't we?'

I nodded. 'I guess so.' I had been thinking about Armando; I had not thought of Lodge since we had left Nocredo. Once the seed was sown though, I felt abnormally sensitised to the surroundings. The sun, almost directly overhead, foreshortened shadows and emphasised colours; sharpening the contrast between the lush greens of the bush, the reds and browns of the road and the greys of waste heaps and outcropping rock. I saw things I would never normally have noticed: a snake slithering behind a rock, a strange lighting effect on a rock face that looked like a witch. I shivered; my thoughts were taking an irrational course, focusing on my own mortality again. I noticed a few places where the road seemed to have changed course over the years, but I couldn't be sure which stretches were relatively recent and which were thirty years old or more. I only realised I had missed the track we'd pulled into the day before, when I noticed we were too close to the island. Sophie was so absorbed in her own thoughts that she did not see it either. I stopped and that is when I spotted it; the faintest hint of an old road running towards the downstream end of the island. It was overgrown, but I was certain that this was the starting point of Lodge's last mile. I said nothing to Sophie, but I turned the car around and went back to where we had parked the previous day.

We made our way to the river using the path I'd hacked so painfully through the scrub. Then we followed the bank until we reached the clearing. It was deserted. Maybe they were working elsewhere? Damn! Where was Muachaquima? He had told us to come.

'Where are they likely to be, do you think?' Sophie did her usual trick of voicing my thoughts.

'God knows. Could be anywhere.'

I took the chance to look around the area and study the operation. It was something I should have done the day before, while the group was working, but the technical stuff had taken a backseat behind persuading Muachaquima to take a chance on us. The miners had taken most of their equipment away with them but there were some worn-out washing baskets lying around; suitable for recovering gemstones. It was a typical ore washing area, like hundreds I had seen around the world, characterised by lots of small pools and a system of channels to supply them with water. The area was small but well established and I guessed it had been in and out of use many times over the years.

'Aqui!' The shout was from near Muachaquima's school, the logs. I grabbed Sophie and pulled her to the ground. I did not know whether the call was a friendly summons or an unfriendly one, drawing unwanted attention to our presence. My unspoken question was answered when a boy stepped into the clearing. He was laughing at us. 'Are you looking for Muachaquima?' he asked.

'Yes, where is he?'

'Follow me.' He beckoned and we moved after him.

He led us into the scrub away from the river, and a few minutes later I was surprised to find us back at the road only a few yards from the track where I had parked the Land Cruiser. He took us to it and gestured that we should get in the front. He climbed in the back seat. I followed his instructions and drove back towards where I had turned the car around earlier. We stopped close to what I believed to be the old road. He got out and went to a bush which he grabbed and tugged. Sophie and I stared at him as though he was mad, but I went to help him when he shouted for assistance. With two of us tugging, the bush moved. It was attached to a flat base which was hidden under loose earth and stones. It concealed the beginning of a track going towards the river. I turned the Land Cruiser onto the track and drove twenty or thirty yards before stopping, so we could walk back and replace the bush.

We hid the Land Cruiser as best we could and covered it with camouflage netting the boy retrieved from close by. We finished the job with some bits of tree from the surrounding scrub, and then we walked to the riverbank. We were opposite the island, about fifty or sixty yards from its downstream end. The boy scrabbled around behind a tree and emerged half a minute later dragging a small rowing boat. Sophie was biting her lip nervously, but she looked set, ready for whatever secrets the island held.

Other than the direction, I had hardly noticed the river flow before; it had just seemed to drift peacefully by. Now, as we climbed into the little boat, it looked more like white water, and the thirty yards to the island seemed like a hundred. The boy passed me a pair of oars and set about fitting his own pair in some rudimentary rowlocks. I followed his lead. Sophie crouched between the seats, chuckling at my efforts. She later explained that she had been a decent lightweight sculler and had represented her college at Cambridge.

As we closed in on the island, the hill seemed to loom over us; it had always looked quite small from a distance, even from the riverbank, but it now cast a deep shadow, despite the height of the sun. The vegetation, though the same as on the mainland seemed somehow secretive and I imagined crocodiles and snakes lying in wait; I said nothing of my fears to Sophie. The only sounds were of water, the flow of the river and my flailing efforts with the oars. The crossing took longer than the boy expected, and we finally made ground, carried by the current, at the downstream tip of the island at least fifty yards from where he had intended. He shook his head and stared at me, squeezing his biceps. His meaning was clear.

Three men appeared out of nowhere. They hauled the boat out of the water and dragged it into cover. The boy led us up through the scrub to the road, cursing because there was no path at that point. The hill rose to our left and I knew we were now on the side of the island hidden from the east side of the river. We were not far from where Jim Lodge had died. Sophie looked agitated but was quiet and I guessed she was looking for a connection to her father. Although it was thirty years since I'd been there, I knew I'd know the exact spot if we reached it, even though the road was partially overgrown. We had only walked a hundred yards or so along the old road when the boy steered us down a path towards the old river course, where Lodge's car had finished up. Muachaquima stepped out from behind a rock and summoned us into a concealed shelter, a hollow in the hillside. There were about twenty people there, some sitting on rocks and logs preparing food, others sorting stones. A little old man stood up with difficulty, using a stick, and I realised he only had one leg. As he moved towards me, I recognised his smile and I moved to him with my arms open. We hugged and grasped each other's hands. We were both laughing and crying at the same time, staring at one another. The trust was still there but I could see that my old friend was not well and that the effort of standing up had taken a lot out of him.

'I've met Muachaquima – David – but where's Esther?' I asked cautiously. A sprightly little woman rushed to his side before I had finished, and she pounded my hand gleefully.

'Obrigada,' she said. 'I never saw you to thank you for … If I'd died that night … David's our only child; I couldn't have any more after …' She hugged me then took Armando's arm and led him back to where he had been sitting when I arrived. She signalled that I should sit down next to him and then pulled Sophie to one side to interrogate her.

'So!' said Armando. 'Is she your wife? She's very beautiful, I think.'

I shook my head.

He laughed again. It was good to hear. 'But you would like her to be.'

Again, I shook my head. I looked down and found myself staring at his foot. 'How did …?' I was not sure whether it was a limitation of my Portuguese or that I did not really want to ask.

'How did I lose my leg?' He helped. 'I was lucky,' he said. 'It was a landmine – one of the millions of them that there are in this country. During the war, I was careless. I could have been killed. It was fifteen years ago now; a nuisance, but I'm used to it.'

'I'm sorry it happened to you.'

'Don't be,' he said. 'It would have been much worse if it had been David. He would have had his whole life still ahead of him.'

'Did David tell you why we're here?'

'Yes.' He smiled again. 'I always knew you'd be back. There was always some unfinished business here for both of us.' He looked over to Sophie. 'The hair … your lady companion looks a lot like that geologist; the one who was killed when everything started to go wrong.'

'She's his daughter.'

He nodded. 'This work you're here to do; it's more than a coincidence isn't it?' Armando may have been unwell, but his mind was as sharp as ever.

'Yes,' I confessed. 'We're here to do what we said, but Sophie also wants to see where her father died. She never knew him.'

'Then she must see.' His face creased with concern and he looked into my eyes. 'How do you feel about going there?'

'Fine,' I said.

'You're a bad liar, David.'

'Maybe, but I'm here and it's time I faced up to it.'

146

Chapter 18

Armando was exhausted. He was struggling to keep his eyes open. The excitement of our reunion had drained him. My elation was now tempered by sadness for his physical condition. He was obviously an extremely sick man. With a huge effort he summoned David to us. He said he needed to rest for a while and asked David to take Sophie and me to the road. He assured David that I would know the place we wanted to see, but I was starting to have doubts.

We went back up the path to the road; it seemed steeper going this way. When I had had time to recover my breath, I asked, 'What's wrong with Armando? Is it a long-term illness, or is it a bug?'

'It's a cancer …' David confirmed my suspicion. '… of the stomach. Papai doesn't have long to live.' His voice was hoarse with emotion. 'I'm glad you came. He's always said you'd be back one day. I didn't believe him, but I'm pleased you got here before he dies.'

'Does he live here on the island?'

'We all do. No one can be bothered to come over and clear us out so we're relatively safe here. Even so, we hide our tracks just in case; we don't want to give anyone an excuse. Have you seen any huts?' he challenged. 'I can see four from here.'

We stopped and, try as we might; neither Sophie nor I could pick out a hut for certain. We made a few wrong guesses before David pointed one out to us. It was well hidden; it had a lower roof than was the norm. It was invisible to the casual observer. 'Even in the dry season they blend into the landscape,' he said.

'And fires?' asked Sophie. 'You must cook stuff.'

'In that hollow where you met papai – the rocks and the vegetation carry the smoke away and disperse it. You can only see the glow from the flames from a few places; places where few people would go.'

'And what about treatment for your father?' I was anxious to return to the subject of Armando's health. 'Is he able to get anything for his …? Painkillers … I don't know.'

'Yes. We're very lucky. He has a friend, a doctor. She's …'

'Maria,' I said softly.

'Yes. Papai told me it was you who introduced him to her. We wouldn't be a family without her help. She's always helped us. She says nothing and charges us nothing.'

That was the Maria I remembered. 'Tell me about her,' I said.

'I don't know much. She was married, but her husband died; I know that. She has a son, João; he's a lawyer. I like him; they've both been good to us, given us help when we've needed it, bringing medicines for papai. It's as though she feels she owes papai something, but he assures me she doesn't. He says it's because of you.'

'We were close once, but …'

Sophie had been listening closely to our conversation and she couldn't let an opportunity pass. 'Where does Maria live?' she asked.

David nodded in my direction and said, 'He knows it. My father always calls it "David's house".'

Everything had moved on, but nothing had moved on very far. It was as though life operated on two levels: the way I lived, where people changed jobs and moved locations; and life in Mumbulo which seemed to have stood still; the same people were doing the same things and living very close to where they had always lived. Maria now lived in the Madhouse, next door to Kevin Dryden who lived where she had thirty years ago.

'Did you know her husband?' I asked.

'No, I know his name was Paulo, but I never met him. He was Portuguese, I think.'

We continued along the old road, making slow progress due to the scrub which had recolonized it over the years, and I was beginning to think we must have passed the spot without me noticing it. Then, there it was. How had I forgotten it? It was so distinctive; my memories had lain dormant but were now triggered by a tall, narrow rock which stuck up from the ground like a twisted spire. We even used to call it Chesterfield. It was only three or four feet tall, but it released a long-suppressed memory. Jim Lodge had died at Chesterfield.

I stopped and stared at it, trying now to remember. Sophie put an arm around me and leaned her head against my shoulder. 'Here?'

'Yes.'

There was no sign that anything had ever happened there. The road looked just the same there as the rest of it that we had seen; it was structurally the same as it had been thirty years before. A channel still traced the uphill side of the road, protecting it from being washed out, and I guessed the culvert would still be where it had always been, to take the water under the road and direct it down the hill to the river.

'There's not much to see is there?' she said, wiping her eyes with a tissue.

'There never was.' Relief almost overwhelmed me as I stared at the rock. I do not know what I had expected. Nothing consciously, but my subconscious had whispered warnings.

A gust of wind blew dust into my eyes. I closed them. Chesterfield, imprinted in my mind, was red. Chesterfield had been red with Jim Lodge's blood that day. How had I forgotten that? What else had I pushed from my mind? I glanced down at the river. It was not as fast-flowing or violent as it used to be because most of the water now took the wider, diversion course round the east side of the island. I looked across at the far bank, the west, where the scrub stretched away over a series of rolling hills into the distance. It was a beautiful, peaceful place and the sound of running water added to its serenity. The sun flashed off something in the middle distance – plastic or corrugated steel sheeting – almost certainly a plant, but not one that I remembered. On closer examination, the sweep of vegetation was not as unbroken as I had first thought; there were some open areas where brown earth carried the fingerprint of human habitation: dwellings and manioc patches. Two grey mounds huddled close to the plant: waste heaps.

'Where was your father's village from here?' I asked David, trying to get my bearings.

He pointed at the waste dumps on the far side. 'Over there. Can you see the plant and those heaps? It was very close to there,' he said.

I nodded. I'd only ever been to Armando's village once, but it had been dark, and Armando had been navigating. From here, I could appreciate it in the context of the surrounding landscape. Cambunda, Armando's plant, had been the only one on that far bank back then, so I had not known the geography there nearly as well as I knew the Mumbulo side of the river. I could see now that I had always been right, that Armando's village could not have had anything to do with Lodge's death; a grave injustice had indeed been meted out. But still the question burned, why, and what other crimes had been committed?

'You know what happened, don't you?' said Sophie in English.

I shook my head. 'No. But I know what didn't happen. I think the main justification for flattening Armando's village was that it was the closest to here, and that's true, as the crow flies. But the river was faster-flowing and impassable back then. The nearest bridges were in Mumbulo and near Nocredo the other way. There were some chain ferries and boats, but not in this stretch; it was far too treacherous.'

I'd forgotten that David spoke English and he said, 'Papai said you were always on our side. But all that's too long ago now. We've come through civil war and countless other setbacks; it's too late to change anything.'

'Perhaps,' I said.

Sophie was picking around at stones and weighing them in her hands. I knew she was wondering if any of them had been instrumental in her father's death. 'Those are much smaller,' I said. 'The ones with blood on them were all bigger I think, unless my memory's playing tricks.'

'But there aren't any bigger rocks here,' she said. 'They're all either this size,' she held up a stone slightly smaller than a golf ball, 'or they're like that.' She pointed at Chesterfield.

She was right. There were very few big rocks by the road, only a range of smaller stones suitable for road surfacing. I checked the ditch to see what was there; it was the same.

'I saw some rocks in your camp, for seats and for supporting cooking pots. Did you get them from here?' I asked David.

'I don't think so. There are plenty of oversize waste dumps around – we collected our rocks from them.'

It was inconclusive but it did raise another uncertainty about Lodge's death, and I could see that Sophie was thinking along the same lines. If there had not been any big rocks here, when Lodge had his accident, then where had they come from and how had they got there.

'We need to get back to Nocredo soon,' I said. 'Do you think your father will have had enough rest yet? There's something I really want to ask him,' I said.

'Not really,' said David, 'but I know he'll happily speak to you whether he's up to it or not. Just keep it brief. I think your visit will do him more good than any harm you can do anyway.'

I promised not to tire Armando and we made our way back. At the camp, Armando had not rested as he should have; he was too excited. 'Did you see what you wanted?' he asked.

'Yes, and more. I never believed your village had anything do with the killing, but today I saw for the first time just how cut off from here it is. But what I really need to know from you is whether you ever heard anything about the other man, the one who Sophie's father hit in the road accident. Who was he?'

'That's the strange thing. I never heard anything. I made widespread enquiries through relatives, friends … I used all my contacts … and no one ever knew of any accident of that kind. As far as I know, nobody was injured or killed by a car at that time.'

There was plenty of food for thought in that, if it was right, but I was sure Armando had enough contacts to be confident about what he had said.

David took us back to the car. He and Sophie took the oars this time and our river crossing was both quicker and more direct than earlier.

We drove the first half of the journey back to Nocredo in silence; both of us analysing what we had learnt and drawing our own conclusions.

'So!' Sophie said, breaking the mood. 'Kevin Dryden must have killed my father. He saw my father on the way to Mumbulo – he had the opportunity. He said that there'd been an accident. He said there were Angolans there … But if they weren't Angolans from Armando's village …? Then the person supposedly knocked down has never been found; and there's the rocks …'

Her stream of thoughts made sense and I had been considering the same idea, but I was shocked to hear it expressed out loud. 'It's a possibility,' I said, 'but I still think it had to be Angolans. Not from Armando's village, but Angolans nonetheless.' Lodge's body was dominating my thoughts; there was something about it that I could not bring myself to tell Sophie, but it was why I believed it was Angolans. 'If Dryden were involved,' I said, 'he wouldn't have acted alone. He's too gutless. And surely, he'd have just kicked us out this last week, especially if he thought there was a chance that we might uncover something.'

'Maybe he thought that would arouse suspicion, or maybe he thought we wouldn't find anything.'

'We haven't really found anything concrete though, have we? Just more questions. I'm certain that Armando would have heard if anyone from the area had been in an accident, but what if it was an outsider your father hit – someone who wouldn't be missed.'

'Why would anyone take revenge for someone they didn't know? Surely, they wouldn't bother. Another thing, even if Armando heard nothing about the victim, he would surely have heard rumours about the murder?'

'True. Maybe they were all outsiders …' I said. 'I never believed the so-called investigation identified the true killers, but, until now, I had always trusted what I saw about the murder itself. I'm sure your father was killed by bigger rocks than those we saw on the island. Where did they come from? The rocks bother me; but I still think it was Angolans as I honestly can't see Dryden overpowering your father. He was a much bigger man, but your father was wirier and tougher.'

'What if I'm right about Dryden being involved, and you're right about him not working alone, who might he have worked with?'

'I've never given it a thought.'

'Humour me please, David. Can we rule out some of those who couldn't have been involved? Let's start with those drinking at your house that day.'

'How many more times ...?' I sighed exasperatedly. I told her I couldn't add any more to what I'd already said; the detail of the afternoon had been overshadowed by her father's death. She urged me to try harder.

For what felt like the thousandth time since she'd elbowed her way into my life, I delved into the recesses of my memory, looking for names and faces but the list remained steadfastly the same: my house mate, Carlos Pereira; the other metallurgist, Steve Vernon; and Chris Howard, the chief engineer. 'Other than that, ...'

'What about those security guys?'

'No. But, like Geoff Morgan and the doctor, they did turn up at your father's body just after me and Carlos. I guess someone thought to raise them. Maybe, Chris or Steve ...'

We completed the ride back to Nocredo in silence.

Chapter 19

Sunday was nominally a day off: a lazy day. We relaxed and caught up with outstanding report writing and planning. I got through to Rachel on Skype, during the afternoon and she was delighted by our progress. We agreed that I would call her again in a week unless there was an emergency. I always felt better after speaking to Rachel.

Early on Monday morning, Sophie and I were sitting on the veranda, waiting for our lift to Mumbulo. The air was fresh and cool, and Nocredo was alive with the sounds and smells of a busy town awakening to a new week.

We had arranged to give ARDCO a progress update that morning. I advised Sophie not to antagonise Dryden if he turned up at the meeting. 'He might be guilty of a lot of things, but he didn't kill your father. That was Angolans,' I said.

'Why are you so sure of that?' she asked. 'There's something you've always kept from me, isn't there, David? You nearly let something slip once. What was it?'

'I can't remember.'

Sophie snorted derisively. 'Anyway, Dryden's all we've got to work on. He's as guilty as hell in my book, whether he threw a stone or not. Why else would he allow an innocent village to be flattened?'

'Maybe he believed all that,' I said. 'Anyway, remember this; if Dryden thinks we're working against him, he'll have us on the next plane out of here and your investigation will end just like that.'

Despite my history with Dryden, we agreed that it would be safer for me to do most of the talking if he was there. Sophie would be less likely to reveal her thoughts that way.

We moved on to talking about the project. Now we had met Armando, David and Esther, and to a lesser extent Sylvestre, the plight of the miners had become as personal to Sophie as it was to me. She had always been genuine in her commitment to the project but now it wasn't just an academic exercise. She had been upset by Armando's illness and she was appalled by the child labour and the lack of proper school facilities where David taught in his makeshift classroom.

'Compared with what they have to put up with, finding out what happened to my father seems trivial, almost spiteful,' she said, 'but I can't drop it.'

'I'm not asking you to. Just go softly, softly. If you're right and Dryden was involved in some way, maybe he'll let something slip. Maybe you'll get something on him that way.'

'I want to nail him. I don't like him, and I believe he robbed me of my father.' She smacked her fist down on the arm of her chair for emphasis.

She simmered for a moment and then confided. 'All this has got me thinking though, and I don't like some of the ideas I've had. My parents were fantastic: they loved me as their own flesh and blood: no one could have been better. I keep thinking that maybe I was lucky that my father was killed, and that my mother died too … Shit! It's confusing. How can I possibly think that? If the Lodges had lived, I wouldn't have known the parents who adopted me – and my life would have been different. Would it have been worse? It could hardly have been better.'

'Stop beating yourself up. There's nothing to be gained from ifs, buts and maybes.' But she had stirred another train of thought. 'You mentioned your mother. You haven't talked about her since our first meeting. Did you find anything out? I've been meaning to ask.'

'Yes. She was relatively easy to research. She had no living family, but I did find some of her old friends, some who had been to their wedding. They recognised who I was immediately, just like you, like Dryden. My mother was intelligent; she had a history degree from Cambridge, Girton College. That's another coincidence because that's where I went too. She was there in the first year that Girton took in men. Men were the norm when I was there. I'll never see the college in quite the same way again, though. I went there a few weeks ago; it was familiar and yet it seemed different. I tried to see it through my mother's eyes, but I couldn't of course. I half expected to learn that we'd had the same room, but it was a relief to discover that she'd lived about as far as it was possible to be from where I'd stayed. I think she was a good woman. People liked her. She never used her degree though; never really worked. My father's money went towards a house and she committed herself to making a home for when he finally left Angola. Dryden screwed all that up of course; and then she was sick and died too. I wonder if she would have lived if my father had been alive. I'll never know of course, but part of me will always imagine that she died of a broken heart.'

'Have you finished looking into her life?' I asked.

'More or less. I keep thinking of odd things, but her life was relatively simple. I like what I know of her and I'm happy with that. I'm sure I would have loved her, and that I'd have been very close to her. There are still a couple of her friends I want to catch up with, but I'm about done. She committed herself to things that were important to her; my father and then, after his death, me. I doubt if she expected to die as young as she did, but she made sure that everything she had would come to me. That was another part of the surprise I got on my eighteenth birthday.'

'Good. I'm not interested in how much, but the estate had to go somewhere, and you were the only living relative as far as I can gather. I'm glad you got it.'

'Thanks, but … you know. It's a shame someone has to die first.'

We had a good view of the town from the veranda, and we watched some children playing football with bare feet in the street. The ball seemed heavy and a protruding wisp informed us that it was stuffed with grass.

'Have you thought of this?' she said, out of the blue. 'If Dryden did kill my father, he might kill us.'

I just laughed. I had never been afraid of Kevin Dryden and I could only feel contempt for him; he was a craven bully. 'No, he didn't do it,' I said. 'You're barking up the wrong tree; it was Angolans. I don't think anyone wants to kill us, except ... I don't know – like Sylvestre – but that was a response to a perceived threat; not premeditated.'

'You really should tell me what it is you're keeping from me. Maybe I'll agree with you if I know what you know,' she said. 'Maybe the doctor will tell me. I want to meet her today.' The words hit me like a bus. 'I can see that you'd rather not come with me,' she continued, 'but I think it's important. It's something I need to do.'

'Do it,' I said.

It had to happen, and I knew I would run into Maria too, eventually. My debate was whether it would be better to get it over with and go with Sophie or wait and risk an accidental confrontation in the street where I would not have a chance to prepare myself.

★★★

Manuel picked us up on time. The more I saw of him the more I liked him. After his initial reaction it did not seem to bother him that I was persona non grata with his brother-in-law. He told me he only put up with Dryden for Teresa's sake and because their paths sometimes crossed at work.

'How did your sister meet Kevin Dryden?' I asked him.

'She's a nurse but she used to help out sometimes as a secretary at the mine; she still does when required; but she did it much more in the past. She worked a lot with Kevin, and, like many young girls, she was seduced by his position of power in the company. He flaunted it of course and, despite me and my family trying to dissuade her from him, she got pregnant and married him. That was more than twenty years ago. In fairness, he's always provided well for her and Rui, he's my nephew; but he's – Kevin that is – is a bastard in other ways. I know for a fact that he's had affairs with numerous other secretaries, and he doesn't make much effort to hide it. It's as though he's always trying to prove what a great man he is.'

'Does your sister still love him?' asked Sophie.

'I don't think she ever did,' he said. 'In many ways, she was as bad as he was. She used him to gain status and she's certainly still happy with that. I suspect the pregnancy was very deliberate on her part. I love her; she's my sister, but I know how she works. She's a good person but she knows how to get what she wants, and that doesn't always reflect well on her.'

'And Rui?'

'He's in Lisbon visiting my parents, his grandparents. He's a student at Bristol University in England – he's going to be a vet.'

'Bristol's okay,' I told him. 'It's a good university, and it's a lovely part of England.'

'Is he friends with João, the doctor's son?' asked Sophie. 'They must be a similar age.' She had a habit of going where I was reluctant to go.

'Maria, his mother lives next door to my sister. João's a few years older, but they get on okay, I think, without being close.'

'And Maria's husband?' asked Sophie.

'Paulo? He died a few years ago; cancer. It was very sad. Maria tried everything. His death hit her hard. And João.'

Nothing more was said until we were almost at the mine offices in Mumbulo.

'By the way.' Manuel sounded embarrassed. 'I haven't been able to secure you the use of that Land Rover again this week, but I've spoken to my bosses and they're going to contact ARDCO to see if they can lend you a car.'

That was bad news. Hitching lifts was not a good basis for carrying out project work and I was much happier with the idea of using transport belonging to Diangola than ARDCO – I suspected that any favours from Dryden would come with undesirable conditions attached.

Chapter 20

As we expected, Kevin Dryden sat in on our meeting, and I had to smile when he sat next to Mitch. Sophie was very subdued, and I could see that she was avoiding any connection with Dryden; either physical or eye to eye. She was struggling to divorce her private thoughts from the needs of the project.

Sophie had done the presentation at our first meeting with ARDCO but this time it fell to me to tell them what we'd discovered, who we'd spoken to, and what we proposed to do next. I reported that we had found a group of artisanal miners that fitted our criteria. I didn't tell them which group it was, but I suspected they would already know. If they did not, it would not be hard for them to find out. All they had to do was talk to the truck drivers who frequented the roads between the mining blocks and the plants; at least one of them must have noticed our parked car, even though it was off the road.

I explained that the miners' group had at least one person prepared to attend the discussions, and possibly more.

'So, what do you want us to do?' asked Dryden.

I patiently summarised our requirements. 'To keep an open mind and consider any suggestions. Ultimately, we'd like to find a way for ARDCO and the artisanal miners to coexist in a mutually agreeable relationship. It might be a subcontract arrangement, or there might be deposits that ARDCO can't work economically, but where a more artisanal approach might be ideal. ARDCO or Diangola would then pay the artisanal miners for their production at a fair price, but with an agreed profit margin. At the moment, because their operations are illegal, the artisanal miners have to sell to buyers who rip them off. As far as I can gather, most of the buyers are from across the border in the

DRC, so Angola's losing diamonds and the DRC is benefiting. If you work with the artisanal miners, Angola will get the diamonds and the artisanal miners will be better off too. You'll also be able to cut back on security costs as the miners will be operating by agreement; a win-win.'

'You really have got it all worked out, haven't you?' Dryden sneered. 'But what about the buyers? They might just cut up rough.'

'True, but we discussed this at the last meeting –' I looked to Harry and Constance for nods of agreement, which were forthcoming – 'and that's a border control issue. You won't need many carats to pay for beefed-up border crossings. Diangola like the idea. They think it could work and they're willing to back it.'

'So, all we have to do is agree to what you say, and everyone is better off; is that what you're telling me?' Dryden looked incredulous. 'You really haven't changed. You still have that blind spot where Angolans are concerned – they can do no wrong in your book.' He smirked.

I refused to be drawn.

Harry and Constance both looked surprised by Dryden's outburst, but Mitch's grin informed me that Dryden had told him a version of my past.

It was Constance who broke the ensuing silence. 'So, what's your decision, Kevin? Are you giving your backing to what we agreed the other day, to work with David and Sophie? You're the boss, but the suggestions all look perfectly reasonable to me.'

'I don't know what he's told you about his past,' Dryden said, 'but he used to work here thirty years ago; left under something of a cloud. It was an Angolan problem.' He stared at Sophie. She looked away.

'Look Kevin,' I said. 'We're here to help the artisanal miners – they're our concern – but no scheme to help them will work if it doesn't benefit you too. You've got nothing to lose. If we can't do our work here, we'll go elsewhere; to Lucapa or Cafunfo; that's our fall-back, and we'll see if they're more receptive.'

'Why didn't you go there in the first place? It would've saved a lot of trouble,' said Mitch.

'Because I know Mumbulo better. As Kevin just said, I used to work here. I know the lie of the land,' I said.

'And this project was my idea not David's,' interrupted Sophie. 'We just want to get on with our work. I'm a social scientist if you're interested, so don't even think of questioning my relevance to the project. Knowing a place gives you a head start. In our line of work there is no project if there are no benefits for the people we want to help; that's what social science is all about, predicting and measuring the effects of the work.'

'Touchy-feely, eh? There's not much scope for the soft touch around here,' said Dryden.

'Look,' I held my hands up. 'Let's cut the in-fighting. Are you going to support our work, Kevin, or should we just pack our bags and cadge a flight to Lucapa?' I hoped my apparent willingness to go would convince him that the project was our sole interest.

It was a good job everyone was looking at me because Sophie tensed visibly. I could tell she thought I was overplaying it.

Dryden pursed his lips and locked stares with me for an uncomfortably long time before he nodded. 'Okay, Let's see what comes out of the first meeting with the garimpeiros – don't ask me to call them "artisanal miners". If I don't like it, you can bugger off to Lucapa. When is the meeting anyway? I want to be there.'

'I think it'll be in a couple of days, in the afternoon, but I'll confirm it with you later. I've asked Manuel to get us a room in Mumbulo, in the edificio público.'

'Okay, and as a show of my commitment I'm going to help you. I know you haven't got transport so I'm allocating a car and a driver to you. Mitch, I want you to take these two wherever they want to go.' Mitch smiled and nodded.

Harry and Constance looked amazed; they couldn't believe that Mitch would accept such a menial task so willingly. It was going to clip our wings somewhat, but we couldn't argue without arousing suspicion. Dryden had outmanoeuvred us. I had no idea how we would get to investigate anything about Jim's death under Mitch's watchful eye.

Dryden then mentioned that Geoff Morgan would be coming to Mumbulo sometime in the next few days. At least Morgan was senior enough for us to meet him without the need for Mitch tagging along.

I was cursing quietly as we left the meeting room, and I could hear Sophie grumbling under her breath too. Mitch was going to be a nuisance. It was about lunchtime and we were due to eat with Manuel and Teresa again. Manuel was waiting in his Land Cruiser for us in front of the offices. Sophie and I spoke to him in Portuguese and it was obvious to us that Mitch did not understand a word – at least we had a code we could use. We arranged with Mitch that we would meet him back at the office after lunch and he reluctantly let us out of his sight. As we turned out of the car park to drive into town, Constance waved us down from the side of the road. Manuel stopped and she climbed into the Land Cruiser with us.

'I wanted to catch you without Mitch in tow,' she said. 'I know all about you, David. Maria told me. I like what you're saying and what you're trying to do here, and I'll support you as much as I can with that, but I can't ...' she struggled for the right words. 'Maria's my best friend here. I can't stand by and watch you screw up her life again.'

It had been Maria who had screwed my life up, not the other way round; she'd deserted me. I was utterly speechless.

'She knows you're here, but I think she's bloody mad. She wants to see you.'

I was shocked. I had not been expecting an invitation. Was she going to laugh in my face at how she had treated me? How had Constance come to believe that I had ever set out to hurt Maria? I was tempted to put Constance right in no uncertain terms, but I could not afford to lose an ally for the project.

'When?' I asked.

'Now. She and I are both joining you at Teresa's. You'd better start working on your excuses. If I were her, I'd ... I don't know what I'd do, but it wouldn't be nice.'

'What have I done to deserve this?' I was mystified, but I could see that Sophie was lapping it up like a soap opera.

She was desperate to know the whole story. I would have to tell her when we got back to Nocredo in the evening; but, for now, it would have to wait as we were just passing the front of the Madhouse, Maria's place.

Chapter 21

Ever since I had learned that Maria was still in Mumbulo it had seemed inevitable that our paths would cross, especially as Sophie was so keen to meet her. I had thought a lot about what it would be like, seeing her again, but I was still unprepared. My feelings were conflicting.

When we arrived at Teresa's, Manuel and Constance wasted no time getting out; they were both keen to get at their lunch. Sophie was eager too, but meeting Maria was her motivation. I dawdled behind, delaying my moment; my hands were trembling, and my mouth was dry. What was I going to say to her? Part of me wanted her to be happy, but another part, embittered by the years of separation, was less charitable; I harboured a grudge.

There was much hugging and shaking of hands on the veranda, as new friendships were made, and existing ones reinforced. My legs felt weak and the wave of laughter and joviality that washed down the path almost overwhelmed me. I reached the bottom step and looked up. She was staring straight at me.

Her eyes drew me in as they always had. I could not look away. My neck muscles relaxed, and the edge of my resentment was blunted. Time had treated her well, physically; wrinkles and creases just served to cement those animated expressions of warmth that I remembered her so fondly for.

'Hello David.' She sounded as confused as I was. 'I had hoped I'd see you before now.' There was accusation in her voice.

'Hello Maria. So, did I ... so did I.'

'Let's go for a walk.' She stepped past me, consciously avoiding any physical contact and I followed without thinking.

'I don't want to hear excuses,' she said. 'I'm pleased to see you're well. What have you done since you left here?' Her words were stilted, as though over-rehearsed.

'I've no reason to make excuses,' I said. 'Why did you never write to me?'

'What? I did. Countless times … Why did you ignore me?'

'You know that's not true. It can't be. The weekly mail was what held the mine together. If anyone even suspected that letters might go astray there would have been a mass walk out. Nobody but Jim knew about us, so …' I was mystified that she would lie to me so blatantly and my anger began to stir again.

'Don't let's argue.' Her tone was conciliatory. 'I just want to know that you're well and that you've had a good life.'

'I have, thank you, but I had hoped for so much better. Maybe I had a lucky escape.' I immediately regretted my words.

She shook her head sadly and tears threatened her eyes. 'I hoped it wouldn't be like this,' she said, 'but I guess it had to be. You always had a savage tongue: right or wrong, but you used to be man enough to admit it when you were wrong, and you'd apologise. It seems you've changed.'

We walked in silence for a while, a chasm between us. I tore up the last vestiges of any dream I might have retained. Why was she lying? I would have forgiven her in an instant if she had been honest. I had written so many letters; at least two a week for months after I had left. I had told her my plans for us and how I could not wait for her to join me. I had not received a single reply. It was possible for one or two letters to go astray but the mail had been sacrosanct; there had been no telephone or email. The mail had kept us all sane: it had been our only link with the outside world.

'I saw Armando and David the other day,' I said. 'Thank you for helping them.' It was a peace offering of a kind. 'David and Esther would both have died that night if …'

'How could I do anything else?' Then she sighed sadly: 'You know Armando's dying?'

'Yes. David told me. I almost wept when I saw him; he's such a wreck. I'm glad I got to see him again though, before ... He was an important part of my life, part of why I am what I am.'

'And what's that precisely?' She turned towards me and glared.

'There was a time when you'd have apologised too.'

'I've tried very hard to forget you over the years, David, but ... You've always been thrown back in my face; I even live in the Madhouse now. Did you know that?'

I nodded.

'Are you married?' she asked.

'I was; divorced.'

'Sorry. Children?'

'No kids. And don't be sorry. Rachel and I are still good friends. David told me about your husband. I'm sorry.'

'He was there for me when I needed someone. He was reliable; a good dad for João. I became a doctor because I wanted to help people, to save them, but I seem to fail those closest to me.'

'Yes,' I muttered. 'But never medically; I can't believe that.' I was sure that Maria would have done everything possible for anybody who was unwell and would have tried the impossible for someone she loved. I know he had the best care possible.'

'Thank you.' She smiled sadly. 'He was a good man. He deserved better than me. We weren't the same as ...'

'But you have João. David said he's a lawyer. You must be proud of him.'

'Yes, very. He's turned out very well, considering. He specialised in mining law and is working for ARDCO. He spends most of his time in Luanda, with Geoff Morgan – you must remember him.'

'How could I forget? I believe he's coming here in a few days.'

She gave a little snort. 'You really pissed him off when you left. He could never understand why you wouldn't back down. I don't know what he'll make of Sophie; I can see that what Teresa told me is true; that she's Jim's daughter. He's bound to wonder what you're up to with her.'

'We're not up to anything; just the project. Why should he think otherwise?' I said.

'That's funny coming from you, David; you were always the conspiracy nut. I know Kevin's already suspicious and all the others from back then will be too.'

'All the others? I know about you, Geoff and Kevin,' I said, 'and I believe those two security guys: Colin and Jug are here too, but who else?'

'That's about it, I think. Isn't that enough?' Maria ran a hand over her chin, deep in thought. 'No, there's one other. I think you knew him, Thys Gerber,' she added.

It was the first time I had heard that Thys was still around, but nothing surprised me anymore.

'I was naïve thirty years ago David.' Her voice had an edge to it. 'But don't take me for a fool now. I might view you more sympathetically than most around here despite everything, but even I find it difficult to imagine that you're here just to do this project thing. You and Jim's daughter together; it's pushing co-incidence too far.'

'It's a genuine project but Sophie did want to see where Jim died. David took us there. Sophie's desperate to talk to you.'

'What have you told her?' Maria's eyes had always been expressive: all I could see in them was fear.

'Most of what I know. I didn't give her the gorier details though.'

'Jim was my best friend until I met you. I was very fond of him,' she said. 'That was one of the worst days of my life. I think that's when everything started to go wrong. I've felt as though I'm being punished ever since.'

'Why?' Her words worried me. 'There was nothing you could have done.'

'I need to speak to Sophie; I want to tell her what you call the gorier details of it.'

We had been walking aimlessly around the streets of Mumbulo. 'Do you realise,' I said, 'that this is the first time we've ever walked around Mumbulo together? We were very secretive thirty years back. Nobody knew about us, did they? Apart from Jim.'

'I don't think so. I never told anyone. If we'd been open, do you think it would have turned out different? Our relationship was secret, but it had to be that way. My community would have banished me if they'd known about us. They wanted a nice clean little Portuguese lady doctor; they didn't want me sullied by an Englishman.'

'You never wanted to leave did you?' I said. 'It was all just a show. If you'd really wanted to leave, all that crap wouldn't have mattered; you'd have been in England or wherever I was.'

'Do you always twist the facts? You know that's not true.' She looked hurt. 'I would have done anything for you; gone anywhere. You forget it wasn't just me though; there was my family too, and how my reputation would reflect on them. If I'd left here, it would have had to appear to be for professional advancement.'

'Sorry. My mind's all over the place: I'd forgotten what it was like then.'

'That's more like it. An apology at last ...'

We both laughed and some of the tension dissipated, though the rift between us still gaped. We carried on walking for a while then she stopped in front of the house, I'd pointed out to Sophie a few days before. 'Jim's house. I remember that day every time I see it. And now, seeing Sophie, it's like yesterday. You said you'd told her almost everything.'

'Yes, except ...'

She raised two crooked fingers.

I nodded. 'I haven't spoken about that to anyone since about a week after it happened; not even to you. But there's something else isn't there?' Something she'd said earlier was still bugging me.

'Yes,' she said. 'That's why I want you there when I tell Sophie about Jim's death. I don't think it's something I can say more than once.'

We were almost back at Teresa's and everyone there was looking out from the veranda, watching us with interest.

'You took your time.' Sophie regarded me as though I had stolen her favourite doll. Teresa and Manuel stared at us curiously and Constance eyed us analytically, trying to read the body language between us. I think I saw a little smile of satisfaction curl her lips.

'We had a lot to talk about,' said Maria. 'It's been a long time.'

Sophie sighed, frustrated.

'We need to talk too, Sophie,' Maria said. 'About Jim, your father.'

Sophie's face lit up. 'Thank you, I thought you might try to avoid me.'

Maria smiled sadly and shook her head. 'You don't know me then, do you?'

Constance stepped forward; she looked irritated. 'Maria, why didn't you tell me that Sophie was James Lodge's daughter? His name's all over the geology here: all the most useful maps and resource estimates. I really wish we had all of them.'

Maria placed a hand on her friend's arm. 'I had my reasons, Connie. And besides, I didn't know for sure until I saw her.' She turned her gaze back to Sophie and smiled. 'When are you free to talk, Sophie? We can't do it now, but … you're welcome to stay at my house … tomorrow night perhaps?' Her eyes did not deviate from Sophie's, which told me the invitation was restricted to one.

I wondered what Maria would tell Sophie and when she planned to tell her the gorier details as she wanted me to be there for that. I knew things from Maria's past that she had never got around to telling me herself; things that would be of interest to Sophie; things that Jim had told me. I could remember one conversation very clearly; it had troubled me greatly at the time but now it was a treasured memory.

★★★

Jim and I were watching a bulldozer with a ripper tearing the life out of an area the size of five or six football pitches. Scrubby trees, which had struggled for years to gain a foothold in the shallow topsoil, were uprooted and dumped unceremoniously, making way for a new mine. I was torn between depression and excitement. A new mine meant feed for my plants; it was my livelihood, but I hated the destruction.

My Land Rover was out of action and Dryden had taken great delight that morning in telling me to stick my thumb out and get a lift if I wanted to see what was going on in the plants. I think he hoped I would get stranded somewhere remote. I was lucky that Jim had overheard our conversation and he offered me a lift provided I did not mind spending an hour at his new mine on the way.

He showed me around the site and talked about the underlying geology before wandering off to speak to his site geologist, and the mining foreman, who was directing the clearance. When he returned, he looked me hard in the face and grinned. 'Maria did a brilliant job on that eyebrow. In a couple of weeks, you won't know you'd ever split it.'

'Yeah, she's not bad,' I said casually.

'Look, I don't know quite how to say this,' he said, 'but there's something you ought to know, and it's better coming from me, or Maria, just in case someone else knows something and blabs. Maria told me about you and her. We used to be together, Maria and I... before I met Gillian.'

I fought hard not to show my disappointment; I tensed and turned my back on him.

'You've got it wrong.' He sounded apologetic. 'Or maybe I have. That didn't come out quite as I intended. There was a time when we both needed someone for company and ... you know what it's like here. We're still close friends but we stopped, you know ... more than a year ago, after I met Gillian.'

'Why are you telling me this? I was happier being ignorant.'

'Because people talk, and they don't always get their facts right. Maria and I kept our relationship a secret — you'll know all about doing that of course — but you can never be a hundred per cent sure that someone hasn't seen something. It's for Maria's sake really. The Portuguese community is very proud of her; she's under constant scrutiny.'

'So, what are you telling me? That it's okay for me to screw your leftovers. Is that it?'

'No, you prat. Maria's nobody's leftover. She's my best friend. We've often talked about the guys in the camp and you were always the one she kept on about. I was beginning to think I'd have to create a situation to get you two together, then lightning struck.'

I grunted.

'Look. For me, I'd rather everyone had known about Maria and me. I'm sure you feel the same way about you and her. I even invited her to my wedding, remember; Gillian wanted to meet her. Unfortunately, she couldn't get away. What I'm trying to say is; she's great and she'll be good for you.'

'I know all that. I'm just not sure I needed to hear someone gloating that they got there first.'

'I'm not. I'm trying to tell you that what's past is past. You might have found out about us some other way before Maria told you. I know she's nervous about doing that. I'm telling you because I want us to be friends and, most of all, because I don't want Maria to be hurt. She's special. So, keep quiet. It would make life very difficult for her if people found out about either of us.'

'Tell me,' I said. 'As we seem to have slipped into man-to-man mode, what is it about Maria that hooked us both? When I look at her, I expect to see perfection, but she's far from that; a collection of interesting but not especially beautiful parts. Yet she is beautiful; I don't get it.'

Jim laughed out loud and his grim expression changed to a grin. 'That's one of the great mysteries. I don't know either, but I've often wondered the same thing. Wonderful eyes: intelligence, warmth, goodness and a face that tells a story, an interesting story. Look after her.'

★★★

'João ... João!' Teresa's voice brought me back to the present. 'Maria está aqui. Your mum's here.'

A young man, about thirty, bounded up the path. Teresa introduced him to Sophie and me before letting him give his mother, Maria, a huge, warm hug. I envied him despite everything. His eyes were dark, and they sparkled like Maria's; he looked like her son. He was a good-looking man, much taller than his mother, and where she was curvaceous, he was more angular. His face, except for his slightly hooked nose, was made to Maria's template.

'I wasn't expecting you until the end of the week,' said Maria. 'I thought you'd be coming in on the Hercules with Geoff.'

'He gave me a couple of days off and told me to lose myself, so I came back early. Luanda's a sauna; it's much better here.'

'Is Geoff Morgan still coming?' asked Sophie. 'I assume that's who you meant by Geoff.'

João turned and addressed Sophie in perfect English. 'Yes Dr Addison. And he's very keen to meet you.'

I wasn't sure whether the 'you' was singular or plural, but his eyes didn't leave Sophie. I could not blame him for that. I was starting to find myself vetting potential suitors for Sophie, as though I were her father. I could not fault João's pedigree.

Chapter 22

Mitch was leaning against his Land Rover when we got back to the offices after our extended lunch; he was drumming his fingers impatiently on the bonnet. He managed to look both angry and relieved; maybe he thought we had found alternative transport. I apologised even though we had not agreed on a time and we certainly were not contracted to any specific hours.

'We'd better get a move on.' I reluctantly unfolded our map on the bonnet and pointed out to Mitch where we were going. Short of bashing him over the head and blindfolding him I could not think of any way to avoid telling him.

He turned out to be a much better driver than I expected. I had stereotyped him as a show-off, but he drove carefully and showed good awareness of the road conditions. When I commented on it, he confided that he had a brother who was confined to a wheelchair after an accident: he'd been driving home to Perth from a remote mine site in Western Australia, too tired to drive safely.

I directed Mitch to park in our usual place but when I suggested that he should wait at the car, he shook his head and told me to lead the way.

We found David in the clearing teaching arithmetic to a group of eight children. He gave a signal that I interpreted as ten minutes, then he continued with his lesson. I watched the miners at work and explained a few things to Sophie. There were twenty or thirty old rice sacks stacked along one side of the clearing: it was the miners' stockpile of dirt and gravel. Sophie's attention was drawn to the women gathered around the washing pools: they were swirling screens, loaded with stones, just below the surface of the water, washing fine dirt away. A small, mixed group sat to one side of the clearing carefully picking through the clean stones, looking for diamonds. It was a lot of hard work for no guaranteed pay-off.

While Sophie and I were observing the miners' activities, Mitch found some shade and played with his phone. I kept an eye on him to make sure he did not raise it to take photos of the miners, but he showed no interest in them.

'Boa tarde.' It was David. He had finished his lesson and come over to join us without me noticing. I was glad he had had the sense to speak Portuguese as Mitch had also joined us.

'How's your pai?' I asked.

'In good spirits but in and out of consciousness. It's the drugs, but it's better than seeing him suffer.'

I nodded sympathetically. It would have been good to see Armando again, but Mitch's presence made that impossible. I thought it unwise even to mention his name. Maybe it was paranoia, but I was sure that Mitch would have been told to listen for any mention of the name 'Armando'.

I looked at my watch: it was already three-thirty p.m. Before leaving Teresa's, Manuel had asked me to let him know by five p.m. whether we would need him to confirm our booking of the edificio público for the following afternoon.

'Have you had a chance to talk to the group about the meeting?' I asked David.

He nodded and glanced at Mitch. 'They're nervous. They don't trust ARDCO. Anyway, I said I was prepared to take a chance, so they elected me as their representative. It's just me, I'm afraid.'

I could see that Sophie was as disappointed as me that there would only be one representative, but Mitch showed no reaction; Portuguese was impenetrable for him. I was delighted that we had David, but I had hoped that at least one other would attend to show that the artisanal miners were serious about the project. I told him that we had provisionally booked a room in the edificio público in Mumbulo for the following afternoon; I arranged to pick him up at the roadside at about three-fifteen p.m. for a four p.m. meeting.

Before we left, David asked if we would like to speak to the children, to explain who we were and what we were doing. Sophie jumped at the chance and soon had the children in her thrall. Her hair fascinated them, but they were soon drawn into the world she described, where they had a future full of hope. I had a feeling that her short time with the children might yield better long-term results than anything else we might do. She had sowed some fertile seeds.

While Sophie was entertaining the children, I searched my pockets and my daysack for my phone; I wanted to call Manuel. Eventually, I borrowed Sophie's, but I got no answer, and I didn't want to leave a message that might be misunderstood. Sophie finished her talk, and we said our farewells before heading back to Mumbulo. I needed to speak to Manuel before five p.m.

Chapter 23

It was the day of the public meeting. I was nervous; I had no feel for how many people we would get, or how we would be received. I had left everything in what I hoped were the capable hands of Manuel. I normally involved myself much more in the logistics but, in Mumbulo, I had allowed myself to be both distracted and hurried. On the drive from Nocredo I quizzed Manuel about his expectations; he shrugged and said it would be fine. There was free beer, courtesy of Diangola so someone was sure to turn up.

Manuel took Sophie and me straight to the edificio público when we got to Mumbulo. I wanted to make sure it was tidy and fit for purpose, not that there was much we could do about it if it was not. We spent the whole morning running around, scrounging screens and flipcharts from Diangola and ARDCO. The edificio was where public gatherings were held in Mumbulo. Its rooms were large and high-ceilinged, and vestiges of grubby, ornate plasterwork hinted at better times. The thirty or so chairs and mismatched tables that we had set out looked lost. It took us nearly two hours with brooms, dustpans and damp cloths to make the room look as though somebody cared. We just had to hope that Manuel, his Diangola colleagues and the free beers had succeeded in generating some interest. I confided to Sophie that these meetings did not always get as many attendees as we would want, but it was important, in the interests of ongoing cooperation, to use and respect any existing organisations and systems.

At about two-fifteen p.m. I phoned Mitch to take me to collect David. He grumbled something about being an Angolan taxi service, but he did do it.

I was relieved when we saw David at the roadside. He was to be the star of our show and, without him, Sophie and I would look silly. He got in the back seat and I joined him so we could talk more easily. Mitch was seething.

The meeting turned out to be small, but everyone there was relevant. Sophie and I had agreed that I would be the chair and she would facilitate the short workshop sessions we had planned. Dryden, Harry, Constance, and Mitch represented ARDCO and I was pleased to see that both Luis Martins and Eusebio Agostinho were there from Diangola, as well as Manuel. Eight Mumbulo residents turned up, but David was the only person there who I knew for certain to be an artisanal miner. I recognised two other people and their presence troubled me deeply.

When everyone was settled, I opened the meeting in Portuguese, welcoming everybody before introducing myself. Sophie then explained who she was and, as there were fewer than twenty there, I suggested that a representative of each group should say a few words.

A young Angolan wearing a Bayern Munich football shirt introduced the Mumbulo residents. He said he was José Neto, a trader in the street market. He and the others from Mumbulo wanted change. They were totally dependent upon ARDCO and Diangola for their livelihoods and they wanted to see more people with money to spend, to broaden the base of the local economy. Manuel introduced the Diangola contingent and Constance did the same for ARDCO, after being given a strong visual cue by Dryden. It was then the turn of the two men I had recognised; the taller of them spoke in English, which I translated into Portuguese. He gave his name as Colin Harris and his companion was John Pitcher. They were the owners of Escutcheon Security; providers of all personnel security for ARDCO. Colin and Jug had come up in the world in thirty years, from foot soldiers to tinpot generals. It crossed my mind that, if there were to be any losers from what we were proposing, it was likely to be them. I had assumed that ARDCO ran their own personnel security and these two were part of it, but Escutcheon was a separate company and, if we were successful, their role in the mine's security operations would be reduced or unnecessary.

I summarised what the project hoped to achieve, and how we planned to do it, then Sophie led an exercise designed to identify how artisanal miners, like David, influenced ARDCO's and Diangola's operations. People called out their suggestions and I wrote them up on a whiteboard. The list included: physical threat to staff; the costs of possessing armoured personnel carriers and employing armed guards; lost potential revenue due to diamond theft; and the costs of resolving environmental damage such as the erosion of riverbanks. The group then discussed the list from David's perspective, looking at the needs of the artisanal miners. David was very open and honest and though it would have been better to have more than just the one representative, he made a strong case. Their needs were simple and boiled down to being able to feed and clothe their families in a safe environment, and to free their children from having to work, so they could have a proper childhood and a decent education – basic human rights.

I then projected a map of the area onto a wall; it was a copy of the one that Constance had marked the suspected artisanal mining sites on. We went through each site in turn and discussed various aspects; ARDCO's mining plans for it, the potential environmental impacts and whether there was any perceived threat of violence from the artisanal miners in that area. ARDCO had no plan to mine where David's group was working, but they did raise concerns about damage to the riverbanks. His group was not considered dangerous, just a nuisance. Sylvestre's group, on the other hand, was well known to ARDCO and Escutcheon. Harry said they had fired on ARDCO personnel transport with AK–47s, and other weapons, several times; they were known to be aggressive. I expected at least Dryden, Colin or Jug to speak up and expand on this, but they offered nothing.

David explained that his group was only interested in shallow gravels or river deposits close to the banks as they had no means to get at anything deeper, at least not safely. He said that a lot of men had tried to get at known, higher-grade gravels by digging deep holes but it had always ended in disaster. The ground was not solid rock, it was soil, sand and gravel so the sides of any hole had to be shored up to prevent them from falling in. In almost every case when the miners had cut corners, the walls of the holes had collapsed, and lives had been lost. David also told the meeting how much he got for selling diamonds to the buyers from the DRC. It raised a laugh from the ARDCO and Diangola contingents as it was less than ten per cent of the market value. David did not divulge how many stones his group recovered in a month.

It was clear to me, although I did not say anything, that there were two big winners from the status quo; the buyers who came over from the DRC and Escutcheon Security whose very existence depended on conflict. If our project succeeded it would be bad news for both.

I spotted Constance glancing nervously in Dryden's direction before straightening her back and raising her hand. She suggested that David's group should be given a trial permit to exploit the area where they were currently working. The proviso would be that all production should be sold to Diangola. To begin with, they would be paid eighty per cent of the average price per carat that ARDCO got, and this figure would be reassessed after three months. Large stones, bigger than ten carats, would be valued individually. ARDCO also agreed to provide David's group with high-quality equipment: picks, shovels and personal protective clothing at cost price. Diangola agreed to the arrangements but the owners of Escutcheon Security remained disturbingly quiet. In fact, neither Colin nor Jug said another word after their introduction, and they left just before the meeting closed, so I had no opportunity to speak to them. I did not see Dryden go either but he was no longer there when I looked around for him, to thank him for attending.

Mitch was another one to disappear before the end of the meeting. I think he was bored because the proceedings were in Portuguese. With him out of the way I was able to borrow Manuel's car. After taking him to Teresa's house, Sophie and I gave David a lift. It was dark by the time we dropped him off close to the island. He was ecstatic, but he could not believe it had been so easy. A few documents would need to be drawn up and a few senior bodies would have to sign on some dotted lines, but he would soon be a legitimate miner, no longer in fear of attack from the mining company.

It seemed too easy to me, but I could not see a catch. The only potential problems were other artisanal miners' groups, the buyers from the DRC, and I had a bad feeling about Escutcheon Security.

I was no longer as comfortable as I used to be, driving on dirt roads at night, so I was glad when we finally got back to Mumbulo. Sophie reminded me that she was staying the night at Maria's but that made no difference to where I had to go. I parked in front of the Dryden's house. Sophie got out and walked to Maria's. I sat in the car, waiting, hoping that Manuel would come out; I did not want to see Dryden. After about five minutes, I gave up and went to the house. Before I even reached the steps, Dryden appeared at the veranda gate; he looked agitated. I feared he was about to go back on everything that had been agreed in the meeting.

'David,' he said, 'I thought you were going to sit out there forever. Come in.' He ushered me to a seat on the veranda then, without asking, he fetched some cans of cold beer. He passed me one then sat down facing me over the table. After a short hesitation, he leaned forward. 'Why do you hate me?' he asked.

The question was so unexpected and so un–Dryden-like that I nearly choked. 'What?'

'You heard. Don't deny it.'

I remembered how he had always opposed everything I suggested or recommended, for no good reason. And I thought of Armando. 'I'm not sure I've ever hated anyone,' I said, 'but you would be near the top of a list of candidates. You undermined everything I ever tried to do. I couldn't do anything right. You blamed me for everything that went wrong.'

'Maybe I was a bit down on you, but you were a cocky little shit. You always had to be right and you were Morgan's blue-eyed boy. I don't think I was unfair though.'

'We'll differ to our dying days on that one. What did you really want to talk about?'

'I know what you're thinking,' he said. 'You think I killed Jim, don't you?' I was too surprised to say anything. 'Well, I didn't,' he continued. 'I don't know who did, but it wasn't me. I want to put the record straight though. I wasn't totally honest about what I saw that day; I made some of it up.'

'What? Why?' I was flabbergasted. His story had been central to everything. 'Which bits ...?'

'Most of it. I didn't actually see anyone else, only Jim. And he was already dead. He was lying where you found him. I don't know how long he'd been there. If you remember, it was a Sunday, so Mining weren't working; the road was deserted. We'd been at the same barbecue in Nocredo, Jim and me, but he left ages before I did. It's really scary, finding a body; he'd so obviously been murdered, the blood, those rocks and ...' he hesitated, 'and I didn't know if the killer was still close by. I felt incredibly vulnerable. I was scared. I fled to Mumbulo as quickly as I could. I was in a right old state. Call it paranoia if you want, but I kept thinking that everyone would suspect I'd done it. That's why I made up all that stuff about the Angolans and the accident. I didn't really try to rescue him as he was already dead. Maybe there was no one there to rescue him from; I don't know. Then people started to talk as though I was some sort of hero and I liked it. I became entrapped in my own lie. It became the truth. It seemed impossible to change the story.' He was almost pleading for me to believe him. 'The lie took on a life of its own ...'

'But the village ...'

'I don't know. I had nothing to do with that. The police investigated and that's what they concluded.'

'But you were their main witness.'

'Look. If I'm guilty of anything, it's that. I'm really sorry about what happened to that village and that's why I'm backing your project, why I let Connie drive things at the meeting, and I've already let you have a Land Rover.'

181

'Yeah. Complete with Mitch. What did he tell you about our trip yesterday?'

'Nothing. Like I said, you're a clever bugger. He doesn't understand much Portuguese. Anyway, it's a waste of a man. You can take a Land Rover without Mitch from tomorrow. I want to put right some of the wrong I did. It might be too late for those from that village thirty years ago but ...' He sighed. 'I'm right though, aren't I? You did come partly to investigate Jim's death, didn't you?'

I nodded; there was no point in denying it any longer. I was shocked and confused. Long-believed facts had turned into fiction; or had they? Why had he chosen to say what he had? Was it true or did he think we might be getting close and he wanted to cloud the issue? My heart was thinking the worst of him, but my head believed him.

'David, what I wanted to say is that I'm truly sorry for my part in that whole sorry affair back then. You were right to defend the Angolans for that.'

'Thank you,' I said. 'I need to think more about what you've told me though. We'll have to have another talk when I've thought it through.' Dryden then got us each a second beer and we passed the time in what, by our standards, was an amicable conversation about the mines, about former colleagues and about the politics of Angola.

I asked him if he could spare Harry or Constance to show Sophie and me some of the mines and plants in the next few days. He jokingly suggested Mitch before agreeing to fix something up for us with Constance.

Manuel poked his head out onto to the veranda to check whether I had returned yet. His face was a picture of amazement when he realised Dryden and I were sharing a joke. Our farewell handshake was in sharp contrast to our previous parting on that veranda. I think it was the first time we had shaken hands since our very first meeting.

I would never like Dryden, but I didn't hate him and, for the first time since he reported Jim's accident, I felt sorry for him.

I pretended to sleep as Manuel drove us back to Nocredo, but my mind churned over the significance of Dryden's words. If he'd just told me the truth, then not only was Sophie definitely wrong about her father's killer, but I was also probably wrong, as my 'understanding' of events was predicated on an act of revenge for the death of an Angolan.

Who had really killed Jim and why?

★★★

That night I dreamed a lot; Maria, Kevin Dryden, Jim Lodge and Sophie all featured prominently. What was it about Maria? Why did I feel drawn to this middle-aged woman even when Sophie, perhaps the most beautiful woman I had ever known, was in the same room as her? Maria confused me. I had no doubt whatsoever that she was the warmest, kindest person I had ever known, but that made her dishonesty all the more hurtful. I knew I still wanted to be with her more than anything, but I couldn't forgive that lie, that accusation.

Then there was Dryden; did I believe him? I had believed his previous story for thirty years – that was what had convinced me that Angolans had killed Jim Lodge. If it wasn't Angolans and it wasn't Dryden, then who had killed Lodge? The question of why it had been necessary to lay waste to Armando's village still persisted. I needed to speak to Sophie, tell her what Dryden had said, and I wanted to talk to Dryden again too, with Sophie there. She was a shrewd interrogator, and I was sure she would be better than me at spotting weaknesses in his new story.

Chapter 24

It felt strange to be alone in Nocredo. I missed Sophie; I was used to her being around. She was good company, intelligent, and I had grown very fond of her. From the beginning I had known I would be vulnerable to her, and I was right, but my feelings were not physical, as I'd expected, they were more parental.

I breakfasted early and, as usual, I was waiting for Manuel to pick me up and take me into Mumbulo. I hoped I would be able to find a vacant room at the mine offices as I wanted somewhere to meet with Sophie to discuss the workshop. I also wanted to Skype Rachel to inform her of our progress. By the time Manuel arrived I was itching to be on the road.

We were well on the way when my mobile phone rang; it jarred like a fire alarm; a sound from another world, another life. I had only made one or two calls since I had been in the mining area and my phone had not rung for more than a week; it was pure chance that I had remembered to charge it. It was Sophie.

'David!' Her voice was urgent and hoarse; she sounded upset. 'Are you on your way yet?'

'Hi Sophie. Yes, we're about halfway. We'll be there in about twenty minutes or so. What's the matter? Did you need me to bring something?'

'Only Manuel. Something terrible's happened. Hurry … please … Maria's …'

'Is Maria okay?' There was a panicky edge to my voice. Manuel turned to look at me; he had picked up on it.

'She's fine and I'm fine, but … Just come straight …' The line went dead.

I tried to call back, but the signal had gone.

'What's wrong?' asked Manuel.

'I don't know, but Sophie asked us to go straight to Maria's.'

'Is Maria unwell?'

When I told him that she was okay he was quiet for a few seconds, but his face betrayed a growing concern. His voice was little more than a whisper. 'Not Teresa. Please God let Teresa be well.' Manuel drove in anguished silence; face white and fingers drumming worry and impatience on the steering wheel.

If nothing was wrong with Maria or Sophie, it had to be Teresa, Dryden or someone else we both knew, and that was a short list. What about Armando or David? No, Sophie would not have mentioned Manuel in relation to them. It had to be Teresa. I knew Manuel had drawn the same conclusion, and I hoped for his sake that we were wrong.

We reached Mumbulo in only fifteen minutes. There were lots of men in uniforms milling aimlessly around in front of the two neighbouring houses and there was an ambulance backed up to the veranda steps of Teresa's, but there was no sign of urgency. There was also a police car parked beside the ambulance.

Manuel dashed to Teresa's, crossing himself and muttering prayers as he ran. Sophie came at me from Maria's and flung her arms around me. Her blouse was splattered, and her arms and legs were splashed and smeared the same colour – red – blood.

'Are you okay?'

I felt her head nodding against my chest, but I knew she was far from all right. She was trembling and she started to sob uncontrollably. I stroked her hair and tried to soothe her as I struggled to make sense of the evidence. Someone was badly hurt or dead in the Dryden's house – that much was obvious – but who? And why was Sophie covered in blood?

João came down the steps from Teresa's, edged past the ambulance and dashed over to us; his face was pale, and his eyes were rimmed with tears. He slipped an arm possessively around Sophie and pulled her from me.

'Mum asked me to get you,' he said, trying to hide the quaver in his voice. 'She's in there.' He pointed at Teresa's.

I ran my hand gently down Sophie's tear-streaked cheek and gave her an encouraging smile before walking the few yards to Teresa's. As I struggled through the gap between the ambulance and the house, I couldn't resist glancing inside it through the open rear doors. It was empty; a bad sign confirmed by one look into the lounge. Blood everywhere. And Kevin Dryden. He was on his side on the floor; there was a gaping wound in his throat. His eyeballs stared at him from a forked twig; they had been gouged out and impaled – a macabre echo of thirty years ago – the gory detail. The acrid smell of vomit triggered a sympathetic reaction from me, and I threw up behind the door; I was not the first.

Several men, some in police uniform, were taking photographs and picking around the body with tweezers and sample bags. It was as though they had seen crime scene investigations on television but could only remember part of the procedure. They had not isolated the crime scene; it was certainly contaminated. I'd been there at least a minute before I was challenged by a man who introduced himself as Daniel something-or-other; he was in charge, but I failed to catch his rank. After I had told him who I was, and that I'd been summoned by Maria, he was quite happy for me to wander around unimpeded.

When I finally dragged my eyes away from Dryden, I noticed a kitchen knife poking out from under a chair, and there was … I retched again. A bloody pineapple, a severed head to my brittle imagination, had rolled under the same chair.

I felt a hand on my arm. It was Maria; she urged me through to the passageway that led to the other rooms.

'Sophie found him …' she said quietly.

'No wonder she's in a state; it must have been a hell of a shock. I'm shocked and I was expecting something; she must have been completely unprepared. Why's all the blood on her, though?'

'She must have tried to stop the bleeding. I was preparing breakfast in the kitchen. I thought she was still in bed. She just burst in, covered in blood and sobbing. When she told me that Kevin was dead, I couldn't believe it; I came straight round …

Well, you've seen him. It's just like Jim. Who could have done that, David?' She squeezed my hand tightly.

'Where was Teresa?' I asked. 'How come she didn't find him?'

'She was out … on a call, I think.' Maria shuddered. 'I'm scared and confused,' she said. 'You are sure you didn't tell her about Jim's eyes, aren't you?'

'Absolutely,' I said. 'I couldn't bring myself to do it.'

'Thank God for that.' Her face relaxed with relief. 'She told me she'd had some questions she needed to ask Kevin; that's why she was there, but I couldn't help wondering …' She drew in a sharp breath and bit down hard on her bottom lip. 'I've just had a terrible thought,' she said. 'What would have happened if Sophie had interrupted the killer? That doesn't even bear thinking about … Where is she now?'

'In good hands,' I said. 'I left her outside with João.'

'Yes. Good hands.' Maria forced a smile. 'Incidentally, I told her to tell the police that she'd gone to see Teresa, not Kevin, to take her some eggs. I've put some fresh ones, from my hens, in her kitchen.'

'Why make up a story?' I asked.

'If the police think she went to see Kevin they might draw the wrong conclusion.'

'Bloody hell! I see what you mean.' There was a lot to think about. 'How's Teresa by the way? I've been thoughtless,' I said guiltily. 'I should have asked after her before.'

'She's a mess, as you'd expect. I sedated her and put her to bed. Manuel's sitting with her, so she's got a friendly face there when she comes to. He looks pretty shaken up too.'

'I guess it's a mixture of shock and relief for him,' I said. 'He was expecting to find something wrong with Teresa, not Kevin.'

My mind kept returning to Dryden's eyes. If they could speak, they had all the answers; they'd seen his killer, their mutilation was the same as Lodge's thirty years before, and … maybe they had seen Sophie.

'Did you tell Sophie everything last night? About Jim?' I asked.

'Almost, but not the eyes, but now … That's no coincidence is it? It can't be.' Her voice, a pitch higher than usual, emphasised her fear. She looked like a frightened child. Without thinking I put a comforting arm on her shoulder. She did not shrug me off. 'There's something very wrong about this,' she went on. 'It's history repeating itself.'

'I think you're right,' I said. 'When Jim was killed, people said the eyes thing was a Chokwe ritual to release the spirits of a killer – absolution. I believed that then because it humanised an inhumane act; it made it more bearable for me, and I think it was the same for all of us. Last night, Kevin told me he had made up that whole accident story. It's just occurred to me that if there wasn't an accident – and Jim hadn't killed anybody – there was no need for a ritual. If not a ritual, what's the mutilation about? Is it a signature? Someone telling us he's still here?'

'Who would do that? David, you're frightening me. I don't know who and what to trust. Who would have wanted to kill Kevin?'

I could think of a few names, but I said, 'Someone who was here thirty years ago, and who's still here now. I can't believe two people would do the same mutilation independently.'

One of the policemen came into the passageway and gave us a look that suggested he wanted us to move. Maria shuddered. 'We can't talk any more now,' she said. 'And Teresa needs me, Sophie too, maybe. And walls … listen.' She struggled for the right English words.

'Have ears,' I said.

She laughed nervously. 'I should have known that. It's the same in Portuguese: as paredes têm ouvidos. When can we have that talk?' she asked. 'Maybe Sophie's in danger too; we should all stick together. She needs to know all that we know. No secrets.'

'The sooner the better,' I said.

★★★

The morning blurred into afternoon. Sophie had cleaned herself up and borrowed a change of clothes from Maria. They were similar in height, but Sophie was slighter and had to wear a belt to keep everything in place. The police had taken Sophie's bloodied clothes away for tests.

Sophie sat with João and Maria in her courtyard, idly tossing grain to the chickens, while I pottered about in the kitchen preparing lunch from what I could find, without disturbing them. The meal of bread and cheese followed by fresh fruit salad tasted better than it looked; food presentation had never been my forte. Maria was just about to go and check on Teresa when Manuel appeared at the courtyard door with her. I admired his good sense in using the back way as that avoided passing through the lounge and the gore that must by then have been feeding a lot of flies. Teresa looked tired and haggard; her gaze was distant, drugged. Manuel ate what was left of our lunch, but Teresa abstained.

Conversation was difficult. Sophie and Teresa were both silent, in shock, but Manuel, João, Maria and I tried to maintain an air of normality. It was an exercise doomed to failure; Kevin Dryden was a magnetic theme. No matter what we talked about, there was always a point where his name insisted on intruding and one or other of us would have to change the subject. Eventually, we all gave up and shut up, each lost in our own thoughts, trying to make some sense of what had happened. Most of my encounters with death had been either remote or sanitised: a telephone call, a handwritten letter or a funeral service. Jim's and now Kevin's deaths were very different; violent and in my face, but it was the mutilation that upset me. Something primeval in me understood revenge – a life for a life, even an eye for eye – but motiveless mutilation was a long step too far, unnecessary. Thirty years ago, we had tried to explain it, to make it bearable, and someone, I can't remember who, said that it was a ritual. That had satisfied our need then, and it had reinforced the general belief that Jim Lodge had been killed by Angolans. Until now I had continued to believe that Angolans had done it, but not the Angolans from Armando's village. Because Kevin's mutilation was the same as Jim's, and the ritual idea – if Kevin had told me the truth – was now discredited, it had to be a signature. Maybe it was because of where I was sitting, in the courtyard of what had been the Madhouse, that another memory stirred.

★★★

It was a typical Sunday afternoon in Mumbulo. Carlos had lit a bar-becue in the courtyard of the Madhouse and its smoke signals had summoned quite a crowd. What had started as a quiet gathering had escalated into a party. Most of the younger men were engrossed in a round or two of the latest forfeit drinking game, the 'beer hunter', based on the Russian roulette scene of the film The Deer Hunter. *Cans of cold beer were the gun, and the loaded chamber was a shaken can. Each player took a turn to open a can against his temple. It was the kind of mindless amusement I used to enjoy on my first contract, but I now had a good reason for staying sober.*

I treasured every moment I spent with Maria, but our relationship was as irritating as it was wonderful. To see her I had to sneak out of the Madhouse under cover of darkness and tiptoe round to her courtyard door and let myself in. I had nearly been caught by Carlos a few times as his bladder capacity was ill-matched to his love of beer and his timing was annoying. I never truly understood Maria's need for secrecy, but I went along with it because the alternative was unthinkable. I loved her and I was proud that she had chosen me, but I also felt sometimes as though I wasn't good enough to be shown off. To my eyes, her family seemed to wear her achievements like medals and that put undue pressure on her; I resented them. I had grown to like Jim Lodge too in the past few weeks and we spent a lot of our social time together. I enjoyed his company and he also knew about Maria and me, which was a bonus; we could talk about her.

Neither Maria nor Jim was at the Madhouse that afternoon. Morgan had hijacked Jim to look at some future mining prospects, and they had taken Thys Gerber along to risk-assess any potential projects from the point of view of personnel security; there was no point opening a mine if the workers could not be protected. Maria had gone to Nocredo to visit her parents. So, I was playing silly games with the boys when I would rather have been with one, or both, of my best friends.

I withdrew to a corner of the courtyard in the shade of a mango tree which grew just outside the wall. I was trying to make my beer last as long as possible without appearing to be slacking. I wanted to be sober when Maria got back.

'You're being a bit antisocial this afternoon.' It was Colin, one of the inseparable pair of ex-British soldiers in the diamond security department. Like many of their ilk, they claimed to be ex-Special Forces. I had no way of knowing whether it was true, but I never challenged it as I did not fancy a fight.

'Not really,' I said. 'I just need a bit of peace. It's been a bit hectic lately.'

'Yeah, same for us.' Jug, the other half of the duo, emerged from behind Colin. After forcing another beer into my hand, they found a couple of deckchairs and sat next to me. I usually managed to avoid them but this time I was literally cornered; I was their captive audience.

They prattled on about the old days: shared experiences in the army and then the macho thing of outdoing one another, in their case, killing more men, more bloodily. I had nothing to contribute to the conversation, but I did occasionally feign interest by asking a question when I felt it was needed in the interests of sociability.

'One thing about us,' boasted Jug, 'is that when we find a body that one of us … you know … we always know who did it. Everyone's got a signature, a unique way of killing.'

I didn't ask what their ways might be, and I seriously doubted the truth of it despite Colin's vigorous nodding.

'Anyway.' Jug put a finger to his lips. 'If you ever need anyone sorting out …' He raised his eyebrows.

I had the strange feeling that I had just been offered the services of a pair of hit men. I was too surprised to comment. I swigged my beer in silence, wondering whether I had misread the implication of their words.

★★★

I had had no idea what the two ex-soldiers had meant by a signature thirty years ago, but now? I needed to discuss it with Sophie and Maria sooner rather than later to share my thoughts. If we were to stay safe, we all had to know who we were up against and what they might be capable of doing.

Everyone knew about the mutual enmity between Dryden and me, but no one seemed to suspect me of having anything to do with his death. Despite that, I felt there was a cloud over my presence. If I had never turned up in Mumbulo he would still be alive. But what could it be about me being here that would trigger Dryden's death? Had he known something incriminating that someone thought he might tell me? What could be so important that Dryden had to be silenced? Who else knew whatever it was? Who else was in danger? Surely it would have been easier just to kill me. It was a sobering thought, but I sensed that I might be protected by my international connections: the charity and its donors. If anything happened to me, I knew that Rachel would stir things up and get to the bottom of it. She was not someone who would allow the death of one or more of her co-workers to fade into history without investigation and, though we were divorced, we were still close. I could rely on Rachel, but did this killer know that?

★★★

After lunch, we discussed the arrangements for the coming night, where everyone should stay. Manuel insisted that Teresa should go to his house in Nocredo. He confided to me that he had found it impossible to pluck up the courage to call Rui, Kevin's son, from Mumbulo, but he hoped he would do better from the comfort of his own home. Maria decided she would also go to Nocredo, to the house she had inherited from her parents a few years before. João said that he ought to stay in Mumbulo as he had the responsibility of ensuring that ARDCO's interests were represented in the light of Dryden's murder.

I was surprised that I had not been interviewed by the police but when I mentioned it to Maria she said not to worry. She told me that they had spoken to her, Sophie and João before I had arrived in Mumbulo that morning, so it didn't look as though I was in their thinking. Indeed, their lack of action suggested that none of us was on their list of suspects, which was a relief.

★★★

The hours passed as they had on a similar day thirty years before. People tried to carry on as though nothing had happened, but their minds were not completely on the tasks in hand. Furthermore, the importance of those tasks was diluted by the context; Kevin Dryden's death. It was like a play, rewritten to exclude a key part, but no one had yet learned their new lines. It was surreal.

Chapter 25

Manuel left us briefly at about four p.m. to have a word with the police officer in charge of the investigation next door. He returned to say that he had told them where we were all going to be that night, and that we had permission to go whenever we wanted. He left almost immediately with Teresa to take her to Nocredo. Maria, Sophie and I stayed a while longer. As soon as Teresa had gone Sophie perked up; it was though someone had flicked a switch. At first, I thought it was the sedatives wearing off, but I sensed it was more than that. She had not engaged in any way with Teresa all afternoon and I had attributed that to a combination of shock and not knowing what to say to the recently bereaved. Now, it seemed different. Was it guilt for being the wrong person to find Kevin, or was it for failing to save his life?

Maria also noticed Sophie's improvement and asked her if she felt up to another talk that evening. 'There's something else you need to know about your father's death,' she said.

Sophie stared at me quizzically. 'Your evasion, David?' she asked.

I shrugged.

'I always knew we'd get there eventually.' She smiled at Maria. 'That sounds good to me, Maria.' She had regained much of her old feistiness and the look she gave me bordered on smug.

'Let's get going then,' said Maria. 'I'll drop you two at the casa de trânsito in Nocredo and give you time to get changed, then I'll pick you up and we'll have that chat at my parent's old house.'

★★★

The house was very similar to most of those in Mumbulo. It was a good design for the climate and most colonial houses in the region showed only minor variations from a limited theme. I had only met Maria's parents once, thirty years ago, introduced as a friend, but I could tell the interior décor here was theirs not Maria's. The furniture was comfortable but heavy and old-fashioned. Sophie lolled in a well-worn leather armchair and Maria and I shared a matching two-seater sofa.

'What is it with you two?' said Sophie.

I looked at Maria. I could see what Sophie meant. We were like bookends. We all laughed, and it lightened the mood somewhat.

We talked for a while about the state of the charity project and our plans to try and get other artisanal mining groups on board. But we could not avoid the inevitable topic indefinitely.

'So, why was Kevin murdered?' I asked at the next pause in conversation. 'A couple of days ago, I believed Jim had been killed by Angolans and Sophie was sure Kevin had something to do with it. Now I'm sure we were both wrong.'

'What?' Sophie was shaking her head, bewildered. She was still unaware of my conversation with Dryden the previous evening.

'Last night, Kevin told me that he didn't do it, and I believed him.'

'What exactly did he say?' she asked. 'And more to the point, why did you believe him?'

'He told me he suspected that we thought he was involved with killing your father. He said he had nothing to do with it, and then he told me he'd made up the story about the Angolans and the accident.'

'And you believed him?' Sophie was white.

'Yes, because of Armando's insistence that his villagers were innocent, and …' I looked at Maria. She nodded. It was a bizarre, wordless dialogue, but we understood it perfectly.

'When you found Kevin this morning,' Maria said, 'you saw the … the mutilation?'

Sophie winced. 'Yes?'

'Well, someone did the same to your father.'

Sophie's hands went to her face; a Munch-like, silent scream. Maria went over to her and perched on an arm of the chair; she put a comforting hand on Sophie's shoulder.

'I'm sorry,' she said, 'but you had to know.'

'Is that what you've been holding back, David?' Sophie asked. 'The thing that convinced you that it was Angolans who killed him. Why would Angolans tear his eyes out like that and impale them on a stick? I could just as well imagine Dryden doing that.'

'We were desperate, shocked; a bit like you must be now,' I said. 'Someone said it was an Angolan ritual to release the troubled spirits from someone who's killed somebody. We were ready to believe any explanation that suggested it wasn't pure evil. I believed it. It diluted the horror, made it tolerable'

Sophie broke down.

Maria and I waited for Sophie to regain her composure. After a few minutes, she nodded and forced a wet-eyed smile to signal that she was ready to go again.

'We need to re-examine your father's death,' I said, 'and colour it with – let's just call it a possibility – that what Kevin told me last night is true. Then we need to think about what happened this morning; I've got a theory.'

'Let's go through the process first, before we hear any theories,' Sophie's fingers dug deep into the leather chair arms; the tension in her was palpable.

I took a deep breath, and I retold the story of the afternoon of Jim Lodge's death. With each telling, the story seemed less plausible to me, but I did remember odd additional details and I no longer needed Sophie to ask questions. Every detail was open to scrutiny now. I told them about the party at the Madhouse, how Kevin Dryden had burst in and told us that Jim had had an accident and was being attacked – stoned – by Angolans.

'And last night,' said Sophie. 'You say Kevin confessed that he made all that up?'

'The bit about the Angolans and the accident, yes. He said he did find your father, but he was already dead, and I believed him. He said he made the story up to deflect any suspicion that he might have had something to do with the killing. By pure chance it made him look good – a hero who stopped to help a friend in a spot. That was why he couldn't change his story. Anyway, going back to that day, I drove to where Dryden said your father was – Carlos was with me. The others went to get more vehicles and reinforcements before driving out to join us. Who went next door to get you, Maria?'

Maria pursed her lips in thought. 'I can't be sure, but I think it was that other metallurgist, Steve ... what was his name?'

'Steve Vernon,' I said and closed my eyes for a second. Yes, I had a clear image of him in my mind, arriving with Maria at the scene, another detail.

'What happened when you got there?' asked Sophie.

'Your father was lying at the roadside, by that rock I showed you, Chesterfield. He was badly battered and there were some hefty looking rocks around him, covered in blood. When we went there with David the other day, I remembered that there'd also been blood on Chesterfield. Your father's eyes were like Dryden's this morning. It was horrendous but the evidence matched the story Dryden told. It looked as though your father had been stoned to death. We had no reason to think that Dryden was lying so we assumed it was a crowd of Angolans getting revenge for the accident, just as he'd said. Colin and Jug arrived just after us and they went off with their guns to check that the place was safe.'

'And Maria, you confirmed that my father was dead. Is that right?'

'Yes.'

'How long after David did you arrive?'

'A few minutes. Not long,' I interrupted.

'And no one checked before Maria turned up? What if he'd still been alive?'

'He was.' Maria's words cut through me like an icy sword. Sophie stared at her in disbelief. I stared too; I knew it was true.

'Jim was one of the best friends I've ever had, and I killed him,' said Maria. 'It was the worst day of my life. His skull was shattered, and his brain was bleeding, exposed. There were bits of rock and grit all mashed into it but there was a very weak pulse and I saw a finger move. He was a dead man breathing … and then there were the eyes … I pressed into his brain with my fingers, hoping to finish him. I didn't know if it would work as he'd survived everything else, but I couldn't bear the thought of him suffering. As it happened, it didn't take long. It was against everything I believe in. I still have nightmares about it, but I'd do the same again. He could never have survived. He'd almost bled out from the head wound and we had no blood to give him, and the brain damage looked way beyond surgery.'

Sophie writhed around, rubbing the heels of her hands against her eyes, as she struggled to control her emotions. I was shocked too. Maria's revelation had unleashed a memory that I had suppressed for thirty years.

'Sophie,' I said. 'No one checked your father's body before Maria arrived. I chose not to because I was afraid he might be alive. I was a coward. I convinced myself that he was dead, sparing myself a difficult decision, the decision that Maria made. I've suppressed that memory for thirty years, but I've always known that I did something terribly wrong that day. I deeply regret not checking and I would have done exactly what Maria did if I'd been brave enough. I didn't know until now that he was actually alive, but he always has been, somewhere deep in my subconsciousness. Maria had the courage to do what I should have done before she even arrived. Don't blame Maria. I'm more to blame. I stood there and did nothing.'

Sophie stared hard at both of us. We were all crying by now.

'When my parents died, the Addisons that is,' she said, 'I blamed myself because they were only on that road because they'd been to visit me. I've always felt guilty about that and that I was glad they'd died instantly; that they hadn't suffered. I hope I could have done what you did Maria if I had been called upon. I do believe you did what you thought was best, and for the right reasons. Thank you for telling me the truth.'

'I've never told anyone about that before and I don't intend ever to say it again. That's why David had to be here too,' said Maria. 'I wouldn't have blamed you if you'd reacted differently.'

I remembered how Sophie said she had reacted when she'd first learned that the Addisons were not her blood parents. She was remarkable and strong-willed; I was proud to know her.

'I don't get it though.' Sophie knitted her brow in concentration. 'How come the police didn't discover that Dryden's story was a lie? They investigated. They must have looked for the other man, the Angolan who's supposed to have died.'

I shrugged. I had no answer.

She carried on. 'It doesn't make sense. If Kevin Dryden just happened across my father's body by pure chance and then made up a story that now looks to be full of holes, how did it become fact? It sounds like a proper stroke of luck for the real killer. I wonder what he would have done if Dryden hadn't made up his pack of lies. And another thing, at least one person other than Kevin has always known that he was lying; my father's killer.'

'I don't know,' I said, 'but I've got a theory about who the killers are.'

'Killers, plural?' said Sophie.

'You remember the two guys sitting at the back of our meeting yesterday, the owners of Escutcheon Security?'

'Yes. I guess they were Colin and Jug,' said Sophie. 'Why them?'

I told Sophie and Maria how the two men had apparently offered me their services as hit men thirty years before. 'I think the eyes might be their signature.'

'So, why did you never suspect them before? It seems so obvious.'

'Because I believed Dryden's story; the accident, the Angolans … It never crossed my mind that anyone I knew could be capable of carrying out that … that atrocity.'

Sophie clenched her fists and clamped her eyes and mouth tightly closed. She sat like that for a minute or so, apparently deep in thought, then she said, 'And those two arrived at the scene just after you and …?'

'… Carlos. Yes. I've been racking my brains, trying to remember if I noticed them behind me while I was driving. There were lots of places, side roads to mining blocks and plants, where they could have parked and waited out of sight until someone drove past. To be honest, I've no idea if they came from town or from somewhere closer, but I'd bet on the closer option.'

'It's not exactly evidence, is it?' Sophie pursed her lips. 'But I suspect you're right. What do we know about them?'

'We know they're trained killers and they were in the vicinity when both your father and Kevin Dryden were killed. There's also what looks like a signature. It's all circumstantial but …'

'But why?' Maria was shaking her head. 'I follow your logic but why Jim thirty years ago, and why Kevin now? What did Jim know? Was it something he saw or was it something professional, geological? Were they both killed for the same reason?'

'In Jim's case, I don't think it could have been professional,' I said. 'He reported all geological stuff to Morgan, nobody else. Anything new would have been under wraps. It had to be something else he knew that threatened them in some way.'

'And Dryden?' said Maria, 'Why would your appearance on the scene make them kill him? If Jim was killed for something he knew about them, they would have killed Dryden back then too if he'd known what Jim knew.'

Sophie butted in. 'As I see it, the only connection between my father and Kevin Dryden is diamonds; it has to be professional. You said my father wouldn't tell anyone where to find diamonds except Morgan. Suppose Morgan was working … is working, with them …'

'They're all here,' said Maria, 'but I can't believe Geoff would have anything to do with Jim's or Kevin's deaths. They were both his friends.'

Maria opened a bottle of Cognac and poured us each a glass as we sat and wrestled with our thoughts. Sophie sucked on her bottom lip in what I now recognised as one of her thinking expressions. Maria tilted her head forward and closed her eyes – she could have been asleep but for a counting action she made with the fingers of her right hand.

'Is it possible,' Maria broke the spell, 'that Kevin's murder was a copycat?'

'Well, the killing itself wasn't,' I said, 'a stoning and a cut throat, but the mutilation could be. Maria, how many people know about what happened to Jim? Was it … is it common knowledge?'

'I don't think so, not now. It's long forgotten for most people; there's been a civil war. I could ask Constance,' said Maria. 'I've never talked to her about that, but she's tuned in to all the gossip and the back stories, and she's always been interested in James Lodge as she's a geologist. If the details of Jim's death are common knowledge, she'll know them. If she doesn't then I doubt whether anyone else does.' Maria fished in her bag, pulled out her mobile and was soon talking to Constance. She put the phone on speaker, so that we could all hear the conversation.

'All I know about that,' said Constance, 'is that Jim Lodge was killed in an accident on the mine road from Mumbulo to Nocredo. It must be at least twenty or so years ago, long before my time here.' She offered nothing about the stoning and nothing about any mutilation. If Maria was right, then nobody who wasn't in Mumbulo thirty years ago was likely to know any of the details.

Maria shrugged and put her phone away.

'Let's assume for the time being that Dryden was murdered by the same person or persons who murdered Jim,' said Maria.

'And let's also assume,' Sophie added, 'that it was because of something he knew, something he might tell you, David. What else did you talk to Dryden about the last night, apart from my father's death?'

'Nothing much; old times and our project. He was actually quite pleasant to me. It was a bit weird. We had a friendly conversation for the first time I can remember. He told me things, as though getting them off his chest. He promised he'd give us a vehicle and pull Mitch off us. He wanted to try and pay back for some of the wrongs he'd done to the Angolan community back then. I can't remember his exact words but that's the gist of it.'

'That's not much help.'

I shrugged. 'I didn't expect that conversation to be our last.'

We talked in circles for another half hour before giving up, and then Maria gave Sophie and me a lift back to the casa de trânsito.

PART 4

Chapter 26

I was awoken by a loud crash and the strident scream of the doorbell. I heard the breakfast steward open the inside door onto the veranda and ask what all the fuss was about.

'Police!' was the response. 'Open up.'

The sound of the steward's key in the lock was followed by the scraping of the wrought iron gate against the concrete floor of the veranda. I had never noticed how noisy it was before. What were the police doing here? There were only two guests. I felt sick. Despite my innocence I could imagine only one answer; I had been fitted up. The thought of a smelly Angolan prison cell turned me to jelly. I waited for the knock on my door, wondering what to say, how to convince them that it was not me. But the knock, when it came, was on a door further along the corridor, the other resident.

'Senhora Addison?'

'Sim?'

'Police! Open up, please!'

'Why? What do you …?' Sophie's voice was weak, lacking her usual confidence, but I heard her door creak open.

'Senhora Addison, we're here to arrest you for the murder of Senhor Kevin Dryden.'

I could not believe what I was hearing. I knew her; I knew she could not have done it. It was rubbish; had to be. I opened my door, wearing only my underpants. Three uniformed Angolans, all with guns, were standing in the corridor. They gave Sophie the time and privacy to dress.

'There's been a terrible mistake,' I said. 'You can't arrest Doctor Addison. She didn't kill Kevin Dryden.'

'And how do you know that Senhor Young? You were here in Nocredo yesterday morning, but Doctor Addison was in

Mumbulo, where Senhor Dryden was killed. She had his blood on her hands.'

'Why would she kill him?'

'Revenge. She believed Senhor Dryden murdered her father.'

'Doctor Addison isn't a killer. You couldn't be more wrong. Even if she had believed what you said she still wouldn't have killed him. She believes in the process of law.'

'Good,' said the senior officer. 'Then this should satisfy her liking for the legal process.'

Sophie emerged looking distraught and frightened. Her eyes were puffy and red. Her cheeks glistened with tears.

I said in English. 'We'll get you out. We'll prove it wasn't you.'

I looked at her in earnest, trying to appear completely confident, but my facial muscles were somewhat paralysed. She nodded dumbly. I think she expected to wake up and find herself in bed, sweating after a bad dream. I tried to get to her, past the policemen, but they barred my way. I wanted to hug her, to let her know I was going to do my best for her. Her eyes, normally so alive, looked dead, devoid of hope, but she managed the faintest of smiles that told me her spirit had only been temporarily knocked out.

'Where are you taking her?' I asked.

'Mumbulo. That's where our enquiries are centred.'

My only previous experience of the Angolan police was their investigation into Jim Lodge's death and that had ended in a gross miscarriage of justice; Armando's village had been bulldozed to rubble. I had to get Sophie released; I had to prove her innocence. The task seemed massive. My fear was that, although Jim's and Kevin's deaths were thirty years apart, another miscarriage was likely to result. Where should I start? Who could I trust?

I had to speak to Maria. Surely, she could give Sophie an alibi and that would be an end to it. No one could doubt the doctor, surely. I was not sure I could find my way to her parents' old house again though; I had not been concentrating when we went there yesterday, and I didn't know its address or her mobile number. Damn! I could spend hours walking the streets without finding it. It did not help that most of the houses looked very similar to one another. I asked the steward if he knew where Maria lived. He did not, but he did suggest Manuel which, if I hadn't been in a state of panic, I would have thought of myself.

He gave me directions to Manuel's house. It was not far so I set off at a fast walk, trying to control my emotions.

'David! What's the matter?' Manuel was eating breakfast with his wife and Teresa on his veranda. He saw immediately that I was distressed. 'Is it Sophie? Is she unwell?'

'It's Sophie, yes, but she's not ill. She's been arrested.' I looked at Teresa. There was only one thing Sophie could have been arrested for and I was encouraged by the look of disbelief on Teresa's face.

'That's ridiculous,' said Manuel. 'Where have they taken her?'

'Mumbulo.'

'Let's go!' He picked up the keys to his Land Cruiser and was past me in an instant.

'No. Not yet. I need to see Maria. She's Sophie's best chance for an alibi. Will you take me there please? Her house here in Nocredo.'

'Of course. Anything for Sophie. I can't believe they think she's capable of doing that. Bloody fools!' He checked that we were out of Teresa's earshot. 'I wasn't keen on having Kevin as my brother-in-law; I didn't like him much and I won't miss him, but I still can't believe he was killed so malevolently. And as for Sophie doing it …' He shook his head in disbelief.

***

It was just after seven when I rang Maria's doorbell.

I was surprised when João answered the door. 'Mum was called out on an emergency. She's a glutton for work. She always lets the hospital know when she's in Nocredo just in case … And she always gets called out. She's been worse since dad died.' He shook his head. 'Come in and wait. Hopefully, she won't be long. Where's Doctor Addison?' He looked at the Land Cruiser as though hoping to conjure her from it.

I told him that she was indisposed. Though I was impatient I had little choice but to wait so I arranged for Manuel to stay at his home in case I needed transport later.

João made coffee for both of us. He told me that the house in Mumbulo had felt lonely without his mother there, so he had driven to Nocredo late in the evening, arriving not long after his mother had returned from dropping Sophie and me back at the casa de trânsito.

'You look worried. If it's about Kevin's murderer, I heard that the police have made an arrest.'

'What if I told you they've arrested Doctor Addison?' I said.

'I'd tell you to be serious and stop messing around,' he had switched to English. 'Where is she?'

'Mumbulo Police Station.'

He looked at me long and hard. 'You are being serious. She didn't do it. She was with mum and me. We went for a walk together in the evening then she sat with mum, talking for an hour or so; very serious stuff, before going to bed. She didn't go out until the morning when she found him.'

'I know she didn't … couldn't … have done it, but how can you be certain she didn't go out?'

'Because I didn't sleep well. I couldn't. I kept thinking about her.' He looked sheepish. 'I even got up to go to her, but my nerve deserted me. I just watched her sleeping from the doorway. I hardly slept. I'm sure I would have woken if she'd got up in the night.'

'Would you be prepared to tell that to the police?' I asked.

'Of course. Maybe I should exaggerate a bit: tell them I spent the night with her.'

'No. Don't do that whatever you do. Sophie's going to have it tough enough. Don't give them an excuse to do an intimate examination, especially if there's nothing to find.'

He sighed. 'They'd never believe me if I said I slept with her without doing anything, anyway,' he said, 'and they'd be right. I don't think I could.'

I understood; I thought of his mother. 'Okay,' I said. 'So, Sophie couldn't have gone out during the night, but Kevin hadn't been dead long when Sophie called your mother. She told me yesterday that she didn't know Sophie had even got up.'

'Mum made up that story about eggs yesterday; she often gives eggs to Teresa. Do you think the police believe it?' he asked hopefully.

'Whether they do or not, does it prove her innocence? It doesn't take long to kill someone. Fuck! What a mess! I hope your statements – yours and your mum's – will be enough to satisfy them,' I said, but I feared the worst.

I'd been thinking about the evidence and, even to me it looked damning: she'd had Kevin Dryden's blood on her; she'd found his body and the police believed she thought that he had killed her father. As far as the police were concerned, she had both opportunity and motive, but what about the means; the knife? Was it the knife I had seen under the chair? It looked like a full set. But how could they have known that Sophie thought Dryden had killed her father? Come to that, how had Dryden known? Probably paranoia from a guilty conscience, I guessed, but that did not explain how the police knew about it.

'It's very odd,' I said. 'The police said something this morning that they couldn't have known unless Sophie or I had told them.'

'What was that? Something from the past?' He gave me a hard stare. 'What is your connection with mum anyway, David? You used to know her, didn't you?'

I nodded.

'Please tell me what's going on? I need to know. Ever since you came on the scene, people have been behaving strangely – and not just in Mumbulo. I was in a meeting with Geoff Morgan, in Luanda, when a girl came in with a message. He'd been his usual relaxed self, but then he got all agitated and drew the meeting to a premature close. Later, I saw the messenger and she told me that she'd told Geoff that you'd been at the Mining Ministry in Luanda. What is it about you and Sophie? And then there's Mum. I've never known her like she is at the moment. She's gone very secretive. She quite pointedly excluded me from her conversation with Sophie the other night, but they've only just met; what could they have in common that required such a long, private conversation?'

'All right,' I said. 'There are things you ought to know as you're involved, and I believe you care about Sophie. I used to work here thirty years ago and so did Sophie's father. He was killed on the mine road between Nocredo and Mumbulo; it was murder.'

'Who did it? The murder.'

'I don't know. Until very recently I thought it was Angolans, but Sophie turned up at my house a few months back and started asking questions. Anyway, we looked at the evidence again and visited the site. I still thought it was probably Angolans who did it, but Sophie was convinced that Kevin Dryden had been involved. When the police arrested Sophie this morning, they said her motive was that she believed Dryden killed her father, which is really odd because only Sophie and I knew she thought that ... and Kevin.'

'Kevin?'

'Yes. I spoke to him briefly at his house the evening before he was killed. He said he knew we thought he'd killed Sophie's father. I thought it was just paranoia; I suppose I still do.'

'Christ!' João was shaking; the full extent of Sophie's plight seemed to hit him suddenly. 'How are we going to get her out?'

'Do you know criminal law?' I asked him.

He shook his head disconsolately. 'No, only commercial and mining law, unfortunately, but ...' he perked up, 'I have a friend. We were at college together. He's in Luanda. I'll phone him now.'

'Wait a minute,' I caught his arm. 'Anywhere else in the world, you and your mother would walk into the police station and make a statement to the effect that Sophie didn't leave your house during the night and didn't have time to kill Kevin Dryden when she went there in the morning. You'd establish the alibi and then she would be released. That might happen, but I have a horrible feeling it won't.'

'And if it doesn't work? What then? We can't just let her rot in prison for something she didn't do.'

'I've no intention of doing that. That's where your mate will come in handy, and I need to contact the British Embassy to get them to apply pressure. They should already be in the loop as Kevin Dryden was British. I assume someone, maybe Geoff Morgan, has contacted them. Can you find that out, please?'

'I'll do whatever I can to help. I'll get in touch with the office in Luanda.'

'Thanks. Meanwhile, when I've spoken to your mum, I think I should go to the police station in Mumbulo and see Sophie if I can. She'll need moral support. I don't want her to feel that I've deserted her.'

'I'll take you,' he said. 'Let's go. I'll tell Mum to meet us in Mumbulo.' He produced a phone from his shirt pocket and was talking to his mother within seconds. He spoke too quickly for me to understand everything, but I heard Sophie's name, the police and Mumbulo. 'She'll meet us at home in Mumbulo. She'll probably get there before us as she's finished her call and the hospital's on the way.'

When I told João to call in briefly at Manuel's so I could tell him I would not need him, he gave me a strange look.

'Don't you have a phone?'

I phoned and sent texts all the time in England, but Angola seemed to anchor my habits in the past. I still remembered Mumbulo as having only six or seven houses with a telephone connection and they only connected to one another, and to the central concentrator plant, which had been the communication hub, relaying hand-written and verbal messages brought in by truck drivers from the pre-treatment plants and the sort house. The only exception was a single line from the Mine Manager's office to the company's office in Luanda. I pulled out my phone and was surprised to find that I had already saved Manuel's number. I rang him and explained that João had taken over the chauffeur duties.

Not for the first time, the drive from Nocredo to Mumbulo was quiet and uncomfortable. I could not begin to guess how much worse it must have been for Sophie an hour or so earlier.

Chapter 27

Maria was not there when we reached her Mumbulo house. João checked his mobile and found a text saying she had been called away on another medical emergency. We decided to go to the police station anyway to reassure Sophie that we were pulling for her. João said it wasn't far, so we walked and used the time to get our thinking straight, something we had failed to do on the drive from Nocredo.

Mumbulo police station was a windowless concrete block on the edge of the town; ugly and jarringly familiar. It took João and me about ten minutes to walk there from Maria's, along roads I had not travelled for thirty years. Some of the roads and buildings were just as I remembered but others were new and there were gaps where things on the fringe of my memory had once stood. All my excursions with Sophie in the past few days had been to the north of Mumbulo, and we had always stayed on the east side of the river. Some rusty steelwork in the distance beyond the police station brought me up short. It was the bridge; the same bridge I had once crossed almost every day. I knew exactly where I was. The old concentrator plant and the sort house should have been near where we were standing. Where were they? I asked João if he knew what had happened to them and he pointed vaguely back the way we had come. Some steel columns and assorted steelwork stuck out incongruously from a ramshackle collection of thrown-together buildings; shanty dwellings constructed from the ruins of the old concentrator. It was almost unrecognisable.

'That would put the police station almost exactly where the old sort house was,' I said.

João shrugged.

We stood, staring at the building, mustering our courage. 'Bloody hell!' I said. 'It's where the old sort house was because it is the old sort house. I thought it looked familiar. It used to have a high wall round it so you couldn't see it until you were inside the gates. I've never seen it from this distance before.'

'So what?' said João. 'What difference does it make that it's the old sort house?'

'Nothing, I suppose. I imagine the cells will be underground where we used to have the strong room. I hated going down there even when I knew I'd be out in half an hour. It's horrible. We need to get Sophie out sooner rather than later.'

The sort house had never been welcoming but now it seemed to ooze hostility from every crack and bullet scar in its walls. The doors were steel plate as they had always been and there was a bell push to attract attention. I pushed the button and we waited. After a couple of minutes I pushed the button again.

There was a metallic scratch then a scrape then the door moved inwards, allowing us to enter. João knew the policeman who let us in: they used to play football together. We did not need to explain why we were there. We were led along the same corridor that had been used for security observation thirty years ago. I felt even more uncomfortable now than I had then, and I wondered if the same rudimentary closed-circuit TV was still in use, monitoring our every move.

We eventually arrived in a waiting area with several mismatched chairs scattered along the walls. We were told to sit and wait. Several short steel stumps stuck up from the floor and I realised it was the old picking room. The stumps were the last vestiges of the long-gone sorting table and the stools where I had shown Jim Lodge how to pick diamonds.

After about half an hour, another policeman took us down to what had been the strong room. It was, as I had suspected, where they were holding Sophie. When she saw us, she tried to get up but was restrained by two male Angolan police officers. Her face was ravaged by fear and tear stains but the set of her jaw and the way she held her shoulders suggested inner resolve. I thought of Boudicca readying herself to face the Romans.

'How are you Sophie? How are they treating you?' I asked.

'I feel fucking shit.' It was the first time I had ever heard her swear. 'The cell's lousy, literally. I'll probably have to shave my head when I get out; but I'm being treated okay.'

'We're trying to get you out as soon as we can, but you'll have to be patient because things don't always happen very quickly here. We're contacting the British Embassy to get them behind us, but we're also trying to prove from here that you couldn't have done it.'

'Thank you,' she said. 'I've done a lot of thinking.' I put my finger to my lips to quieten her. Although I didn't think the Angolans could understand English, I didn't want to take any chances. 'How long do you think they'll hold me for?' she asked.

I shook my head. 'I don't know, but we'll get you out. Trust me.' I felt a huge psychological weight settle on me and my legs felt wobbly. Could I keep my promise? There was no choice.

João was staring intently at her. 'I'll be helping too. I'm going to provide a statement that you didn't leave the house during the night and so you had no time to do anything in the morning.'

Sophie let out a huge sob. 'I've done something really stupid. I panicked … When they were questioning me …'

'Tell me about it,' I said. 'It can't be that bad.'

'Worse,' she said. 'They showed me a knife and asked me how I would hold it. All I could think of was that if I helped, they'd be more likely to let me go. I picked it up. It's got my finger-prints on the handle – it was probably the knife that killed Kevin Dryden.' She sobbed noisily and tears streamed down her cheeks. 'I'm stuffed,' she blubbed.

I had to hide my fear at this turn of events. 'No, you're not,' I said, as steadily as I could. I tried to exude confidence but my voice had a reediness that sounded nervous even to me. 'We'll prove who really did it.'

João was stunned, silent. His dream was sitting there, un-touchable and fading. He looked distraught.

214

We told Sophie that Maria was on an emergency call-out, but she would make a statement that would strengthen Sophie's defence, as soon as possible. One of the policemen pointed at his watch and gestured for us to leave. Our farewells were awkwardly optimistic; forced smiles and promises with no foundation. Nobody was fooled. João and I were taken back up to the old sorting room where Maria was now waiting. I watched as they hugged.

'I have to make a statement,' Maria said. 'João too. It'll be Sophie's alibi. The sooner we do it, the sooner she'll be out.' I hoped she was right.

She went over to the desk and I heard her explain to someone that she and her son both wished to make formal statements regarding the death of Kevin Dryden. One of the officers then opened a door granting access to the office, which used to be the jurisdiction of the Chief Sorter, and they went inside.

An hour later, the three of us left the police station together, but without Sophie.

'What else can we do?' I asked when we were back in the fresh air. I felt helpless, out of my depth. 'Do you trust the police here to get the right answer, find the real killer? Has it changed since ...?'

'Things have changed,' Maria said. 'It is better than it was when you were here before, but ...' she sounded unsure. 'There might be outside pressures.'

'From where, or from whom?'

'God knows,' said Maria. 'I just can't get over the similarities between the two murders. Either the same person killed them both or there's a copycat.'

'Bloody hell! Did someone cut Sophie's father's throat as well then?' João asked. 'Or do you mean the eyes?'

'The eyes,' I said. 'It's why we always believed it was Angolans who killed Sophie's father.'

'But why? I didn't have you down as a racist, David. Why would you think Angolans would be any more likely to do that than the British, Portuguese or anyone else for that matter?'

I told him about the ritual theory, and how we willingly latched onto an explanation that softened the evil of the mutilation. João's headshake spoke volumes. He had many Angolan friends.

'Maybe, that's the key,' he said. He had become more animated, stretching his hands in front of him and bringing them together to suggest a reduction of options. 'Who suggested the ritual? Perhaps it was meant to throw you all off. It certainly succeeded.'

'I've no idea,' I said, 'It was all very confused. In the first few days afterwards, there were lots of pet theories, but that was the one that stuck. As time passed, Jim's death became a taboo subject. No one talked about it for fear of upsetting anyone else. It could have been anyone and not necessarily someone who went out to the body.'

'So, what do you suggest then?' he said. 'You're the one who seems to know everything; everything that doesn't matter, that is.'

I could understand his frustration at me; I shared it. I wished I could remember more. 'We have to identify Kevin's real killer and prove it unless we're really lucky and they release Sophie on your alibi; I'm not hopeful of that. I think we'll have to come up with something the police can't ignore.'

'Like what?' asked Maria.

'I haven't a clue yet.'

'Do you have any idea of who might have done it?' asked João.

I looked at Maria for permission to go ahead. She nodded reluctantly.

'Sophie believed Kevin Dryden killed, or helped to kill, her father, but I'm sure she was wrong about that. I do think her instincts were leading her in the right general direction though, towards someone at the mine, and I've got a bad feeling about those guys from Escutcheon Security: Colin and Jug; then there's Thys Gerber and Geoff Morgan.'

'Geoff? You're joking. He's still in Luanda. So's Thys for that matter. Neither of them could have killed Kevin,' said João. 'It's impossible.'

'I know,' I said, 'but that doesn't mean they're not involved. Geoff was somewhere else when both murders were committed but he might still have authorised them.'

'I spoke to him yesterday, on my cell phone after Sophie found Kevin's body. I even sent him a picture,' said João. 'Was I wrong to do that?'

'No,' I said. 'You weren't to know. You did what you thought was right. Besides, I doubt if you're Morgan's only source of information.'

João told me that he had phoned the ARDCO office in Luanda earlier and asked them to contact the British embassy. 'Do you think they'll do it?' he asked; his confidence was fragile. 'I don't know what to believe, or who to trust, anymore.'

I told them I ought to contact my boss, Rachel, in the UK, as soon as possible and get her to chase the embassy from there. She would soon find out if ARDCO had already made contact. When I asked if either of them had a laptop I could borrow, with Skype on it, Maria said she did, back at her house.

'Isn't Rachel the name of your ex-wife too?' said Maria; she did not miss much.

'Yes, my ex-wife is my boss.'

'Another of life's little ironies then,' she said.

'Why do you two always talk in riddles?' João sounded confused.

Maria stared challengingly at me, but I wasn't sure whether the challenge was to say something or to keep quiet.

In the end she said, 'David and I were friends once.'

'Tell me something I don't know,' he muttered wryly.

Chapter 28

The rest of the day was a blur of disbelief and deepening depression. I had no clue what to do, and I doubted I could achieve it even if I knew. Maria had given me her home office to use, but it only made the situation even more surreal; it was my old room from when I had lived in the Madhouse. It had changed, but something of the past seemed to linger, in my mind at least.

When I eventually managed to raise Rachel on Skype she was stunned when I told her of Sophie's arrest, and almost speechless when I told her it was for murder. She knew nothing about Sophie's father except that I had once worked with him. But Rachel always rose to a challenge and, once she had recovered from the shock, the prospect of clearing an employee of murder was a catalyst for her. She was a tigress with a cub to protect. I knew I could trust her absolutely to mobilise people and organisations to do the job. It was what she thrived on and enjoyed. The one thing I had underestimated though was the extent to which she identified with Flourish. Any threat to its reputation would also be fought to the death.

'Let me get this straight,' said Rachel. 'Tell me again why it is that the Angolan police think Sophie killed this man, what's-his-name, Dryden.'

'Because they think she thought that Dryden had murdered her father.'

'That's what I thought you said. So, are you telling me that you and Sophie went to Angola specifically to find out what happened to her father? Aren't you supposed to be concentrating on artisanal miners? Or had that slipped your minds? You'd better be making some progress because when this gets out, and it surely will, the press will have a field day if you two appear to be ploughing your own furrow at our donors' expense. They'll flush our name into the gutter that drains skid row. I'll fight for her, but you'd better be doing what you're meant to be doing, or else … I dread to think of the consequences. And send me a progress report; I'll have to fend off the donors – they'll be asking questions when they get wind of this. It'd better be good. I don't like being pissed around, even by you.'

'Well, it was you who insisted that I went to Angola again,' I said defensively.

'Why did you never tell me about what went on there? I knew you had demons there; I thought it'd be good for you: cathartic. If you'd told me …'

'I wish I had. I should have.'

'Anyway, there's no point going over that now. You'd better tell me again … everything you know about how and why Sophie was arrested. I'm recording the conversation, so I've got something to refer to in the short term.'

I gave Rachel a condensed version of everything we knew about Jim Lodge's death and its aftermath, and then I told her what we had discovered since we'd been in Mumbulo. I explained that Sophie had stayed in Mumbulo with Maria on the night of Dryden's murder as Maria had been the doctor who had pronounced her father dead, and she had also been a personal friend of Sophie's father. When I described the details of Kevin's mutilation and that Sophie had seen it, Rachel immediately said she would arrange counselling for Sophie as soon as she got back.

'That's about it,' I said when I had finished.

'So, what's wrong with her alibi?' asked Rachel.

'Maria lives next door to the murder victim and the police will probably reckon that Sophie could easily have slipped out at any time and got back before anyone would miss her. She also had blood on her.'

'Bloody hell! Why?' asked Rachel.

'I think she tried to stem the blood flow from Dryden's neck wound. The police were still doing their investigation when I got there, and it didn't look very thorough to me. The forensic work, such as it was, looked haphazard. People, including me, were just wandering around contaminating the scene. Maybe they finished the critical stuff before I turned up – I had to travel from Nocredo – but that would have only given them an hour or two at most.'

'Tell me,' she said, 'why did Sophie think this Dryden character killed her father?'

'Because he was the obvious suspect in her view: he reported the incident, and he was the only person we know of who saw Jim between when he left the party in Nocredo and when his body was found. Also, the body of the Angolan that Dryden said Jim hit … There's no evidence that it ever existed.'

'Is there anything else I need to know? I don't want more surprises.'

'Maybe one thing … I spoke to Dryden about Jim's death the night before he was murdered.'

'You did what? Can this get any worse? Were you planning to keep this from me?' Rachel's voice was pitched higher than I had ever heard it before. 'I'm surprised you're not the one in an Angolan gaol. Why?'

'I was dropping Sophie off at Maria's house and I went to pick up Manuel from his sister's, next door to Maria's. Manuel's the Diangola guy who's been giving us lifts between Nocredo and Mumbulo. His sister is … was married to Kevin Dryden.'

'This is doing my head in, David,' she interrupted. 'Oh, what a tangled web …? I'm almost afraid to ask what happened next.'

'Dryden was there, and he invited me in for a chat. He brought up the subject of Jim's death; he told me that he believed we thought he'd killed Sophie's father. He then said that he'd made up the story about the accident and that Sophie's father was already dead, stoned, when he arrived at the scene. He was scared and he was afraid of being suspected of the killing – it was so obviously murder.'

'He was a proper piece of work then. So, who might actually have killed Sophie's father? Could it have been Dryden?'

'It could, but I don't think so; his death wasn't suicide and I think the same person killed both men. There's only a short list of possibilities, assuming it wasn't an Angolan. The body mutilation's the clincher; the same in both cases.'

'The eyes?'

'Yes.'

'Bloody hell, David. Who's next? What are you doing to ensure your own safety?'

'What can I do? I'm the only person staying in the casa de trânsito in Nocredo now that Sophie's in a Mumbulo gaol. I don't think Manuel would want me at his house; he's got his family to consider and he's already lost his brother-in-law.'

'What about this Maria character? She put Sophie up that night, you said ...'

Under any other circumstances I would have found the irony of that suggestion hilarious, but I took it completely seriously. 'I'm making this call from Maria's, but I don't want to put anyone else at risk. Besides, I don't actually know that I'm a potential target.'

'Oh, I think you are,' she said. 'Do you think Sophie's been set up to make sure both of you leave Angola?'

'If it were that simple, at least she'd be free, and we'd be out of here. I don't know what the aim of any such set-up might be.'

'I always thought your behaviour was irrational where Angola was concerned, but now ... Let's get both of you out of there then we'll assess what we've got so far on the project and work out how to progress things. When can I have a progress report from you?'

'I'll send you one tomorrow.'

'Make it early. I don't know when people are going to start asking questions, but, when they do, I want to be in a position to give straight, honest answers; I don't want to have to flannel my way through.'

'I'll send it first thing. I'll also sketch out some notes about the murder to augment your recording of this conversation.'

'Thanks David. I'll get on with chasing the embassy and anyone else I can think of who might be able to help us. Good luck and for God's sake come home safe with Sophie. Flourish has never lost anyone yet and we're not going to start now.'

We closed our Skype session, and her image went from the screen.

'So that was Rachel.' It was Maria. I had not noticed her come into the room. 'She sounds like a good, strong woman and she obviously cares a lot about you.'

Chapter 29

I had made good progress on the report, but my worries kept interrupting me. I did not want to be alone. What if I was a target? They, whoever they were, had got rid of Kevin Dryden for no apparent reason … I believed there to be more people to be afraid of in Mumbulo than in Nocredo but at least I would not be alone in Mumbulo.

Manuel had brought Teresa back to Mumbulo earlier in the afternoon. I was expecting him to come looking for me, to pick me up, at any moment, so I wasn't surprised when I heard Maria's doorbell. I saved the report to a flash drive, gathered up my things and switched off Maria's laptop. I would finish the report off on my own laptop when I got back to Nocredo.

'David!' It was Maria: her voice urgent.

'Just coming,' I shouted, 'Is it Manuel?'

'No. It's David.'

I dropped everything and dashed through to the lounge. I heard Maria invite him to sit down but he was mooching around, fidgeting, clearly disturbed. We shook hands cursorily, both of us distracted. His brow was furrowed – he looked angry – and he was staring me hard in the face without saying anything.

'What's wrong, David?' I asked. 'Is it Armando?'

He shook his head. 'Where were you today, David? Did you set us up? Mine security came and gave us an ultimatum. Twenty-four hours to get out.'

'What?' I was stunned. I slumped in a chair, head in hands. Everything I touched was a disaster. Everyone I tried to help would have been better off not knowing me. I had no idea how I was going to help Sophie and now it seemed that I had jeopardised the livelihoods of the very people I had come to help.

I straightened up and looked at him. It was the first time I really registered his physical similarity to a young Armando. And it had been in the very same room thirty years before that Armando had attacked me on a similar pretext; déjà vu. Things had turned out badly then; how could I make them turn out better now?

'You'd better tell me what happened because I honestly don't know,' I said.

'That's the truth,' said Maria. 'He's been here all day, trying to help Sophie.'

'Sophie? Why? What's the matter with Sophie?'

When I told him about Kevin Dryden's murder and Sophie's arrest, he was amazed. He questioned how the police could possibly think she had done it. I told him how she had suspected Dryden of her father's murder and that somehow the police had found that out and they believed it gave Sophie a motive.

'And did he, Kevin Dryden, kill her father?' he asked.

'I don't think so. Dryden's body was mutilated in the same way as Sophie's father's, though. His eyes were gouged out and impaled on a stick.'

David grimaced. 'So, they think Sophie killed Kevin Dryden then hacked out his eyes to get full revenge? She's not capable of doing that; the police must be mad.'

'I hadn't thought of the eyes as a revenge thing,' I said. 'We,' I looked at Maria, 'thought it must be a signature, showing that it was the same killer who did both.'

Maria spoke up. 'That makes more sense to us because we know Sophie, but I also know how Angolans think, and the police here are all Angolans. They understand revenge. There's been a lot of it in these parts over the years and they'll see it as a powerful motive. The police aren't stupid though. I'm sure they'll realise soon that they've got the wrong person.'

'I bloody hope so,' I said. 'Tell me what happened to you today, David. Who gave you the warning?'

'An armoured personnel carrier drove straight into the clearing; smashed through the bush direct from the road. They knew exactly where we were – they didn't need to look around like you had to. They used a megaphone to tell us to get out or they'd take drastic action. It was early afternoon. They came while I was teaching. There was a lot of noise on their approach, so we cleared the area and hid in the bush – it's something we practise. I don't understand how they were able to drive straight to us. Who told them exactly where we were? I know they could find us whenever they wanted, like you did, by following the river, but they didn't need to do that. We're not set up to defend our-selves against a direct assault from the road.'

'GPS,' I said slowly. 'Shit! I bet that bastard Mitch was run-ning a GPS app on his phone when he was playing around with it the other day.'

'What's GPS?'

I told him it stood for Global Positioning System and that it used signals from satellites orbiting Earth to calculate exactly where it was on the surface to within a few metres. I explained that Mitch would only have had to save the coordinates while he was there and anyone else could drive straight in through the bush.

'I'm sorry David but I didn't know; I didn't think. But it shouldn't have happened anyway – ARDCO and Diangola both agreed …'

'What can we do?' asked David.

A car pulled up outside.

'That'll be Manuel to pick you up.' Maria was staring at the floor, slightly flushed. 'Make an excuse for not going with him,' she said. 'We've a lot to talk about.'

'Boa tarde.' Manuel poked his nose through the wrought iron gate. 'Is there any news about Sophie?'

I shook my head. 'They want to interview me early in the morning, so it'll be easier if I stay here in Mumbulo tonight. Maria's kindly offered to put me up.' I was not certain that she had but I was happy to push my luck.

Manuel gave an encouraging smile. 'I'll pray for Sophie and I hope your interview goes well in the morning.' I thanked him and he walked to his car and drove off towards Nocredo.

I watched him disappear, then I shuddered as reality hit home; I would be spending the night in my old home, the Madhouse. When I had recovered my poise, I noticed Maria staring at me with the suggestion of a smile on her face.

'Where's João?' I asked.

'He had to go to Nocredo to pick up Geoff Morgan from the airport. He changed his plans; brought his visit forward.'

'With everything that's happened, I'd forgotten he was coming at all. Where does he stay when he's around?'

'In the Manager's house, same as always. I don't think he's ever spent a night in Mumbulo anywhere else.'

I had the feeling that things were coming to a head, but was Morgan the brains or an innocent dupe? 'Let's get started,' I said.

Maria went out and fetched some beers from the kitchen. We sat quietly for a short time, enjoying the palate-achingly cold beer.

'I've been thinking,' said David. 'The most likely murderers are people who are used to killing and, if they killed Sophie's father too, they've been comfortable with killing for a long while. To me, that implicates anyone with a link to the military, Angolan, British or South African, maybe.'

'That's pretty much the way I see it too,' I said. 'Those two British security guys are top of my list as they were here thirty years ago. It was probably them who gave you the warning this afternoon, too. I used to think Angolans had killed Jim, but not from your father's village. When we went to where it happened the other day, I could see that I was right about that. The village was physically close but logistically remote. But there was something wrong: it was Sophie who noticed it. The rocks there: they were all much smaller than the ones used to kill Jim. How did they get there and where did they come from? Of course, the road was in use back then and the obvious conclusion is that they fell off a truck, but I don't think so. The only trucks using that stretch of road would have been carrying gravel to the concentrator. The biggest stone would have been an inch across, that's twenty-five millimetres, at most. It's hard to believe, but maybe someone took the rocks with them and they'd have needed transport for that, which rules out most Angolans at that time.'

'We also used to believe Jim was killed because of an accident.' Maria spoke slowly, deep in thought. 'And the killers used the weapons that were handy – the rocks. Then Kevin admitted that there had never been an accident, and if there weren't any rocks at the site …' Realisation dawned on Maria's face. 'Do you think Jim's death was premeditated?' She looked horrified.

'I don't know,' I said. 'It's possible – I don't like it.'

'If it was those security men,' said David, 'do you think we can prove it before they raid us tomorrow and clear us away from the area? Papai's in no state to move far and I want the family to be with him.' David was close to tears as he looked at Maria.

'I haven't seen Armando for a couple of weeks. How is he?' asked Maria.

'He's deteriorating as you said, maybe a little faster than we thought. He's very weak and rarely lucid now, but I think that's the drugs. I'm sorry; I forgot to thank you for the last lot you sent. Thank you, Maria.'

She looked away, embarrassed. She said, 'Bring him here, and your mother; there's plenty of room. You can stay in one of the spare rooms and I can take proper care of Armando.'

'That sounds like a good idea,' I said to David. 'He'll be in the best hands and you and Esther can be near him. But how will people like Geoff and the Escutcheon guys react if they find out?'

'I don't want to put you in any danger, Maria,' said David. 'They might come looking for me and it won't be good for you if they find out that you've been harbouring us.'

'I don't care anymore. Jim was a dear friend. Kevin Dryden was never that, but he didn't deserve what happened to him. I just want whoever did it caught and put away.' She looked at me. 'Do you really think Geoff's involved? He's always been a friend, and he gave João his job.'

'I hope not. I always liked him too and …' I stopped. 'Maria, you never left did you? You were here all through the war?'

'Yes. Why?'

'Who else was here for all that period? I'm thinking of Colin, Jug, Geoff and let's throw Kevin in for good measure.'

'None of them. Kevin was married to Teresa – she stayed; but he went back to England for a year or so at the height of the fighting. He came back when things settled down a bit and helped UNITA to run the mines until the war ended. Geoff and the others were gone for years; maybe ten or fifteen. I guess they kept in touch with Kevin though.'

'And Teresa? She a nurse, yes?'

'A very good one; works at the hospital. She does a lot of home visits though. She's very conscientious. UNITA realised she was useful, and they were only too happy to please her by letting Kevin come back. Anyway, he helped them too; he managed the plants. Do you think there's a UNITA connection here?'

'Who knows? But I'm getting an idea. What state were the mines in after the civil war? Were they operating well?'

'You must be joking,' said Maria. 'They were hardly running at all. The plants were held together by string; old mining trucks were scattered around like dead hippos and no one had done any prospecting or exploration to find new reserves since Jim. I expected the mines to close but then Geoff came in with ARDCO ... like the cavalry.'

'Shit,' I beat my fists against the wall. 'I haven't been asking the right questions at all have I? How long did it take ARDCO to get things going when they got here?'

'They brought in a couple of mobile processing plants from South Africa as a temporary measure, along with a few second-hand trucks, dozers and other stuff that I don't know the names of. They were in production within three or four months I think, probably less.'

My mind was awash with questions that didn't quite follow one another but I was sure the answer was there somewhere.

We talked and talked, testing theories and considering courses of action, but nothing concrete came of it.

We were just starting to relax and think about bed when João arrived. He had Geoff Morgan and another man in tow. We only just had time to send David into one of the back rooms before Geoff crashed, half-drunk through the gate of the veranda.

'Long time no see, boyo,' Morgan was redder, rounder and balder than he used to be, but his voice and smile had not changed; he seemed genuine. 'It's good to see you. Shame about the circumstances, though.'

'Hello Geoff,' I said. 'You're looking well.'

We shook hands and he slapped me on the back. The other man, who had been loitering by João's car, finishing a cigarette, stubbed it out and came up the path. He was still as tall and as terracotta red as he had been when we had first met at Nocredo airport, but his waist had inflated like a lifebuoy.

'Hello Thys,' I said as he climbed the steps to the veranda. We shook hands; his grip was not what it used to be.

'David. Good to see you.'

'We've got some catching up to do,' said Morgan, 'but first things first.' His face hardened. 'This girl who's with you. Is she really Jim's daughter?'

I nodded.

'What were you thinking of, bringing her here? It was always going to be trouble. You are not stupid. You must have known that someone going to where their father was killed could only be out for revenge.'

I shook my head. 'Sophie's not like that. Even if she wanted revenge, why would she kill Kevin? He didn't kill Jim, and I'm sure it wasn't the Angolan villagers either.' It might have been my imagination, but I thought I saw the muscles around his eyes clench for an instant.

'Of course, he didn't,' he laughed. 'I don't have murderers as friends. So why did she kill him?'

'Like I said, she didn't. Somebody's stitched her up, somebody who knew about Jim's eyes. Probably the same person who killed Jim. Anyway, why haven't you asked why I don't believe it was the Angolans who killed Jim? You were convinced it was them at the time. Are you still?'

229

Maria was watching Morgan's face as closely as I was and I wondered if she'd made the same interpretations.

'I was trying to get a handle on this girl's motives,' he said. 'Of course, it was Angolans who killed Jim. I've seen and heard nothing that overturns the evidence given at the time.'

'Which was?' I tested.

'I wouldn't reveal it even if I could, but the report was lost in the war.'

'Very convenient,' said Maria.

'That's as maybe, but you can't accuse me of starting the civil war.'

I realised we were not going to get anything useful from him. 'Do you have any suggestions,' I asked, 'about how we might get Sophie released from prison. Do you have any influence?'

Morgan laughed. 'I never thought I'd ever hear that. You've changed, David. You of old would never have asked for strings to be pulled. I don't know what agreements exist between Angola and the UK, but I believe it often happens that prisoners, sentenced where a crime was committed, can be allowed to serve their time in their own country. I can certainly suggest something like that if it comes to the worst. The fact that she killed another Briton could work in her favour for that, but I'm just speculating; I don't really know.'

'But she didn't do it,' said Maria. 'She stayed here that night; she was with João and me the whole time. She couldn't have done it.'

'That's right,' João contributed.

'Of course, she could, and you know it. And Kevin only lives … lived next door; your old house if I remember rightly, Maria.'

'If you met Sophie, you'd know she couldn't have done it. She's so small.'

'I'll speak to the police tomorrow,' he said.

I looked at Maria; she seemed to share my doubts. Yes, he might speak to the police, but would he plead Sophie's innocence? I doubted that.

'Are you going back to Nocredo tonight David?' asked Morgan.

'No, he's staying here,' said Maria.

'So, it's just like old times for you two is it?' said Thys. Morgan glared at him. 'I mean you're back in your old house; Maria's house now,' Thys explained.

His cover-up did not fool me.

Morgan feigned a yawn and glanced at his watch. 'It's time I was getting home. I'm starving and I need my beauty sleep. We do need to catch up though, David. Sometime tomorrow okay, after I've spoken to the police?'

I nodded reluctantly. We exchanged farewells then he left.

'What was all that about?' It was João.

I had forgotten he was there and so, clearly, had Maria; she looked nervous and confused. 'Not now,' she said.

He squinted at both of us in turn. 'I think there's quite a lot you haven't told me, Mum, but it's waited a long time. A bit longer won't make any difference, but don't think I'm going to let you off the hook.' He smiled. He seemed amused that his mother had had a life before his father, and I was reassured that he did not seem to disapprove of me.

There was a knock on the door from the hallway. Maria opened it and ushered David back into the room. João was surprised but not upset by David's presence; the two obviously knew one another well. They shook hands and the first question João asked was about Armando's health.

'He's coming here to stay,' said Maria. 'Just so you know.'

'Good. It's the best place for him. He'll be as comfortable as he can be.' Both men looked downcast.

I think João was remembering his own father's death and David was thinking about the inevitable outcome of Armando's condition.

We decided that we would all benefit from a good night's sleep. The rooms were all made up, ready to go. I was given the office, my old room, which had a bed in the corner and David was given what had been the spare room. Maria's room was what had been Carlos's.

I struggled to sleep. I wanted to go to Maria but, more than that, I wanted her to come to me. She had always led our relationship and now, thirty years later, it still felt as though she should make the first move if there was to be one. I realised that I was still just as frightened of rejection as I had always been, perhaps more so.

Chapter 30

I could not sleep, and my watch kept telling me it was only five minutes since I last checked. The night seemed endless. Eventually, I gave up. I got up and finished my progress report for Rachel. I sent it to her at four-thirty a.m. then I went back to bed. I was confused and overwhelmed by everything that had happened over the last two or three days. I seriously doubted that I had the character or the ability to overcome the obstacles ahead. Who had killed Kevin? How could I find out and prove it to the satisfaction of the police? Yes, I had my suspicions, but I'd been wrong before and my confidence was dented. Then there was David and Armando; how could I ensure that history would not repeat itself? I could not let them be uprooted again; my conscience wouldn't allow it. And what was the connection between Lodge's death and Kevin's? The same perpetrator? Probably, but why? I'd thought a lot about who might have killed Lodge, but it occurred to me that, since the accident story had been discredited, I hadn't given much thought to why he'd been killed. Jim's death was the first event in the sequence. A new idea was starting to germinate.

It was six-thirty a.m. I got up, dressed, and put on the coffee maker in the kitchen.

'Ah! Fresh coffee, lovely!' Maria had slipped in without me noticing and was sniffing the air appreciatively. She looked vulnerable with her hair untended. I wanted to hold her. Instead, I poured coffee into a mug and passed it to her. 'I'm sorry,' she said.

'What for?' I tensed.

'For doubting you. You did write to me, didn't you?'

'Of course, I did.' I could hear my own irritation. 'You already know that; you must have got the letters ...'

'I didn't, but ... I think I know what happened – it came to me last night. Remember what Thys said? It was something about us ... us together. But how did he know? We thought nobody knew. He, or someone else, must have read our letters – intercepted them.'

The room seemed to go cold. I shivered. The mine's postal service had been a cornerstone, one hundred per cent trustworthy. Yes, it would have been physically easy to interfere with it, but no one ever would as it was the only link between workers and their loved ones. The mine would have collapsed without a reliable postal service; no one would have been prepared to work there, totally cut off from family and friends. We didn't have email and Skype, that we take for granted today. It had never occurred to me that anyone would look at who was writing to whom; why would they? But I knew Maria was right. I felt sick; sick that we had both had more faith in the integrity of the mine's postal arrangements than in one another. What did that make us? We probably both got what we deserved. I closed my eyes.

I felt something against my chin; it tickled. Maria's hair. I felt her arms slide around my waist. She was crying.

We stood like that for an age, not moving or saying anything, until we heard other movements in the house. Maria dabbed at her face with a tissue, but the tear streaks were still plainly visible when João came in.

'Mum! Are you all right? Has he hurt you?' He glared at me.

'No. David would never do that. Not on purpose.' She rubbed her eyes. 'It's just everything that's going on right now. It got too much for me. I'm all right João.'

He nodded and his face softened. 'I've got to see Sophie. She needs to know we're working to get her out,' he said. 'Are you coming too, David?'

'Not now. I've had some thoughts and I want to see Constance. I'm hoping it'll help Sophie. Tell her that I'm doing my best for her and I'll drop in later. Can you give me a lift to the mine offices on your way, please? It'll save me some time.'

'Sure. Let's go. Mum, tell David – Muachaquima that is – that I'll take him to pick up Armando and Esther as soon as I get back.'

He poured some cold water into the coffee he had helped himself to and downed it quickly. He then gave Maria a peck on the cheek and dashed off towards his car. I ran after him.

We were both quiet until we had almost reached the mine offices. He kept glancing across at me, measuring me up. I knew he wanted to say something.

'You and mum?' He had just turned into the office parking area. 'I know you were friends, but were you … you know … more than that?'

'Yes.' I could not lie to him; I didn't want to.

He nodded. 'I don't know what I'd do if Sophie … I've only known her a few days but … I'm scared David. I'm no expert in criminal law. I know she didn't do it, but this doesn't look good.'

'It'll be all right. She's innocent. They can't touch her.' I bluffed.

As I got out, I reminded him to tell Sophie that I'd be visiting her later.

I was still confused by the maze of containers and I had to ask the way to Constance's office. She was in early, which was a relief. I half expected her to be either still in bed or out in the field doing what Lodge used to describe as real geology.

We greeted one another.

'Constance, the other day, at Teresa's, when you realised that Sophie was Jim Lodge's daughter, you said something. I didn't think much of it at the time but …'

'You've lost me … What?'

'You said something about Lodge's maps or resource estimates … documents of some sort. I got the impression that you didn't have them all.'

'Ah that. Lodge was very systematic; he cross-referenced everything. We've got a lot of documents referring to maps and reports that we don't seem to have; at least, the geology department doesn't.'

'But you think someone else does?' I fished.

'I don't know.' She shrugged. 'But we do seem to mine in an awful lot of places we've got little or no geological data for.'

'Do you have a map of … where you've mined without back-up geology?'

'That map I gave you has a lot of it. That river diversion – Mitch told me where your miners are working – was done on an apparent whim. And the pipe.'

'The pipe? Kimberlite? I thought you were still working alluvial stuff.'

'We are, but most of the production's from the pipe now.'

I felt goose bumps prickle. 'Can you show it to me, on a map, please?'

She nodded and went to a map cabinet in the corner of the office where she opened and closed a few drawers until she found the one, she wanted. She returned with a much larger version of the map she had marked up for Sophie and me; she spread it on her desk. It took me a few seconds to adjust to the different scale, and the colouring, but it was all there: the river, the island, the hills on the far side, the plant and what was quite clearly a very big, almost circular hole. It was so obvious I could not believe I hadn't noticed it either on the map or, on the ground, from the island.

'Can you see the pipe from the river diversion?' I asked.

'I don't know.' She stopped to think for a moment. 'No. I don't think so. The hills on that side of the river aren't high but they're big enough to obscure it; you have to get quite close to see it. You can see the plant from there though.'

I tried to remember the details of that field trip I had taken with Jim Lodge; I was sure he'd said something but …

★★★

Jim tapped my arm and pointed at his watch. We were watching the water slowly covering the fabulously rich sand and gravel in the Txicaca river diversion. 'It's time we were heading back,' he said. 'There's somewhere I need to stop at briefly on the way.'

He pulled up on a stretch of the mine road I knew well. We both got out. He wandered to the side of the road nearest to the river and looked out over the rolling hills on the far side; his lips pursed in thought. I walked about twenty yards up the road and perched my backside against the rock that I knew as Chesterfield; I waited. After about five minutes he returned to the VW and I walked back to join him. He muttered something.

★★★

I reran the scene in my mind's eye, over and over again. What had he said? The only inkling, I had was that it was something incongruous, a non sequitur.

'Are you still staying in Nocredo?' Constance's question derailed my train of thought.

'No, I stayed at … That's it!' I felt a surge of excitement. A place name!

'What? What is it?'

'Constance, have you got a general map of the province, Lunda Norte?'

'Of course. What do you want: geological, road map or …?'

'Just one with all the towns and villages marked. I've just remembered that Jim – Lodge, that is – mentioned a place name to me once. I can't remember what it was but I'm sure it was a town; one from a different mining area. I remember thinking it was strange at the time.'

I pored over the map she produced, systematically running my eyes from one side to the other, working down the sheet, but nothing leapt out at me. I had another idea. 'Constance, I'm going to read out the place names. Tell me if any of them has any geological significance.'

'How do you mean?' She looked at me as if I had gone mad.

'I don't know but humour me.' I read out the names of towns and villages in other mining areas, slowly and clearly. 'Andrada, N'zargi, Maludi, Chitotolo, Cassanguidi, Cafunfo, Luzamba, Ponte Cuango, Lucapa, Mafuto, Calonda …'

'Calonda! It's in the Lucapa mining area. It's also the name of a geological formation; a partially weathered kimberlite deposit that hasn't yet got into the river system.'

'Bingo!'

'What's going on, David? Calonda formations aren't that rare.'

'But they're diamond-bearing; they're from kimberlite, aren't they?'

'Yes, but …'

'Is there any Calonda close to that pipe?'

'Yes, but …'

At last, I felt I was getting somewhere. I was sure Jim Lodge had known about the Calonda and the pipe, but it still didn't explain why he was killed. I knew he reported all that kind of information to Morgan, but did he tell anyone else? I doubted it. He had told me that the Company wouldn't consider mining kimberlite while there was a war on but now, when the war was over, a different company, ARDCO, was mining and treating kimberlite. What did that tell me? I was not sure, but a lot of faces from the past were in important positions with companies that were making a lot of money from that kimberlite.

My mind shifted from Jim to his daughter. Why had she been fingered for Kevin's murder? I had been so engrossed by how I was going to get her out that I hadn't really thought about that before – surely it would have been more logical to pin the murder on me – I had history with Kevin, and everyone knew it. I needed to talk to Maria again.

I persuaded Constance to give me a lift back to Maria's.

I ran up the steps and flung open the veranda gate.

'What's the matter?' Maria looked worried. 'Has something else happened?'

'No. Nothing physical. I had an interesting talk with Constance. I've worked a few things out … I had a thought … it's not a nice one. Why did they pick on Sophie? What if they had a different plan and it went wrong?'

'I'm not with you,' she said. 'What other plan?'

'What if they were really after me? We know Thys knew about us, so Geoff probably did too; maybe the killer expected me to stay here with you the other night, not Sophie.'

'You're saying Geoff's behind it? I had hoped he wasn't, but …'

'I don't know. Maybe,' I said. 'My thoughts are all mixed up. We thought nobody knew about us, but, if one person knew, maybe everybody did. I can't believe Geoff actually killed anyone but he's good at pulling strings.'

'But why?' Maria's face was imploring me to arrive at a different conclusion. 'Geoff and Jim used to be friends and Kevin was Geoff's right-hand man. Hell! João works with him every day. I don't get it.'

'Nor do I, but …'

'What about Colin and Jug? I thought you were homing in on them.'

'I am but … okay. My chat with Constance. I'm now fairly certain it was Jim who found the kimberlite pipe that ARDCO's mining. He must have told someone about it and that someone wanted it hushed up. I know he reported any finds to Geoff, but I don't know who else would have been told; it's unlikely to have been Colin and Jug though. They wouldn't have understood the significance anyway, nor would they have known how to exploit it. They might have done the killing, but under orders; Geoff's.'

Maria shook her head slowly. 'Do you think he intercepted our post then?' she paused to think. 'The out tray and all the pigeonholes were in his secretary's office. Yes, he definitely had the opportunity. But, if it was him, why did he do it? I don't get it.'

'Think about it,' I said. 'I was a nuisance, but I'd gone, never to return, as far as he was concerned. Imagine his feelings when he found out about us; he knew I'd be back to see you and he daren't let that happen. He knew I was like a dog with a bone. He had the means to make us both think we'd been taking advantage of one another.'

'If you're right, Geoff judged you well,' she said. 'You've been nothing but trouble since you got back. Sophie told me about the other day, when you were captured, and she thought she was going to die. She said you took a beating before they recognised you and let you both go. You certainly made some odd friends.'

'Yes, I did,' I winked at her. We both laughed. 'Anyway, back to my theory. I think they, whoever they are, expected me to stay at your place the night that Kevin was killed. I think my being in Nocredo must have given them a serious headache, especially as Manuel could vouch that Kevin was alive and well when I left with him for Nocredo. It must have required a serious re-think to cast Sophie as the killer.'

'It seems plausible,' she said. 'If you're right, their case against Sophie won't be nearly as sound as it would have been against you. Everybody knew that you and Kevin couldn't stand one another. But what I don't understand is why they need a case against anyone: you or Sophie.'

'I don't know either, but I wonder what would have happened if two different people had come to Mumbulo to do the Flourish project. Probably not a lot … on any front. It feels as though everything that's happened since we set foot in Mumbulo has been because I am who I am, and Sophie is so obviously Jim's daughter. I was a nuisance before so I'm likely to be a nuisance again. And Sophie? Well, there's something about Jim's death that they don't want anyone to know about and, as far as they're concerned, she's only got one reason for being here – to dig into the circumstances of her father's death.' I glanced at my watch; it was half past nine. 'Has João been back yet?'

'About half an hour ago; they wouldn't give him much time with Sophie. He's gone off with David to fetch Armando and Esther from the island. I'm really worried about Armando …'

'I guess it'll be an hour or so before they get back. I think I'll take a walk and to do my bit for Sophie's morale.'

Chapter 31

I had no legal right to visit Sophie without permission from the police. Would they allow me to see her again? Part of me hoped they would not as I dreaded seeing what that dismal dungeon might have done to her. The building had always been soul-destroying, but I couldn't begin to guess what it was like as a gaol. If I'd ever been locked in there, I knew I'd have been looking very seriously at my bootlaces and anything else that might bring it to a quick end. I hoped Sophie was blessed with greater optimism than me.

I tried to banish these thoughts as I walked to the door. I rang the bell and waited. As before, I had to ring a second time before someone came and opened it. It was the same policeman who had let João and me in the last time; I wondered if his job description stretched beyond door duties. He took me to the same waiting area as before, and I sat in the same chair. I noticed rusty streaks on the concrete floor, running from the rotting steel stumps of the long-gone sorting table; they looked like blood. I wanted to be out of there.

The detective who had been in charge at the murder scene saw me and he invited me into his office. The name plate on his desk said 'Coordenador de Investigação Criminal: Daniel Chimica'. Maria told me later that this was roughly equivalent to Chief Inspector. He offered me coffee, then, after I had taken a big gulp, he leaned forward, resting his elbows on the desk.

'Things don't look good for Doctor Addison. She found Senhor Dryden's body. Her fingerprints are on the murder weapon and we know she believed Senhor Dryden killed her father – she had a motive.' His summary was disturbingly similar to my own interpretation. 'Cards on the table,' he said. 'I look at Doctor Addison and I see a very small, beautiful lady and I ask myself if she could

241

have killed Senhor Dryden. I've seen children with guns, killing men in the civil war; by that standard, she's capable. Then I look at what Doctor Addison is doing here, and I see a lady who is trying to help some of the neediest of my people. Senhor Young, I like her, and I hope the evidence will eventually prove her to be innocent, but at the moment ...'

I almost laughed. 'But she was entrapped into handling that knife and ...'

'Entrapped? No. Did she handle the knife? Yes.'

'I don't understand.'

'There were two knives in the interview room: the murder weapon and an identical knife, a carving knife, to demonstrate with. She was asked how she would hold the knife and she was offered the demonstration knife by the interviewer. Instead of taking that, she reached over and grabbed the murder weapon. Fortunately, we'd already taken the fingerprints from that or she'd have compromised it. It wasn't entrapment; it was either a misunderstanding or a foolish attempt by her to compromise evidence.'

'And were her fingerprints on the murder knife when it was first checked?'

'No. It had been wiped clean. It didn't even have senhor Dryden's prints on it and he'd been using it, or senhora Dryden's; it was her knife.'

'So, you don't have any real evidence that Doctor Addison handled the knife.'

'Her action in the interview room makes me very suspicious. She might have been afraid that her prints were on the knife and she wanted to contaminate the evidence. We still have the knife; it has her prints on it and I'll use it if I feel I need to.'

'Let me get this straight. Are you admitting to me that you would use false evidence to convict her?'

'Not exactly. I'm saying that, if everything else points to her, and I'm convinced that she did it, I'll use it to secure a conviction if I feel the weight of the other evidence isn't enough to sway the court.'

'Why are you telling me this?'

'Because I want her to be innocent. I went to school here in Mumbulo with João; we're old friends and I can see how he feels about her. But I also want to warn you that if I believe she's guilty I'll do whatever is necessary to nail her.'

'Well, she's not guilty. What about Senhor Dryden's eyes? They were torn out and impaled in the same way as her father's, but she didn't know about that until after Senhor Dryden's death. If she didn't know about it, she couldn't have done it.'

He smiled. 'We only have your word for that. She clearly knows about it now; she knew about it when we questioned her. I have to assume she knew about it all along.'

I closed my eyes and swore inwardly. Why had we told her? If we hadn't, her ignorance would have been in her favour.

'Senhor Young, I would like you to make a statement about the eyes, explaining why you are so sure that she didn't know about them.'

He called in a second detective who made notes as I told them about how I had first met Sophie and how I had told her about her father. I emphasised that I had failed to provide her with any contact details for anyone else who had witnessed her father's death. I stated that it would have been impossible for her to know about Lodge's eyes unless she had spoken to another witness. Chimica suggested I get Maria to go in again to add to her statement and corroborate my assertion that Sophie had been shocked when we told her about her father's eyes.

I read my statement carefully and initialled some minor changes before I signed it. I then asked if I could see Sophie. I wanted to reassure her.

Chimica rang a bell on his desk and the officer who had let me into the police station came in. He was given instructions then he took me down to see Sophie.

She looked surprisingly well. She was obviously wearing borrowed clothes and I apologised for not thinking to bring some of her own from Nocredo.

'I had a shower this morning,' she said. 'It was pretty horrible, cold, but better than nothing. How are you getting on? João said you had some ideas.'

243

'I have …' I put a finger to my lips; I did not want to take any chances. Sophie looked disappointed. I thought she was going to cry, but then she pulled herself together, forced a smile, and nodded her understanding. 'I think my investigations will help,' I said, 'and I've spoken to Rachel. She's pulling strings from the UK and with the embassy in Luanda. Everyone is doing their utmost for you. We have to succeed. After all, you're innocent.'

'Is that enough?'

'I think it's enough anywhere; we just have to prove it or prove someone else did it. João's desperate to get you out.'

Sophie blushed.

The policeman tapped his watch. 'You've had your time. You have to go now.'

I said goodbye to Sophie and assured her that she would be free soon. I only had about two minutes with her and two minutes later I was out in the fresh air. I dragged my feet all the way back to Maria's; weighed down by the growing burden of my self-doubt. If I couldn't cheer myself up and find something positive to take into the fight, I was going to be worse than useless.

Maria had always been able read my body language. My heavy tread and hunched posture must have screamed my state of mind at her from the end of the road. As I entered the house, she handed me a beer and gave me a brief hug.

'Not good then.' It was a statement of fact.

'I don't know. Sophie seemed remarkably well – she'd had a shower – but I had a chat with the Coordenador de Investigação.'

'Daniel Chimica? I've known him for years. He's a good detective, a friend in other circumstances; went to school with João. But he's a crafty blighter. What did he say?'

'He denied that they'd set Sophie up with the knife.' I told her all about the strangely nuanced conversation.

'Daniel's straight,' she said. 'I don't think he'll use that knife as evidence. He's just putting pressure on you to do his detective work for him. He has very limited resources. As I said, he's crafty. I don't think they've got a strong case against her: the blood is easily explained, and it can only be speculation that she thought

Kevin killed her father. João seemed more confident when he got back, and I trust his judgement in legal matters.'

When I told her that Chimica wanted her to go to the police station and add a bit to her statement she said she would go in the afternoon.

'The only thing that worries me,' she said, 'is why did she go to Kevin's house that morning? I think the police believe the egg story I gave them, but we all know it's a lie. I know she didn't kill Kevin because I know her, but I lied in my statement. I lied for Jim and for João.'

I had not thought much before about why Sophie had gone round to Kevin's. I had assumed she just wanted to talk to him, or maybe to Teresa. What difference did it make anyway? What was done was done. Perhaps I was better off not knowing; that thought worried me somehow. I turned my mind to identifying who had really killed Kevin.

I helped Maria with some housework as we waited for João to return with Armando, Esther and David; there would be plenty to do when they arrived. We had just sat down for a short break when Teresa walked in. She was carrying a 'Chivas Regal' cardboard box; it had been Kevin's favourite tipple. We said our greetings. Maria took the box from her and set it down on the table before probing her about how she was coping.

'I've started to clear up the house; sort things out, throw stuff away,' said Teresa. 'I can't sit around doing nothing in Nocredo when I can be doing something useful here. I found this box among Kevin's things. It's yours.' I expected her to focus on Maria, her neighbour, but her eyes included me too.

'Obrigada. What is it?'

'Letters. I don't know … English.' Her cheeks were crimson.

She hurriedly looked at her watch, said she had to get back to her work and dashed off before either Maria or I had the chance to ask her anything. From the look on Maria's face, she was thinking the same as me. Her eyes were fixed on the box, as were mine. Did the content of those letters matter anymore? I knew my own writings followed a trend from cringe-inducing expressions of love to desperation and, ultimately, something akin to bereavement. Thirty years on, did I want Maria to read my embarrassingly frank expressions of love and lust? I wanted her to know I had been true to her but, even in middle-age; I could not bear the thought of her laughing at the young me. What was she thinking? Probably much the same.

'So …' Maria was always better at facing up to things. 'Something else we got wrong. It wasn't Geoff, it was Kevin. They did share the same outer office and secretary, remember?'

'Now you mention it, yes.' The image of that outer office sharpened in my mind from a fuzzy room with a desk to a white-walled office with two oak interior doors to Kevin's and Geoff's offices. The postal pigeonholes were bracketed to the wall between the doors and there was a table with an open tray on it for outgoing letters. 'But it doesn't mean Geoff wasn't involved just because Kevin kept the letters. Anyway, we're assuming here; they might not be our letters.'

She opened the box and lifted out a bundle of envelopes.

'Mr. David Young, 67 South Meadow Road, Glazeby …' She put the bundle on the table next to the box then she took out another bundle. 'Dr. Maria … Bastards! How could they?'

'I don't know.' I sighed. It just added to my sense of general woe.

'You've a right to read my letters,' she said. 'After all, they're addressed to you and there are some things in there that you ought to read. But can I make a request?'

'That sounds very formal. Of course. Name it.'

'May I look through them first and pick out the ones I'd still like you to read. I was very upset when I wrote some of them and some of my words might not be fair, knowing what I now know.'

'If I can do the same.'

'Deal. Can we leave it though, until after all this is over?' she said. 'We need our minds to be clear to get Sophie out. Shall I lock all these away in my safe for the time being?'

I nodded reluctantly but I knew she was right.

Chapter 32

João was taking longer to get back with Armando than we expected, and Maria was on edge. He eventually arrived at about midday and drove straight round to the back of the house where he parked by the courtyard gate. He only had two passengers: Armando and Esther. Maria produced a folding wheelchair from somewhere and I pushed it to the gate. Esther's damp eyes were a window to her thoughts as she watched João and me manoeuvring Armando out of the back seat of the car. Once he was out, I lifted him easily, on my own, into the wheelchair; there was nothing left of him. I thought he was unconscious, but a small eye movement and a barely intelligible murmur told me otherwise. I put my ear close to his mouth so I could hear him better.

'… be okay,' was all I could make out.

'What'll be okay Armando?'

He smiled feebly and I sensed he was making a huge effort. 'David … Trust him.'

'Where is he? David? I thought he'd be here with you and Esther.'

'No. Work … Preparing …' He closed his eyes.

I was not sure whether he was asleep or avoiding interrogation; I suspected the latter. I wheeled the chair the short distance to the outbuilding that Maria had had converted to accommodate guests. She told me where I would find a camp bed in the house and she sent me to fetch it for Esther so she could sleep next to her husband. I had only rediscovered my old friend a few days before, but I knew we would have little chance to talk again. I was saddened to the point of despair; I had to sit down in the kitchen to gather myself before returning with the bed. I wanted to appear strong for Armando and Esther.

Maria asked me to sit with Armando for a few minutes while she took Esther into the house to talk to her.

'She means well.' Armando's voice was barely audible. 'Doesn't want me to hear days, hours …'

'Shhh. You'll wear yourself out.'

'Few words left … ten minutes … ten days.' Speech was an effort; I struggled to catch what he said, even with my ear close to his mouth. 'Our last … Listen … Thank you … David, Esther … Help David …' His eyes closed and he drifted into unconsciousness. I wanted to ask more but it would have to wait; I feared it would never happen.

I took his hand, and I gave it a gentle squeeze before sitting down to wait for Maria and Esther. When they returned, Maria and I left Esther alone with Armando and we went to sit on the veranda until it was time to eat. Maria called João out to join us and she coaxed me into telling him about my conversation with Daniel Chimica.

It did not seem to worry him; he laughed. 'The knife episode was a misunderstanding; she wasn't meant to touch it. They had another one that she was supposed to pick up, but she took the wrong one, the murder weapon. The forensics had already been done on it before and there were no fingerprints; it had been wiped clean on a cushion.'

'But the murder weapon has her fingerprints on it now and they're keeping it. That's what Chimica said,' I told him.

'That's true, but he won't use it. I know him … I trust him as a friend. Anyway, Xavier, my criminal lawyer friend from Luanda will be here tomorrow; he'll make mincemeat of that.'

I asked João where the murder weapon had come from and he told me it was one of Teresa's kitchen knives. Dryden had been using it to cut up a large pineapple, so it was handy.

He then asked me directly, 'How was Sophie when you saw her David? You did see her?'

'Yes. I only had about two or three minutes with her and she was in better spirits than I was.'

We talked about Sophie for a while and Maria said she would contact a friend in Nocredo to go to the casa de trânsito and bring our bags over to Mumbulo. João asked if I had made any progress with the idea I'd discussed with Constance in the morning. I told them that I was still working on it but that I had identified a possible motive behind Jim Lodge's murder. The next step was to prove who carried it out, and who was behind it.

'Jim Lodge discovered that volcanic pipe near Armando's island,' I said. 'He reported it to Geoff, and I think Geoff wanted to keep it a secret. I don't know, but I suspect Lodge wasn't prepared to go along with that and he was silenced.'

'But why would Geoff want it hushed up? I don't understand,' said João.

'There was a civil war going on …'

'I know; I was brought up here. What difference did that make? The war hadn't reached Mumbulo at that time.'

'No, but supplies weren't getting through so the mining company had a policy of not exploiting hard rock like kimberlite, not even looking for it seriously. I think Geoff guessed it would not be long before UNITA captured Mumbulo and the company would be forced to evacuate. The mine had very few proven reserves left so it was unlikely that the company would be interested in returning after the war; they would go where there were richer pickings. If they had known about the pipe, they would almost certainly have come back but, instead, Geoff came back with ARDCO and reaped the benefit.'

'So, you really do think Geoff had Sophie's father killed then?'

'It seems likely. I want to talk to him. See if I can wheedle something out of him. There are lots of strange details that don't add up.' I trusted João instinctively. I felt happy to confide in him. Was it just because he was Maria's son? I wondered.

Talking things through had liberated a lot of memories for me in the last few weeks and months, and João had a pair of ears that were not yet fed up with listening to me. I went through the details of Jim's death again for him: how Kevin Dryden had told me, the evening before his own death, that he had made up most of his story.

'It can't be denied,' I said, 'that Jim Lodge was stoned. Kevin told me the other night that Lodge was already dead, so why did everyone buy into Kevin's story at the time; unless, by some quirk of coincidence, it suited them. It got the real killers off the hook as the crime was blamed on Angolans and it made it look like Jim's death had nothing to do with diamonds. There was the added bonus that Geoff had an excuse to clear an Angolan village away from the area he intended to mine one day. Then there's the rocks: how did they get there? And there's another thing ...' I stopped.

'Yes?' João was anxious to hear more.

'I'm sure Geoff didn't want me ever to come back here.'

'Why would you anyway? You'd left.'

I stared at Maria; I wanted her to be sure how I had felt back then. 'If things had turned out differently, I would have come back, but not to work or to live.'

Maria blushed; she turned her attention to the floor.

'I don't get it,' João gave me a puzzled frown. 'Why would you have come back here for any other ...?' He had spotted his mother's embarrassment. 'Aaah! I see.'

I felt my own cheeks redden too. 'Yes, I'd hoped to come back to visit my in-laws.'

'But what's Geoff got to do with it?'

Maria sensed I was flagging. 'David and I wrote to each other, but we never received one another's letters. I thought David wasn't writing and that he had taken advantage of me, and he must have thought the same.'

'Why didn't you just phone?'

'There weren't any phones. We couldn't even call Nocredo or Luanda.'

'Yes, I forgot that. So, Geoff intercepted your post? Maybe neither of you really wrote but you won't admit it.'

'No.' Maria shook her head vigorously. 'That's what we both thought for years, until now. Thys said something last night; then Teresa brought a box full of letters round this morning. They were in Kevin's stuff; our letters.'

'If Kevin had the letters maybe Geoff had nothing to do with it, then,' suggested João.

250

'I think they both must have been in on it. We kept our relationship secret, your mother and me. It would have been awkward for her otherwise. We didn't think anyone knew about us except Sophie's father. But, when we saw Geoff and Thys yesterday, Thys forgot that he wasn't supposed to know, and he said something. I guess either Geoff or Kevin must have seen an envelope, addressed to me, in your mother's writing, in the mail out tray, and they couldn't resist taking a peek. Once they knew about us, they had to intercept all our mail. Even if I was living in England with your mother, we were bound to come back to visit your grandparents and I was the one person they thought might put two and two together when their plans unfolded. I really want to talk to Geoff. I need to ask him some questions.'

'Be careful.' Maria clenched her fists tightly. 'If it's like you say … Look what happened to Kevin.'

'Colin and Jug; Escutcheon Security,' I said. 'I can't see beyond them as killers now, but I'm sure Geoff's behind it. Those two offered themselves to me once … as hit men, and they talked about … Oh shit! Why didn't David come back with you, João?'

'He said he needed to work. And the kids …'

'Armando mumbled something to me about David preparing. That ultimatum … it's about up. I have a nasty feeling. I've got to get to the river clearing before Escutcheon. Maybe I can talk them out of whatever they mean to do.'

'Don't be such a fool, David,' said Maria; her eyes were wide. 'Don't give them the excuse to shoot you in a situation they can dress up as an accident.'

'I have to try; I let Armando down thirty years ago. I should have worked it out then. I should have stopped the village being bulldozed. I can't allow it to happen again. I'm going out there now. May I borrow your car please, João?'

'No. I'm driving. I'm coming with you.'

Maria's face crumpled.

Chapter 33

João drove like a mad man; his inner rally driver seemed to take him over as soon as we left town. Every bend was an invitation to put the car into a slide and braking was a game of dare.

'I hope you didn't drive like this when you had Armando in the car, João; you'd have finished him off.'

'Sorry. It's something I do when I'm nervous; it takes my mind off things.'

'You're not kidding.' He reduced speed a little.

'Where is it we're going exactly – the island?'

'Close to it. Park as though you're going there; it's probably the best hiding place in the area. I don't want any passing trucks or the Escutcheon vehicle to spot us. I hope we're ahead of them.'

He kept his speed down for a while and I found myself looking at him as he concentrated on the road. There was something familiar there, not just Maria, someone else. I thought of the letters. What was Maria so keen for me to read? Why did we have to wait, and why did João seem to quiz me at every opportunity about my relationship with his mother? I had one answer in mind; his age was right, but I would have to wait for Maria.

I returned to reality with a jolt. He had speeded up again and I had to dive for the grab handle on a tight right-hander.

'Sorry,' he muttered and slowed down again.

João found the parking spot more easily than I would have done but he had used it many more times, when delivering drugs to David and Esther for Armando. We hauled the sections of camouflage scrub out of the way together and João drove into the hiding place. He helped me to replace the camouflage and cover our tracks before we headed on foot towards the island. When we reached the river, we turned north and followed the bank. After about half a mile I recognised where Sophie and I had previously broken through to the river. We continued along the bank and I started whistling to warn of our coming. João was as mystified as Sophie had been until I explained.

As we approached the clearing, David stepped out from the scrub and blocked our way; he was frowning. 'What are you two doing here? It's not a good time.'

'That ultimatum runs out soon and I thought we might be able to talk to them.'

He laughed nervously. 'Thank you for thinking of us, but it's too late for that. There won't be any talking.'

'Have they already been? Are we too late?' I felt my energy drain; surely, I hadn't let them down again?

Just then, another man stepped out. My jaw dropped; I hadn't expected to see Sylvestre. What was he doing with David? He looked at me, shook his head in surprise and asked David, 'todo bem?' David said that all was well and Sylvestre, seeming satisfied, walked towards the clearing.

'I thought you didn't get on with Sylvestre and his group,' I said after he had gone.

'Needs must,' said David enigmatically.

'What's going on here?' João put my thoughts into words.

'Nothing.' David was a poor liar. I was surprised he hadn't taken us to the clearing; I knew he was hiding something.

'What time does the ultimatum expire?' João asked.

David glanced at the sun. 'About now.' He fidgeted. 'I need to get back to work. Go home. Please leave us and go home,' he implored; his eyes reinforced the message. He stiffened and I could see he was listening intently. I listened too. There was a distant growl; it sounded like the diesel engine of a mine truck on the road. I continued to listen. The noise was getting closer; it was not on the road.

'Just go!' said David. He dashed towards the clearing.

João looked at me, uncomprehending.

'I've got to do something,' I said. We were crouching on the bank listening to the engine noise intensifying. 'It must be

Escutcheon. They'll be using the track they made through the bush yesterday when they gave the ultimatum.' As I said it, I remembered something else that Colin and Jug had once told me …

★★★

We were driving back to Mumbulo with three Angolans tied up in the back of the Land Rover. Colin and Jug were in high spirits after playing soldiers and they poked fun at me for allowing an Angolan, Sylvestre, to escape. Their conversation moved on to land mines.

'A lot of vehicles get blown up by mines because drivers are stupid,' said Colin. 'They follow fresh tyre tracks, thinking that there can't be a mine there. Big mistake. Mine layers are clever; they dig up fresh tracks and lay mines under them. Then they disguise their work by rolling a wheel over the disturbed earth; nowhere near heavy enough to set off an anti-tank mine. They're quick. They've been known to blow up the vehicle, which made the original track, on its return journey.'

'That's right,' said Jug. 'If you see fresh tracks on a dirt road, steer away from them.'

★★★

'Sylvestre worries me, João. I've got to stop them,' I said. I stood up and started to run towards the clearing. I could hear João behind me.

'Stop who?' shouted João, 'David or Escutcheon?'

'Both. It might be an ambush.' I stopped and turned so suddenly that João nearly ran into me. I was very afraid. 'João, go back to the car now! Leave this to me.'

I started off again, checking every few yards that he was not following me.

The clearing was empty. All I could hear was my own panting, overlaid by the river and the ominous growl of the approaching vehicle. Where had everyone gone?

I dodged around numerous heaps and holes until I reached the centre of the clearing. I took out a handkerchief – white enough –

and held it in the air. It was no good waiting. I had to stop them; I ran on. I hoped they would see me in time. They would have to stop and talk. I was at the edge of the clearing; the noise was very close. Then I saw it. I had never paid much attention to the mine's personnel carriers before; I'd assumed they were ex-South African army Casspirs; armoured, with a V-profile bottom to deflect blasts from land mines and roadside bombs. This was just a truck armoured against attacks from the front, sides and back. I waved my handkerchief furiously, willing it to stop, but it came on relentlessly. Then the world stopped. A millisecond of action expanded to a minute in my mind. Dust and rocks blew out from under the truck, then flames. The truck was lifted and dumped on its side. I stood transfixed, then a mighty wind and a wave of debris smashed me to the ground. It went dark.

I looked up. I could not focus; confusion was everywhere. My head hurt and I could not hear. I think João was looking down at me; he was spinning. I reached for his hand; missed. I felt sick; something foul-tasting and gritty in my mouth. I closed my eyes. Something gripped my arm and pulled. My chest burned.

I opened my eyes again. I was on my side, coughing and vomiting. The world slowly stopped spinning; I started to register my surroundings. David and João were crouching over me; their faces lined with worry. João kept checking my mouth with his fingers. I was sore and ached all over, but I sensed I had no serious injury. I tried to ask what had happened but, even to my ears, it didn't come out as words. I gave it a few minutes then I tried again.

'He's back with us.' João's voice sounded very distant but at least I could hear again.

'Good.' It was David. 'You'd better get him out of here. I'll get one of the men to help you with him. When you get back on the road, call the mine on your mobile and report the accident. Get them to send their medics but keep your mother away from here.'

'What happened?' I asked.

'Anti-tank mine,' said João.

'Aaagh!' It was what I had feared; Sylvestre. 'Where are the ...?'

'Shush.' João was adamant. 'I need to get you back to town; get you to bed. You're probably in shock. I want Mum to check you out.'

'Was anyone hurt?'

He shrugged. 'I was worried about you.'

I nodded my thanks. It was a mistake; it hurt.

'They won't let me near,' he said. 'Let's get out of here. Put your arm around my shoulder and the other around our friend here.' He gestured at the man David had sent to help him. 'We'll get to the road then I'll get the car and take you back to Mumbulo.'

They hefted me to my feet. I felt surprisingly well; groggy but strong. I shook off their arms and turned to look back at the clearing. It was so unnaturally quiet. I thought my hearing had been affected, then I heard the moaning. I moved as quickly as my hurting body would allow to the end of the clearing and I saw the wreckage of the truck. It was a shock. David was running around, trying to organise a group of Angolans but it was the line of bodies that held my attention. There were five or six men, some Angolan and some European in appearance, lying side by side in the track; they were obviously dead. One looked like Jug. Then I saw Colin. He was walking wounded, but his right arm was badly broken; David had just finished fixing him up with an improvised splint and was helping him to the school area to sit on one of the logs. There were two other survivors: they looked battered.

I realised João was standing next to me, taking in the view of the carnage. 'Are you okay?' he asked.

'Blinding headache and my chest is killing me.'

'You were lucky. When the Escutcheon vehicle hit the mine … Bang! You were knocked off your feet and blown into one of the washing pits – I thought you'd drowned.'

'Maybe I did. This is hell. It's like an abbatoir. João, some of those guys came here yesterday and they didn't hit a mine. I don't like it. Did David say anything? Did he say why Sylvestre was here? Was it an old mine or …?'

David was still helping the surviving security men and offering them water. He gave me an exasperated look as I approached, then he took me to one side.

'That landmine,' I said, 'did you or Sylvestre lay that?'

'No.' He shook his head. 'It must have been there for years, a leftover from the war.' I wanted to believe him.

'I want to speak to that British guy, David: the one who was at the meeting the other afternoon. I have to ask him something.'

He gave me a long, hard look. 'Go ahead,' he said eventually.

Colin looked dazed; he was leaning against another man. They were sitting on the logs. He was holding his shirt to a cut on his forehead with his left hand. His chest glistened with sweat and blood and his right arm was splinted and supported by a makeshift sling. He was a sorry sight. A group of Angolans, including Sylvestre, stood guard over the survivors, holding automatic rifles. Sylvestre nodded his permission for me to talk to Colin.

Colin tried to smile when he saw me. 'I might have guessed you'd turn up,' he said.

'I came to stop you before anything happened.'

He coughed. 'As if you could … Bastards laid a mine. Are those the kind of people you want to help?'

'Colin, I'll make sure you get to hospital as soon as possible but I've got to ask you something first before I go. I can't remember whether it was you or Jug who told me once that you should never drive with your wheels in fresh tyre tracks.'

'Could have been either of us. We didn't though; we straddled the tracks we made yesterday.'

I almost collapsed with relief. 'It was an old mine then.'

'What do you know about such things?'

'These guys didn't lay that mine.' I hoped I was right. Why was Sylvestre here? 'You must have missed the mine yesterday and you'd have missed it today if you'd followed the tracks you made then.'

'Quite a soldier now aren't you? How did you imagine you were going to stop us? You can see from this lot that it's a war.' He gestured with his good arm at Sylvestre and his men.

'I don't read it like that.' I sat down on the teacher's log as a wave of giddiness threatened to floor me. I waited for the spinning to stop. 'It's not a war,' I said. 'You came here as an armed force; that's not very friendly. You just happened to run over an old landmine with your vehicle. These people have treated you well; your arm's been attended to. They've done all they could for the injured and the dead.' I stopped. I couldn't just ignore what had happened to Jug; I knew they were close. 'About Jug,' I said. 'I'm really sorry about what happened to him.'

'Thanks,' he said. 'We joined the army together nearly forty-five years ago; we've always been together. I'll miss him. I didn't especially like him, but I always knew I could trust him with my life.' I thought I saw a tear in the corner of his eye.

'Tell me, Colin, what were you intending to do here today?'

'Garimpeiros have been the bane of my life for as long as I can remember. We were going to move them on … Let someone else deal with them.'

The blast had performed one useful service at least; it had cleared my mind of superfluous detail.

'Rubbish Colin. You need garimpeiros. Without conflict you don't have a job. It's not in your interest to be rid of them. You need mine workers to feel insecure, so they'll pay for your services to keep them safe. These guys were no threat. Yes, they mine diamonds, but not from where ARDCO's mining, or ever intend to mine. They're just eking out a livelihood. If you come in with guns blazing, they have no choice but to fight back; you're the aggressors not them.'

'So, why are they armed?'

'They knew you were coming. You charged in here yesterday and told them. You needed them to be armed. I bet you were hoping for the *Gunfight at the O. K. Corral* to prove your worth to ARDCO, so they keep on paying for you. Did Geoff know you were wading in here today?'

He said nothing.

'What about Kevin?'

'He'd gone soft. I was surprised; I never thought he'd ever sympathise with anything you proposed, but he was willing to buy into your project.'

'Is that why you killed him?' I asked.

'I … We didn't kill him. We had nothing to do with it. The girl killed him. The evidence points to her.'

'Did you kill Jim Lodge then?'

'Jug and I arrived on the scene after you did if you remember. It's more likely that you killed him.'

'But you don't believe that. Do you remember when you took me with you once … playing soldiers? Do you remember leaving me to guard an Angolan?' I pointed at Sylvestre.

He laughed. 'You let him go.'

'Small world,' I said.

Colin chuckled drily. 'You're right though. You're too soft. Wouldn't harm a fly.'

'As a matter of interest,' I asked. 'If it wasn't you, who do you think killed Jim Lodge? And Kevin for that matter?'

'This lot probably. It was Angolans. That thing with the eyes; it was an Angolan ritual.'

'Says who? I think it was you or Jug who came up with that theory. It fitted the evidence at the time, and you had a gullible audience. We were all looking for a justification and it fitted the bill a treat. I believed it then but not now.'

'It was Thys,' he said. 'He came up with that theory; said he'd seen something similar when he was in the South African Police.'

Now it had been said, I had a clear mental image of Thys explaining it to us at the roadside as we all struggled to come to terms with the death and mutilation of our friend.

I got up; I needed to speak to Geoff. 'I've got to go. I'll make sure the mine medics are sent out and we'll make sure you get to hospital okay?'

He nodded his thanks. I walked across the clearing to the river where João was waiting to take me back to Mumbulo.

Chapter 34

When Maria was satisfied that I was not concussed or in shock, she washed the grit from the lacerations on my face and chest, then patched me up with a variety of bandages and plasters. I looked a mess, but I was in running order after swallowing a handful of painkillers, antibiotics and antidiarrheal tablets. When she had finished, João gave me a lift to the mine offices. I guessed Geoff Morgan's office would be close to Constance's, so I went to her office to ask for directions. She no longer saw me as someone out to hurt her friend; she was friendly and genuinely concerned about my battered appearance. She directed me to a door two containers further along; it was open.

'David boyo, how are you doing?' Morgan rose, pensive but smiling; he held out his hand.

I shook it. 'A bit beaten up, but otherwise fine. There was a bit of a bust-up. Did you authorise Escutcheon to go in?'

'No. Not specifically. They have a general remit, and they work autonomously within that. I had a conference call with them yesterday, before I left Luanda, and I made it plain that I wanted to put a stop to you playing silly buggers. Kevin should never have committed ARDCO to your ridiculous little project.'

'Have you heard what happened?'

'Nasty business. Bloody garimpeiros laid a mine. João asked for us to send the medics and ambulances out there, but I knew about it anyway.' He waved his mobile phone at me. 'A blood-bath by all accounts. What happened to you? How did you get bashed around? You weren't with Escutcheon, were you?'

'I was there before them, with the artisanal miners, waiting for them. I hoped I'd be able to stop anything from happening, but ...'

'Still bloody Superman!' Morgan grunted. 'I guess the Escutcheon mission was a total failure as they seem to have lost most of their men – at least they weren't Brits.' He sighed. 'But there's always another day.'

'Jug was one of the dead; he was a Brit. What bloody difference does that make anyway? A life's a life.'

'Paperwork, boyo. Bugger! That'll be even more drama with the embassy. First Kevin, then Lodge's girl and now Jug. It'll keep the legal team busy anyway – they'll have to earn their money.'

I saw the callous side of Geoff Morgan for the first time then and it shocked me. 'For the record,' I said, 'the artisanal miners didn't lay that mine; it was a left over from the civil war.'

'Whatever. They're still garimpeiros.'

'What have you got against artisanal miners? I expected Kevin to be against our work but you …?'

'How long have you got? I've spent a lot of my working life here in Angola. Illegal miners have always been a problem. We've lost a lot of workers in incidents like today's: Angolans and ex-pats; some of them were close friends like Jim Lodge.'

'But he wasn't killed by Angolans and you know it.'

'So you seem to think.'

I decided to attack. 'Tell me, Geoff, why was it necessary to have Jim Lodge killed?'

'Whoa! Steady on! That's a bit strong.' He raised his hands in a defensive gesture. 'I didn't have him killed as you put it. Why can't you take anything at face value? You always have to have someone to blame, don't you? Jim was a friend; there's no way …'

'Tell me what happened then. Tell me about that kimberlite.'

'Ah that.' He clicked his tongue. 'He showed me it about a week or so before … It would have prolonged the life of the mine for years. Well, it's still going – you can see. The company was never going to invest in exploiting kimberlite, a hard rock, back then.'

'Not during the war, but after …'

He laughed. 'You were always looking for the conspiracy, David. That's why I wanted you out. You were off target then, but it was only a matter of time. You were going to work and

261

rework what you knew, and you'd eventually chance upon the right answer.'

'That you were keeping a major diamond deposit a secret?'

'It didn't start like that.' He sighed heavily. 'Jim took Thys and me on one of his monthly geological tours of future prospects. We stopped by that funny rock, the one some of you called Chesterfield, and he told us what he'd found on the other side of the river. He was excited and keen to do some drilling to confirm his conclusions. When we got back, the three of us had a beer at my house and we speculated about keeping the find a secret and waiting to see how the war panned out. The published reserves were small so it was unlikely that the company would bother to come back here. There might be an opportunity.'

'I assume Jim wasn't keen.'

'It was only hypothetical, none of us was serious, but he made it clear that he would never entertain such an idea. And that's how we left it. A week or so later, he was dead.' He looked genuinely downcast at the memory. 'The hypothetical became reality by chance. I can't deny that Jim being out of the way was commercially fortuitous later, but I didn't kill him or have him killed.'

'Who else knew about the kimberlite?'

'Just Thys.'

'Could he have killed Jim?'

'I don't know. I've never thought about it because of Kevin's story.'

'Me too. I never considered him as he was with you when you turned up at the body. I never really believed you could have killed Jim and you were Thys's alibi.'

Morgan was quiet for a moment, deep in thought. 'I'm sure Thys only turned up at my house a few minutes before someone else came banging on the door to tell me about Jim's accident. Yes, we did drive to the body together.'

'How was he when he arrived at your place before you went out?'

'I honestly can't remember. Even if he had behaved oddly, I'd have forgotten in the shock of what we saw afterwards.'

I nodded; I believed him. 'So, what about Kevin …' I pressed.

'What about Kevin?' he echoed. 'Thys certainly didn't kill him: he was in Luanda.'

'So, if Thys did kill Jim, Kevin's murder must have been a copycat. Why would anyone do that?'

'Revenge. The evidence points at Sophie Addison and …'

'But she didn't know about Jim's eyes until after Kevin was killed. You can't copy something you don't know about. It wasn't Sophie. Did you speak to the man in charge of the investigation – Chimica – as you promised?'

'I did my best. As far as the police are concerned, she had the opportunity and the motive. The eyes are against her as she knew about all about that when she was interviewed.'

'Yes, she did, but we only told her after she'd found Kevin's body. I've made a statement to the police about that. Because of the eyes, we – Maria and I – assumed that Jim's killer was active again and Sophie needed to know that for her own safety, so we told her everything.'

'Your mistake then. Tell me, David, who do you now think killed Jim and Kevin?'

'Do you really want to know, Geoff? I spoke to Colin earlier and he had some interesting things to say. I had Colin and Jug at the top of my list of suspects before that, but not anymore. I think I believe what he said.'

'And what was that?'

'That'd be telling. I want to talk to Thys,' I said. 'Where's his office?'

He hesitated; I could see that he was considering his options, but eventually he said, 'Follow this line of containers to the end. There's a gap of about twenty metres before the next block. That's the security complex. Thys's office is on the far side, number eight.'

'Thanks. I might be back.'

Chapter 35

I walked as quickly as I could to the security complex; my legs were beginning to stiffen, and I was feeling generally sore. Thys's office was where Geoff had described. I knocked and went in without waiting to be invited. He was putting his phone down; he looked guilty.

'So, what is it you want, David?' he asked.

'Good afternoon to you too, Thys. Just a chat about old times.'

'You'd better sit down then. Coffee?' He gestured towards the percolator, spluttering noisily on an electric ring sitting on his filing cabinet.

I shook my head. 'December '84,' I said. 'Ring any bells?'

'Jim Lodge.'

'That's right. Tell me what you remember.'

'It's a long time ago. It's all a bit hazy now. Ask me another one.'

'No. We'll stick to this. Where had you been before you went to Geoff's that day? Geoff said you went together to the body, but you only turned up at his house a few minutes before you heard about Jim's so-called accident.'

'I can't remember. Like I said, it's a long time ago. Anyway, I don't have to answer your questions.'

'That's true. Okay, I'll tell you what I think happened, but feel free to correct me. I know Jim had told you and Geoff about the kimberlite pipe not long, a week or so, maybe, before he died, and he showed you where it was. I think you went there again that day, probably just to have another look, and to think about what to do. I think Jim turned up unexpectedly, driving back to Mumbulo, and he stopped when he saw you there. You talked about the kimberlite, you probably tried to persuade him to keep it quiet; have it as a possible investment after the war ended. Jim wouldn't go along with it, you argued, and you killed him. That would ensure his silence.'

'You make it sound like murder,' said Thys.

'Wasn't it? I'd really like to know.'

'No. I was there. Jim did turn up. But his death was an accident. Not the kind of accident it was thought to be, but an accident, nonetheless. We had a discussion; it got heated and I shoved him. He tripped, fell backwards and hit his head on that funny looking rock. He was dead. I was using a Geology Land Rover that I'd borrowed from Jim that morning. There were lots of biggish rocks – samples, I guess – in the back. It gave me the idea. When I was in the South African Police, I once investigated a tribal execution, a stoning, where the victim had his eyes gouged out and stuck on a stick. I mimicked it – the eyes were for authenticity. Then I drove back to Mumbulo. I only wanted to deflect attention from my involvement. I didn't know Kevin would be along shortly afterwards and I couldn't believe my luck when he came up with that accident story. Everyone bought it.'

'What if I told you that Jim was still alive when I got there? I think that does make it murder because you deliberately did things to him that resulted in his death.'

'Don't talk shit David. He was dead.'

'The doctor says otherwise, and she should know.' I was not going to tell him what Maria had actually done. 'Tell me Thys. Why are you owning up to all this now, after thirty years? Are you planning to kill me too?'

'Don't be silly. I'm not a killer. I'm telling you this because it's the truth. I used to be a policeman, living a lie's been hard for me. The story back then just grew and gained substance. Everyone had their own reasons for wanting to believe it. I've always wanted to confess my part in the accident, but the eyes … No one would have understood that; that was my mistake. Anyway, everyone believed Kevin's story and nobody apart from Jim got hurt.'

I snorted. 'What about the people living in that village? All innocent people – women, kids – you ruined their lives. Nobody hurt? You've got a convenient way of judging things.'

'I meant nobody was physically hurt.'

'I know what you meant. I doubt if I can prove anything. As you say, it was a long time ago. I hope that policeman's conscience of yours will dwell on the fact that Jim wasn't dead though. That should be enough to guarantee you sleepless nights for the rest of your life.'

'I believed he was dead. I still do. I've never had a conscience about that; never will. At worst, it's manslaughter. He died as a result of his fall; it was an accident.'

'He didn't. Maybe he did fall and bang his head, but that didn't kill him. Think about it. What about Kevin Dryden? He knew his story was a lie so he must have known that there was another set of circumstances that could explain the scene, even if he didn't know what it was. Was he starting to suspect you? Maybe he was blackmailing you.'

Thys shook his head emphatically. 'You're forgetting I was in Luanda with Geoff. I knew Kevin had lied of course, because I knew the truth, but I don't think Kevin ever suspected me of anything. He was committed to maintaining his own story; it wasn't in his interest to look elsewhere. I know absolutely nothing about Kevin's murder – and that is murder – except that the evidence points to the Addison girl.'

'But why take the trouble to create a cover scenario if Jim's death was an accident? Surely, as an ex-policeman your instinct should have been to tell the truth?'

'It was. But it would have drawn attention to the geology of the area; the kimberlite. That was why Jim and I argued, why he died where he did. It would have been a waste not to take advantage of the situation and turn the "pie in the sky" into reality.'

I was baffled. Should I believe him? Thys's story certainly fitted the evidence of the time, such as my memory and contemporary notes represented it. Why tell me the logic for removing Jim's eyes if it was not the truth? When I had arrived at the body thirty years before, my decision not to check for signs of life had been influenced by the eyes, but did that make Thys a murderer? The blood I had remembered on Chesterfield the other day fitted. It had been out of keeping with the other rocks, which lay on the ground, but not with Thys's explanation.

But who really killed Kevin Dryden? Thys Gerber had admitted killing Jim Lodge; I was happy with that. Whether it was an accident, manslaughter or murder was probably irrelevant now and I had no wish to draw attention either to Maria's action or to my own inaction. Kevin Dryden's death was certainly murder so there was still a murderer to be found. That murderer had known about Jim Lodge's eyes, so it was probably someone who had been at the scene. My list of possible killers was getting shorter and I was starting to doubt whether anyone on it had killed Dryden. What was I missing?

I went back to Geoff Morgan's office; the door was still open. I walked in and sat in one of his visitors' chairs uninvited. He watched me carefully, waiting.

'Let's cut the crap,' I said. 'We both need to do a deal. I need Sophie released and you need a clean reputation.'

'I have a clean reputation,' he said.

'You and Thys hushed up the kimberlite pipe. Without it, this mining area wasn't worth bothering with. You came in here unchallenged after the civil war and immediately started mining it.'

'And your point is?'

'You're guilty of some kind of fraud; falsifying reserves by not declaring their existence. Quite a long gaol sentence for that sort of thing and you're not in the first flush of youth.'

'You can't prove anything.'

'Maybe not,' I said, 'but can you afford to take the chance? Besides, if I stir the dirt, some of it'll stick; always does. Someone'll start digging where you don't want. They'll start asking questions. How did you find that kimberlite so quickly when others had been in the area for tens of years without finding it? Fluke? I don't think anyone'll believe that.'

'All right. Let's talk. For a start, who killed Jim? Do you know?'

'Yes. It was Thys. He confessed to it just now. But he maintains it was an accident.' I told Morgan most of what Thys Gerber had said to me.

'So, what do you intend to do about it?'

'Probably nothing, as long as I get what I want – Jim's death is inextricably linked to the kimberlite. I either tell all or I tell nothing.'

'Let me guess what you want. Sophie Addison's release, a licence for the garimpeiros to rob me and some sort of payment?'

'If this weren't so serious, I'd be laughing. You hide a diamond deposit, you flatten a village on false pretences, then you have the nerve to accuse the artisanal miners of robbing you. I bet you've made thousands of times more money than all of them put together have ever made. You're the worst kind of hypocrite.'

'Stop being so bloody self-righteous. How much are you asking for?' he snarled.

'Let's start with Sophie Addison,' I said. 'You are going to get her released.'

'How exactly? I've no influence over Angolan law.' A little smile touched his lips; it worried me.

'Oh, you'll have your ways, I'm sure.' I hoped I had interpreted his smile correctly.

'Now for the big question,' he said. 'How much?'

'I've never thought about it before,' I said, 'but, since you're offering: a donation of, say, £ 250,000 to Flourish's *Diamonds for Good Not Blood* project would be very welcome. You'll be able to keep an eye on our progress from close hand and, who knows, it might even pay back one day.'

Morgan laughed; he had always enjoyed irony. 'If I find out it's a pocket-liner for you, our agreement will be null and void – you'll be in the same gutter as me. And the garimpeiros ... what do you want for them?'

'Just honour what Kevin agreed to do: let us carry on with our project, open talks with selected artisanal miners' groups and see where it leads. I think you'll be pleasantly surprised. Oh. And get rid of Escutcheon, what's left of them – you won't need them anymore.'

'We'll see.'

Chapter 36

I felt physically shattered: stiff, sore and sluggish. My dressings needed changing; my shirt stuck to me, damp with blood and sweat. I could not decide whether it had been a good day or a bad one. I had certainly achieved a lot, but men had died, and Sophie was still in gaol.

Maria's house was in darkness. Why were there no lights on? There was not a power cut; light was leaking from the windows and doors of Teresa's house and others along the road. It was eerily quiet. What was wrong? I approached warily. The veranda gate was unlocked and so was the front door. A thirty-year-old memory took my hand to the light switch. Something like a ball of flame hurtled at my chest, nearly knocking me over. Sophie's arms were around me, hugging me tightly. Her shoulders heaved; she was sobbing and laughing at the same time. My battered chest hurt, but I did not mind. She was out! Free! João and Maria stood together, watching, grinning. Evil sods!

'When?' I asked.

'About an hour ago,' said João. 'Daniel Chimica called me. He told me he didn't have enough to justify holding her for any longer. I think he was under pressure too, from Luanda; your embassy.'

'Brilliant!' I hugged Sophie's head to me. I wanted to jump up and down, and shout and scream. It was as though I had been lugging a load around on my back for the past couple of days and someone had now taken it off me. 'We knew you didn't kill Kevin,' I stroked her hair affectionately. 'You couldn't, and you didn't know …' Sophie sobbed deeply and bored her face harder into my chest. I winced. 'Did Chimica tell you anything?' I asked João.

'A bit. Sophie was arrested because she was the obvious suspect: she was there, she found the body and she had Kevin's

269

blood all over her. Even though they thought she knew about the eyes they never really believed she was capable of that. And they couldn't legitimately tie the knife to her.'

'But what about the motive?' I asked. 'How did they know that Sophie thought Kevin had been involved in Jim's murder? Was someone bugging us or something?'

'No. It was something they found on Kevin's desk; a note to himself. Chimica gave me a photocopy of it while I was waiting for Sophie.' João passed me a sheet of A4 with Kevin's handwriting on it. Sophie still had her arms around me, so I rested it gently on her head and looked at it.

Lodge

Innocent – how to convince …

» talk – Young/Lodge(?) – explain?
» truth: accident invented
» village – don't know – Morgan?
» Investing → Morgan?

Wrong (as bloody usual) – bastards!

'I don't think I could draw any conclusion from that; it's all hints but nothing concrete. It certainly doesn't explain how Kevin knew what we were thinking though, does it?' I said. 'Let's leave it as paranoia, shall we? He seems to point the finger at Morgan for the village clearance and the investigation.'

Sophie let go of me and went to cuddle up to João. She looked freshly bathed, but she was still dressed in ill-fitting clothes; clean except for some bloody blotches she'd just picked up from me. It looked as though Maria's friend hadn't turned up with our bags yet, and it crossed my mind that Xavier, João's criminal lawyer mate was also late for the party. Who cared anyway? Time in gaol had not robbed Sophie of her beauty but it had put a good five years on her, at least temporarily. I hoped a few days' rest would sort her out.

'It's been a long day,' I said. 'I need a beer.'

'That'll have to wait a few minutes.' Maria pointed at my shirt. 'You can't stand around looking like that for long in my house; I've got a reputation to uphold. Bathroom! Now! I'm going to change those bandages. Then you can have a beer.' She led the way.

When she had finished dressing my wounds for the second time, and was putting everything away in her bag, I moved towards the door.

'Where are you going?' she asked. 'I haven't finished with you yet.' She reached an arm round my neck and pulled my head to her; she kissed the eyebrow she had first kissed thirty years before. 'I did a good job there,' she laughed. 'I thought I was kissing the wrong one for a minute.'

'My prized reminder. I'm glad it didn't fade away completely.'

She glanced at her watch. 'Damn. I'm half an hour late with Armando. I have to go and check on him.'

'How is he?' I dreaded the answer.

She shook her head. 'Come with me. Talk to him; tell him about today. He might not hear or understand but, if he does …' she smiled wanly.

Armando was completely still. Esther held his right hand; she was murmuring gently, soothingly; resigned to the inevitable but committed to making her husband's passing as peaceful as possible. She smiled at me and gestured for me to take over. It was strangely formal the way she placed Armando's hand in mine.

'Boa tarde, Armando. It's me, David.' My words were stilted. I felt shy; overawed by the responsibility of occupying so much of my old friend's little remaining time.

'Just talk,' said Maria. 'Don't worry about the words.'

'Armando, you said I should trust David. I did and you were right. He behaved perfectly when mine security raided their work area. ARDCO has agreed to let David continue working and I'll be with him. I don't know about Sophie – maybe she's had enough of it. But David and Esther are safe here now. You don't need to worry. It won't be like thirty years ago.'

I thought I felt some movement and maybe I imagined the smile on his face, but I had a strong feeling that he'd understood.

Maria finished her checks then Esther took over from me at Armando's side.

When we were out in the courtyard Maria said, 'I'm going to send João to fetch David as soon as it gets light in the morning; it won't be long now.' I did not have to ask what.

'I'll go with him. There's something I need to talk to David about and it might be difficult once we get back here.'

We went back into the house where João was impatiently holding a bottle of champagne. 'To celebrate Sophie's release,' he said and set about easing out the cork with well-practised thumbs.

We toasted Sophie's freedom then I told them about my meetings with Geoff Morgan and Thys Gerber. They listened intently. I explained how Jim Lodge had found the kimberlite pipe and how his death had resulted from a fracas with Thys over its disclosure, his death subsequently enabling Geoff and Thys to make their fortunes by exploiting the kimberlite exclusively. It was obviously taking a while for the details to sink in with Sophie.

When I suggested that Jim's death had probably been an accident or manslaughter rather than murder Sophie stiffened visibly.

'I'm sure Thys didn't intend to kill your father, Sophie,' I said.

She glared at me, shaking her head. 'No ... No, I'm not having that. I'd happily kill the bastard and rip his own bloody eyes out,' she said. 'It's what he deserves. He robbed me of my father, probably my mother too. I'm sure she wouldn't have died if my father had been alive.' Her face contorted with rage; she looked demented. Not for the first time, I fretted about the effect of that depressing gaol.

'Even if it started as an accident,' she continued emphatically, 'that bastard deliberately smashed my father's head with rocks and then ... that stuff with the eyes. If he hadn't done that, maybe he could have been saved. You said it yourself, David, that you didn't check because of the eyes. If he hadn't done that, you'd have tried to save him. Maria, were the head injuries – the ones that made you sure he could never recover – caused by his fall or the stoning, Thys's cover up?'

'I really don't know. I saw a stoning – it's what I'd been told I'd see. The foul play was so obvious; I didn't look for anything more innocent.' Maria shrugged. 'But I think David's right; intent is the important issue. I don't think Thys set out to kill your father.'

João put his arm on Sophie's and looked at her compassionately. She held his gaze. It had the desired effect of calming her down.

I carried on; I had a lot to get off my chest. 'I'm happy that we now know the details of Jim's death: who killed him, why he was killed and how he was killed; but I'm none the wiser about Kevin Dryden,' I said. 'Now Sophie's out, I'm not sure that I care anymore. It might be wise not to dig any deeper. Maybe we should draw a line under it and leave that one to the police. I'm sure Geoff and Thys are involved in some way, but we have a hold over them now. I don't think they'd dare do anything against us. If the police find something on them, that'll be great, but otherwise ... I think we should just get on with the job. That's what I'm going to do anyway. Morgan's agreed to back us in exchange for his reputation. I sort of blackmailed him; told him that I'd rake the muck if he didn't help.' I remembered something else. 'I'd better phone Rachel. Tell her that Sophie's free; call off the hounds. I think it's probably best if we send you back to England, Sophie, and we'll get another social scientist sent out here. Rachel will fix you up with counselling and any other support you might need.'

'No way. I'm staying here now. It's my project. I'm not letting you take all the glory for my idea. I also want to see this Thys Gerber character squirm every time he sets eyes on me. Besides ...' She smiled shyly at João. 'I've got support.'

'I can't force you to go,' I said, 'but I do strongly recommend it. If you do decide to stay, I'll back your decision, but I'll expect your total commitment and ...'

'I'm as committed as you are. I'll be ready for work in the morning,' she said.

'No, you won't,' Maria said gently. 'You need some proper rest and a good few feeds before you do anything. And I want to keep an eye on you; make sure you didn't pick up anything nasty while you were inside.'

'I'll do the paperwork then. I can't sit around doing nothing,' she said.

'You've got a deal,' I said, 'but if I think you're struggling to cope ...'

★★★

Maria warmed up some food in the microwave and we washed it down with champagne before moving on to beer. After we had finished eating, Maria gave Sophie a sedative and put her to bed in the office where I had slept the previous night.

When Maria returned, she was carrying the 'Chivas Regal' cardboard box.

'Are you ready for this?' It sounded like a test; Maria's voice was edgy. Why was she nervous? I was looking forward to it and I found myself smiling at João.

I nodded. She scrabbled around in the box and produced several bundles of envelopes. I felt both satisfied and vindicated when she'd finished dividing them; if love could be weighed, we had loved one another equally.

João was stretched out on the sofa, supping another beer; he watched us, bemused.

I looked at the pile I had written. Did I really want to read them? No, but I wanted to read what Maria had written to me. I shoved my letters towards her.

'I trust you to understand the tone, the anger and frustration,' I said.

She smiled and passed me all the ones she had written. 'That's how I see it too,' she said. 'I think everything that's important is in the first few letters I wrote anyway. It's just rehashed and angrier later.'

I had thought a lot about Maria over the last few days and, since the letters had turned up, about João too; I couldn't keep the smile off my face.

Maria's first letter was full of love and optimism; I wanted to go to her and sweep her off her feet; I felt sublimely happy. The second and third letters were similar, but there was an undercurrent of disappointment that she had not yet received anything from me. I read on; not expecting any surprises, only feeling growing impatience for news of João.

I glanced across at her. She was not reading; she was watching me, her face taut with concern.

Her next letter started on an angry note; why hadn't I written? My euphoria turned to shock, then incredulity and anguish. Maria had been desperate for my support; more desperate than I could ever have imagined. I thought of myself thirty years ago. What kind of a person had I been? How would I have reacted then to what I was now reading? She was pregnant, she was from a devout Catholic family and she needed a father on the birth certificate. She also had to maintain appearances within her community. Yes, I would have married her like a shot if that had been the full story, but …

★★★

Two weeks after I climbed onto the plane in Nocredo to leave Angola, Geoff Morgan had thrown a party at his house. Everyone there got very drunk and, unusually for her, so did Maria. After the party, she had walked home and, on the way, she'd been attacked and raped by a man wearing a mask. She had no idea who it was except that he was a young European. I read Maria's words over and over again. If Maria and I had embarked on a life together all that time ago, would I have been able to raise João, knowing that he was the son of an unknown rapist? I got up and went out onto the veranda to get some air and to get my mind straight. Could I have raised and cared for João if I had known that? I honestly did not know. Maria had been forced by circumstances into marriage, but at least she had been lucky: she had married a good man and he had stood by her. Maybe I would have pushed her to have an abortion. Maybe our relationship would have fallen apart because I was incapable of giving Maria the support she needed. That is how she must have interpreted my apparent failure to write.

I felt a hand on my shoulder; it was Maria. I was blubbing; confused, disappointed, upset. She stroked my head and I slowly pulled myself together. I did not know what to say. I thought about João; imagined him playing with his father as he grew up. Paulo had obviously been a good father. Maybe they had all been lucky.

'Would you have married me and done what Paulo did?' Maria went straight to the point.

'I like to think I would, but I don't know. I would now, but now I can see the result; João's a son any parent would be proud of. Paulo must have been a good man, but I wish I'd been there for you.'

'I'd better show that letter to João,' she said. 'He's always known that Paulo wasn't his father, but I was never able to tell him who his real father was because I didn't know; I still don't. I think he started putting two and two together and getting five when you turned up.'

João was as shocked as I had been. I was honoured that he seemed disappointed that I was not his father, but he was worried.

'My real father was a rapist. What if I'm like that? If he could do that, what else could he do? What else is in me that I don't know about?'

'You're not like him, João. You've nothing to worry about.' I put my arm around his shoulder. 'Remember how you feel about Sophie. You told me you wanted to go to her the other night – the night Kevin was killed – you didn't; you resisted. You're not a potential rapist and the very fact that it bothers you means you're not going to be like that.'

Maria hugged me. 'When everything's done, I think we should go away somewhere, away from Angola; not England, but spend some time together. Let's see what happens. No strings. It's not going to be easy, but …'

Chapter 37

David rode in the front with João and I sat in the back. I'd spent half the night and all the morning worrying about how to broach the question I had to ask. In the end I said, 'David, what was Sylvestre doing with you yesterday? Was that landmine really from the civil war?'

'We didn't lay the mine. I swear it. As for Sylvestre … I was in an impossible position. I'd made an agreement with ARDCO; I'd told everyone in my group about it; I'd assured them that we could trust ARDCO, and then … they broke the agreement before it was even a day old. Enough was enough. I was cornered; I spoke to the group and we decided to fight. I knew Sylvestre would help. It wasn't your fault but …'

'So, what happened? Why didn't you fight? You had the perfect opportunity to deal with them once and for all, to finish them off.'

'It was tempting but after the explosion those who survived were helpless – they offered no further threat. Sylvestre wanted to kill them, especially that man you spoke to, but we were on my territory … We bandaged them up as best we could and helped to get them back to Mumbulo. It'll probably turn out to be a mistake, but we'll see.'

'You behaved perfectly. No one can say they can't trust you. I expect they'll conduct an enquiry into the landmine but, when they've confirmed that it had been there for years … I need you to trust me David,' I said. 'Don't interfere with their investigation. Let them do it.'

'Why should I help them? They were attacking us, not the other way round.'

'I've got another agreement from ARDCO,' I said.

'No.'

'Hear me out, David. Please. I know things that can send ARDCO's bosses to prison for many years. I've persuaded Geoff Morgan to invest a lot of money in this project, so he's now got a vested interest in its success. They'll help you. They won't like it at first, but they have no choice. In time, I'm sure they'll realise they should have been doing it all along. I'll also make sure they get rid of Escutcheon.'

'It'll be hard to convince the others.' David sighed. 'I told you when we first met that you'd only get one chance to earn their trust, but ... they saw you yesterday, walking out to face that armoured personnel carrier. That takes courage; they respect that. They might just give you a second chance. I'll do my best.'

'Thank you, David. I spoke to your father last night. I don't know whether he heard or understood me, but I think he did. I told him that we'd be working together and that you and your family would be secure here.'

'I hope you're right. I guess this is the end; he'll be dead when I next see the island.'

'I didn't know your father for long – a year, at most – but I always liked him. I always found him to be intelligent, hard-working and honest. I wanted to promote him, to give him more responsibility. Then Sophie's father was killed, and everything went wrong. The village was flattened, he lost his job and was forced to go away. I've always felt guilty for not being able to prevent all that from happening.'

'Don't worry, Papai always spoke well of you, David. He knew you'd be back one day. Like you said: he's intelligent – he was right.'

Epilogue

Lisbon was beautiful in November; still warm enough in the early evening to walk around without a coat. Life had been hectic in Mumbulo in the last few months, but Maria and I had at last found the time to take the break we had promised ourselves. The project was going better than either Sophie or I could ever have dreamed. Morgan's contribution meant we could both spend more time on the project than we had originally budgeted. Rachel had protested strongly that we should return, but she had surprisingly caved in after speaking to Maria. Neither would tell me what had passed between them. Numerous other miners' groups were now working with ARDCO, including Sylvestre's. David had given up mining to run a school built for him by ARDCO in Mumbulo; it was made from shipping containers, like the mine offices, and was called 'Escola Armando Muachaquima' in memory of his father.

'Where did you arrange to meet?' Maria asked.

'Somewhere on the Avenida de Liberdade, a fish restaurant. He chose it …' I laughed at the memory of the conversation. 'It's called "Something Fishy".'

Maria chuckled. 'He hasn't changed then. Trust him to choose one with an English name, and a sort of joke.'

'I wonder what he looks like now, probably bald and fat after all these years. I didn't tell him about you – I'm keeping you as a surprise – I just told him I'd have a lady friend with me.'

'No wonder you're always getting into trouble.' She punched me playfully on the arm. 'Do you have directions? I'm starving.'

'We're looking for the Sofitel. It's supposed to be close to that.'

We ambled along happily, arm-in-arm, along the broad boulevard that is the Avenida de Liberdade. It brought back memories of stopovers; odd nights in the Hotel Tivoli when there was no same day connecting flight to Luanda. It had all been a long time ago – thirty years.

'There it is! The Sofitel anyway.' Maria nearly yanked my arm off in her hurry; the prospect of fish was always irresistible to her.

I gave the waiter the booking name; he consulted his seating plan then he beckoned us to follow him. A tall, deeply tanned man with unnaturally dark hair rose from a window table. He advanced, wearing a huge grin, and he almost killed me with the power of the bear-hug he gave me.

'David. Thirty years. It's wonderful to see you.'

'And you, Carlos. You look well. Teaching English obviously suits you.'

'It does.' He looked in Maria's direction. You'd better introduce me to …' He stopped. His face told a wordless story; pleasure at meeting an attractive lady, realisation that she looked familiar, and finally, recognition. It was the only time I ever saw Carlos blush. Eventually, he said, 'Maria?'

She nodded. He gave her a tentative hug. 'What are you two doing here together?' It was comical the way his eyes moved back and forth between us. I could imagine his brain working, joining the dots. 'You're a sly one David. I used to wonder why you were always dressed, and wearing a guilty look on your face, when I got up for a pee in the night. I must have been stupid not to see what you were up to.' He laughed again; he had regained his composure. I had always liked Carlos Pereira and I regretted the years when our friendship had lapsed.

In between the eating and the drinking, we talked about shared experiences in Mumbulo and what we had all been doing since we last met. It was a thoroughly pleasant evening, and I was glad that I'd taken the trouble to contact the language school in Porto where Carlos had been teaching when we lost contact. They had told me about his move to Lisbon and, after that, he had been easy to find.

We were rounding off the evening with a coffee and a cognac when Carlos said, 'I had an even bigger surprise about a year ago. I thought I'd seen a ghost. Jim Lodge's daughter, Sophie Addison, turned up to see me. She told me she'd spoken to you, David. Talk about a tough interrogator. She wanted to know everything about Jim, and you know …'

I nodded. 'She didn't say she'd seen you. What did you tell her?'

'Jim was her father; she'd a right to know. Everything.'

The room felt icy.

Maria was as white as I knew I was. Carlos frowned, confused; his expression emphasised the slight hook of his nose, something I could not ever remember noticing before. I looked at Maria; she had stiffened visibly; she did not say another word, except for the most perfunctory of goodbyes to Carlos, until we were outside, walking back to our hotel.

'What should we do?' She sounded panicky. 'Sophie, Sophie, Sophie … She'll be my daughter-in-law in a month. She couldn't have … could she?'

'Of course not,' I said. 'Just because she knew, doesn't mean she did it. Nothing's changed. We should just forget it.'

'Thank you.' She tucked her head into my chest. 'You're a rubbish liar though.'

'Believe it or not I'll happily forget about it …' I hesitated, 'especially if Sophie's my daughter-in-law too?'

Maria looked me up and down and gave me one of those you-must-be-mad looks that I was now familiar with.

'I don't want any diamonds,' she said. We hugged and kissed like teenagers. 'Right!' said Maria when we had settled down again. 'Carlos. It wasn't my imagination, was it?' She sounded very edgy. 'You noticed too, didn't you? I saw your reaction.'

I nodded. 'Yes. How sure are you?'

'It makes complete sense. His embarrassment when he recognised me … He hardly looked at me directly … I had a funny feeling all the while we were in the restaurant, but I couldn't explain it, then … That look – it was pure João.'

'What do you want to do? I'm with you whatever you decide, but that has to be your decision.'

'Thank you, David. It was a long time ago. I think he knows that I know, though. Why else would I stop speaking to him so suddenly? Maybe that's enough, and knowing the answer, of course. Let's just leave it at that for the moment and see how I feel when I've had time to think. We'll keep it between the two of us.'

The author

John Simpson was born in 1956. He has degrees
in Metallurgy and Environmental Diagnostics,
which prepared him for a career in the mining
industry. John has performed various metallurgical
roles on gold and diamond mines in South Africa,
Angola and other countries. He was an Area
Metallurgist on a diamond mine in Angola when
that country's first free elections took place.
During the subsequent recommencement of the
civil war he was captured by UNITA rebels and
evacuated to Brazil on release. He spent several
years as a Mining Specialist for an international
development charity, running projects in
Zimbabwe, Mozambique, Madagascar, Kenya,
Ghana, Sri Lanka and Guyana. He has also been
the Metallurgical Manager of a gold mine in
Greenland. Since 2014 John has worked as an
SAP ERP training consultant. He loves reading,
writing, walking, watching sport, enjoying wildlife
and listening to classical music. He is single and
has no children.

The publisher

> *He who stops*
> *getting better*
> *stops being good.*

This is the motto of novum publishing, and our focus
is on finding new manuscripts, publishing them and
offering long-term support to the authors.
Our publishing house was founded in 1997, and since
then it has become THE expert for new authors and
has won numerous awards.

**Our editorial team will peruse each manuscript
within a few weeks free of charge and without
obligation.**

You will find more information about
novum publishing and our books on the internet:

w w w . n o v u m - p u b l i s h i n g . c o . u k